PERFUME

"*The Name of the Rose,* the last literary sensation from Europe, crept up on America by stealth. *PERFUME* . . . arrives with fanfare . . . *PERFUME* GIVES OFF A RARE, SINFULLY ADDICTIVE CHILL OF PURE EVIL. SÜSKIND HAS SEDUCTIVE POWER AS A STORYTELLER."
—*Connoisseur*

"*PERFUME* IS ONE OF THE MOST EXCITING DISCOVERIES IN YEARS . . . A SUPREMELY ACCOMPLISHED WORK OF ART, MARVELOUSLY CRAFTED AND ENJOYABLE, AND RICH IN HISTORICAL DETAIL, WITH AN ABUNDANCE OF LIFE . . . AN ASTONISHING PERFORMANCE, A MASTERWORK OF ARTISTIC CONCEPTION AND EXECUTION . . . CONSTANTLY FASCINATING . . . WITH HIS VERY FIRST NOVEL, PATRICK SÜSKIND HAS ASSURED HIMSELF A PLACE BESIDE THE MOST IMPORTANT . . . WRITERS OF OUR TIME."
—*San Francisco Chronicle*

"BEAUTIFULLY RESEARCHED . . . BRILLIANT."
—John Updike, *The New Yorker*

(more)

D0112199

Also by Patrick Süskind

The Pigeon

Published by WASHINGTON SQUARE PRESS

Most Washington Square Press Books are available at special quantity discounts for bulk purchases for sales promotions, premiums or fund raising. Special books or book excerpts can also be created to fit specific needs.

For details write the office of the Vice President of Special Markets, Pocket Books, 1230 Avenue of the Americas, New York, New York 10020.

PATRICK SÜSKIND

PERFUME

The Story of a Murderer

*Translated from the German
by John E. Woods*

Originally published in German as *Das Parfum*

WASHINGTON SQUARE PRESS
PUBLISHED BY POCKET BOOKS
New York   London   Toronto   Sydney   Tokyo   Singapore

This book is a work of fiction. Names, characters, places and incidents
are either products of the author's imagination or are used fictitiously.
Any resemblance to actual events or locales or persons, living or dead,
is entirely coincidental.

WSP

A Washington Square Press Publication of
POCKET BOOKS, a division of Simon & Schuster Inc.
1230 Avenue of the Americas, New York, NY 10020

Copyright © 1985 by Diogenes Verlag AG
English translation copyright © 1986 by Alfred A. Knopf, Inc.
Cover illustration copyright © 1991 by Kinuko Y. Craft

Published by arrangement with Alfred A. Knopf, Inc.

Originally published in German as *Das Parfum* by Diogenes Verlag

All rights reserved, including the right to reproduce
this book or portions thereof in any form whatsoever.
For information address Alfred A. Knopf, Inc.,
201 East 50th Street, New York, NY 10022

ISBN: 0-671-74960-9

First Washington Square Press trade paperback printing
November 1991

10 9 8 7 6 5 4 3

WASHINGTON SQUARE PRESS and colophon are
registered trademarks of Simon & Schuster Inc.

Printed in the U.S.A.

PART

1

❧ One ❧

IN EIGHTEENTH-CENTURY France there lived a man who was one of the most gifted and abominable personages in an era that knew no lack of gifted and abominable personages. His story will be told here. His name was Jean-Baptiste Grenouille, and if his name—in contrast to the names of other gifted abominations, de Sade's, for instance, or Saint-Just's, Fouché's, Bonaparte's, etc.—has been forgotten today, it is certainly not because Grenouille fell short of those more famous blackguards when it came to arrogance, misanthropy, immorality, or, more succinctly, to wickedness, but because his gifts and his sole ambition were restricted to a domain that leaves no traces in history: to the fleeting realm of scent.

In the period of which we speak, there reigned in the cities a stench barely conceivable to us modern men and women. The streets stank of manure, the courtyards of urine, the stairwells stank of moldering wood and rat droppings, the kitchens of spoiled cabbage and mutton fat; the unaired parlors stank of stale dust, the bedrooms of greasy sheets, damp featherbeds, and the pungently sweet aroma of cham-

3

ber pots. The stench of sulfur rose from the chimneys, the stench of caustic lyes from the tanneries, and from the slaughterhouses came the stench of congealed blood. People stank of sweat and unwashed clothes; from their mouths came the stench of rotting teeth, from their bellies that of onions, and from their bodies, if they were no longer very young, came the stench of rancid cheese and sour milk and tumorous disease. The rivers stank, the marketplaces stank, the churches stank, it stank beneath the bridges and in the palaces. The peasant stank as did the priest, the apprentice as did his master's wife, the whole of the aristocracy stank, even the king himself stank, stank like a rank lion, and the queen like an old goat, summer and winter. For in the eighteenth century there was nothing to hinder bacteria busy at decomposition, and so there was no human activity, either constructive or destructive, no manifestation of germinating or decaying life that was not accompanied by stench.

And of course the stench was foulest in Paris, for Paris was the largest city of France. And in turn there was a spot in Paris under the sway of a particularly fiendish stench: between the rue aux Fers and the rue de la Ferronnerie, the Cimetière des Innocents to be exact. For eight hundred years the dead had been brought here from the Hôtel-Dieu and from the surrounding parish churches, for eight hundred years, day in, day out, corpses by the dozens had been carted here and tossed into long ditches, stacked bone upon bone for eight hundred years in the tombs and charnel houses. Only later—on the eve of the Revolution, after several of the grave pits had caved in and the stench had driven the swollen graveyard's neighbors to more than mere protest and to actual insurrection —was it finally closed and abandoned. Millions of

bones and skulls were shoveled into the catacombs of
Montmartre and in its place a food market was
erected.

Here, then, on the most putrid spot in the whole
kingdom, Jean-Baptiste Grenouille was born on July
17, 1738. It was one of the hottest days of the year.
The heat lay leaden upon the graveyard, squeezing its
putrefying vapor, a blend of rotting melon and the
fetid odor of burnt animal horn, out into the nearby
alleys. When the labor pains began, Grenouille's
mother was standing at a fish stall in the rue aux Fers,
scaling whiting that she had just gutted. The fish,
ostensibly taken that very morning from the Seine,
already stank so vilely that the smell masked the odor
of corpses. Grenouille's mother, however, perceived
the odor neither of the fish nor of the corpses, for her
sense of smell had been utterly dulled, besides which
her belly hurt, and the pain deadened all susceptibili-
ty to sensate impressions. She only wanted the pain to
stop, she wanted to put this revolting birth behind her
as quickly as possible. It was her fifth. She had
effected all the others here at the fish booth, and all
had been stillbirths or semi-stillbirths, for the bloody
meat that had emerged had not differed greatly from
the fish guts that lay there already, nor had lived much
longer, and by evening the whole mess had been
shoveled away and carted off to the graveyard or down
to the river. It would be much the same this day, and
Grenouille's mother, who was still a young woman,
barely in her mid-twenties, and who still was quite
pretty and had almost all her teeth in her mouth and
some hair on her head and—except for gout and
syphilis and a touch of consumption—suffered from
no serious disease, who still hoped to live a while yet,
perhaps a good five or ten years, and perhaps even to
marry one day and as the honorable wife of a widower

with a trade or some such to bear real children . . .
Grenouille's mother wished that it were already over.
And when the final contractions began, she squatted
down under the gutting table and there gave birth, as
she had done four times before, and cut the newborn
thing's umbilical cord with her butcher knife. But
then, on account of the heat and the stench, which she
did not perceive as such but only as an unbearable,
numbing something—like a field of lilies or a small
room filled with too many daffodils—she grew faint,
toppled to one side, fell out from under the table into
the street, and lay there, knife in hand.

Tumult and turmoil. The crowd stands in a circle
around her, staring, someone hails the police. The
woman with the knife in her hand is still lying in the
street. Slowly she comes to.

What has happened to her?

"Nothing."

What is she doing with that knife?

"Nothing."

Where does the blood on her skirt come from?

"From the fish."

She stands up, tosses the knife aside, and walks off
to wash.

And then, unexpectedly, the infant under the gutting table begins to squall. They have a look, and
beneath a swarm of flies and amid the offal and fish
heads they discover the newborn child. They pull it
out. As prescribed by law, they give it to a wet nurse
and arrest the mother. And since she confesses, open-
ly admitting that she would definitely have let the
thing perish, just as she had with those other four by
the way, she is tried, found guilty of multiple infanti-
cide, and a few weeks later decapitated at the place de
Grève.

By that time the child had already changed wet

nurses three times. No one wanted to keep it for more than a couple of days. It was too greedy, they said, sucked as much as two babies, deprived the other sucklings of milk and them, the wet nurses, of their livelihood, for it was impossible to make a living nursing just one babe. The police officer in charge, a man named La Fosse, instantly wearied of the matter and wanted to have the child sent to a halfway house for foundlings and orphans at the far end of the rue Saint-Antoine, from which transports of children were dispatched daily to the great public orphanage in Rouen. But since these convoys were made up of porters who carried bark baskets into which, for reasons of economy, up to four infants were placed at a time; since therefore the mortality rate on the road was extraordinarily high; since for that reason the porters were urged to convey only baptized infants and only those furnished with an official certificate of transport to be stamped upon arrival in Rouen; since the babe Grenouille had neither been baptized nor received even so much as a name to inscribe officially on the certificate of transport; since, moreover, it would not have been good form for the police anonymously to set a child at the gates of the halfway house, which would have been the only way to dodge the other formalities . . . thus, because of a whole series of bureaucratic and administrative difficulties that seemed likely to occur if the child were shunted aside, and because time was short as well, officer La Fosse revoked his original decision and gave instructions for the boy to be handed over on written receipt to some ecclesiastical institution or other, so that there they could baptize him and decide his further fate. He got rid of him at the cloister of Saint-Merri in the rue Saint-Martin. There they baptized him with the name Jean-Baptiste. And because on that day the prior was in a good mood and the eleemosynary fund not yet exhausted, they did not have the child shipped to Rouen, but instead pampered him at the cloister's expense. To this end, he was given to a wet nurse named Jeanne Bussie who lived in the rue Saint-Denis and was to receive, until further notice, three francs per week for her trouble.

❧ Two ❧

A FEW WEEKS later, the wet nurse Jeanne Bussie stood, market basket in hand, at the gates of the cloister of Saint-Merri, and the minute they were opened by a bald monk of about fifty with a light odor of vinegar about him—Father Terrier—she said "There!" and set her market basket down on the threshold.

"What's that?" asked Terrier, bending down over the basket and sniffing at it, in the hope that it was something edible.

"The bastard of that woman from the rue aux Fers who killed her babies!"

The monk poked about in the basket with his finger till he had exposed the face of the sleeping infant.

"He looks good. Rosy pink and well nourished."

"Because he's stuffed himself on me. Because he's pumped me dry down to the bones. But I've put a stop to that. Now you can feed him yourselves with goat's milk, with pap, with beet juice. He'll gobble up anything, that bastard will."

Father Terrier was an easygoing man. Among his duties was the administration of the cloister's chari-

9

ties, the distribution of its moneys to the poor and needy. And for that he expected a thank-you and that he not be bothered further. He despised technical details, because details meant difficulties and difficulties meant ruffling his composure, and he simply would not put up with that. He was upset that he had even opened the gate. He wished that this female would take her market basket and go home and let him alone with her suckling problems. Slowly he straightened up, and as he did he breathed the scent of milk and cheesy wool exuded by the wet nurse. It was a pleasant aroma.

"I don't understand what it is you want. I really don't understand what you're driving at. I can only presume that it would certainly do no harm to this infant if he were to spend a good while yet lying at your breast."

"None to him," the wet nurse snarled back, "but plenty to me. I've lost ten pounds and been eating like I was three women. And for what? For three francs a week!"

"Ah, I understand," said Terrier, almost relieved. "I catch your drift. Once again, it's a matter of money."

"No!" said the wet nurse.

"Of course it is! It's always a matter of money. When there's a knock at this gate, it's a matter of money. Just once I'd like to open it and find someone standing there for whom it was a matter of something else. Someone, for instance, with some little show of thoughtfulness. Fruit, perhaps, or a few nuts. After all, in autumn there are lots of things someone could come by with. Flowers maybe. Or if only someone would simply come and say a friendly word. 'God bless you, Father Terrier, I wish you a good day!' But I'll probably never live to see it happen. If it isn't a beggar, it's a merchant, and if it isn't a merchant, it's a

10

tradesman, and if it isn't alms he wants, then he presents me with a bill. I can't even go out into the street anymore. When I go out on the street, I can't take three steps before I'm hedged in by folks wanting money!"

"Not me," said the wet nurse.

"But I'll tell you this: you aren't the only wet nurse in the parish. There are hundreds of excellent foster mothers who would scramble for the chance of putting this charming babe to their breast for three francs a week, or to supply him with pap or juices or whatever nourishment . . ."

"Then give him to one of them!"

". . . On the other hand, it's not good to pass a child around like that. Who knows if he would flourish as well on someone else's milk as on yours. He's used to the smell of your breast, as you surely know, and to the beat of your heart."

And once again he inhaled deeply of the warm vapors streaming from the wet nurse.

But then, noticing that his words had made no impression on her, he said, "Now take the child home with you! I'll speak to the prior about all this. I shall suggest to him that in the future you be given four francs a week."

"No," said the wet nurse.

"All right—five!"

"No."

"How much more do you want, then?" Terrier shouted at her. "Five francs is a pile of money for the menial task of feeding a baby."

"I don't want any money, period," said the wet nurse. "I want this bastard out of my house."

"But why, my good woman?" said Terrier, poking his finger in the basket again. "He really is an adorable child. He's rosy pink, he doesn't cry, and he's been baptized."

"He's possessed by the devil."

Terrier quickly withdrew his finger from the basket.

"Impossible! It is absolutely impossible for an infant to be possessed by the devil. An infant is not yet a human being; it is a prehuman being and does not yet possess a fully developed soul. Which is why it is of no interest to the devil. Can he talk already, perhaps? Does he twitch and jerk? Does he move things about in the room? Does some evil stench come from him?"

"He doesn't smell at all," said the wet nurse.

"And there you have it! That is a clear sign. If he were possessed by the devil, then he would have to stink."

And to soothe the wet nurse and to put his own courage to the test, Terrier lifted the basket and held it up to his nose.

"I smell absolutely nothing out of the ordinary," he said after he had sniffed for a while, "really nothing out of the ordinary. Though it does appear as if there's an odor coming from his diapers." And he held out the basket to her so that she could confirm his opinion.

"That's not what I mean," said the wet nurse peevishly, shoving the basket away. "I don't mean what's in the diaper. His soil smells, that's true enough. But it's the bastard himself, he doesn't smell."

"Because he's healthy," Terrier cried, "because he's healthy, that's why he doesn't smell! Only sick babies smell, everyone knows that. It's well known that a child with the pox smells like horse manure, and one with scarlet fever like old apples, and a consumptive child smells like onions. He is healthy, that's all that's wrong with him. Do you think he should stink? Do your own children stink?"

"No," said the wet nurse. "My children smell like human children ought to smell."

Terrier carefully placed the basket back on the ground, for he could sense rising within him the first waves of his anger at this obstinate female. It was possible that he would need to move both arms more freely as the debate progressed, and he didn't want the infant to be harmed in the process. But for the present, he knotted his hands behind his back, shoved his tapering belly toward the wet nurse, and asked sharply, "You maintain, then, that you know how a human child—which may I remind you, once it is baptized, is also a child of God—is supposed to smell?"

"Yes," said the wet nurse.

"And you further maintain that, if it does not smell the way you—you, the wet nurse Jeanne Bussie from the rue Saint-Denis!—think it ought to smell, it is therefore a child of the devil?"

He swung his left hand out from behind his back and menacingly held the question mark of his index finger in her face. The wet nurse thought it over. She was not happy that the conversation had all at once turned into a theological cross-examination, in which she could only be the loser.

"That's not what I meant to say," she answered evasively. "You priests will have to decide whether all this has anything to do with the devil or not, Father Terrier. That's not for such as me to say. I only know one thing: this baby makes my flesh creep because it doesn't smell the way children ought to smell."

"Aha," said Terrier with satisfaction, letting his arm swing away again. "You retract all that about the devil, do you? Good. But now be so kind as to tell me: what does a baby smell like when he smells the way you think he ought to smell? Well?"

"He smells good," said the wet nurse.

"What do you mean, 'good'?" Terrier bellowed at her. "Lots of things smell good. A bouquet of lavender

13

smells good. Stew meat smells good. The gardens of Arabia smell good. But what does a baby smell like, is what I want to know."

The wet nurse hesitated. She knew very well how babies smell, she knew precisely—after all she had fed, tended, cradled, and kissed dozens of them. . . . She could find them at night with her nose. Why, right at that moment she bore that baby smell clearly in her nose. But never until now had she described it in words.

"Well?" barked Terrier, clicking his fingernails impatiently.

"Well it's—" the wet nurse began, "it's not all that easy to say, because . . . because they don't smell the same all over, although they smell good all over, Father, you know what I mean? Their feet, for instance, they smell like a smooth, warm stone—or no, more like curds . . . or like butter, like fresh butter, that's it exactly. They smell like fresh butter. And their bodies smell like . . . like a griddle cake that's been soaked in milk. And their heads, up on top, at the back of the head, where the hair makes a cowlick, there, see where I mean, Father, there where you've got nothing left. . . ." And she tapped the bald spot on the head of the monk, who, struck speechless for a moment by this flood of detailed inanity, had obediently bent his head down. "There, right there, is where they smell best of all. It smells like caramel, it smells so sweet, so wonderful, Father, you have no idea! Once you've smelled them there, you love them whether they're your own or somebody else's. And that's how little children have to smell—and no other way. And if they don't smell like that, if they don't have any smell at all up there, even less than cold air does, like that little bastard there, then . . . You can explain it however you like, Father, but I"—and she crossed her arms resolutely beneath her bosom and cast a look of disgust toward the basket at her feet as if it contained toads—"I, Jeanne Bussie, will not take that thing back!"

Father Terrier slowly raised his lowered head and ran his fingers across his bald head a few times as if hoping to put the hair in order, passed his finger beneath his nose as if by accident, and sniffed thoughtfully.

"Like caramel . . . ?" he asked, attempting to find his stern tone again. "Caramel! What do you know about caramel? Have you ever eaten any?"

"Not exactly," said the wet nurse. "But once I was in a grand mansion in the rue Saint-Honoré and watched how they made it out of melted sugar and cream. It smelled so good that I've never forgotten it."

"Yes, yes. All right," said Terrier and took his finger from his nose. "But please hold your tongue now! I find it quite exhausting to continue a conversation with you on such a level. I have determined that, for whatever reason, you refuse to nourish any longer the babe put under your care, Jean-Baptiste Grenouille, and are returning him herewith to his temporary guardian, the cloister of Saint-Merri. I find that distressing, but I apparently cannot alter the fact. You are discharged."

With that he grabbed the basket, took one last whiff of that fleeting woolly, warm milkiness, and slammed the door. Then he went to his office.

❧ *Three* ❧

Fᴀᴛʜᴇʀ Tᴇʀʀɪᴇʀ was an educated man. He had not merely studied theology, but had read the philosophers as well, and had dabbled with botany and alchemy on the side. He had a rather high opinion of his own critical faculties. To be sure, he would never go so far as some—who questioned the miracles, the oracles, the very truth of Holy Scripture—even though the biblical texts could not, strictly speaking, be explained by reason alone, indeed often directly contradicted it. He preferred not to meddle with such problems, they were too discomfiting for him and would only land him in the most agonizing insecurity and disquiet, whereas to make use of one's reason one truly needed both security and quiet. What he most vigorously did combat, however, were the superstitious notions of the simple folk: witches and fortune-telling cards, the wearing of amulets, the evil eye, exorcisms, hocus-pocus at full moon, and all the other acts they performed—it was really quite depressing to see how such heathenish customs had still not been uprooted a good thousand years after the firm establishment of the Christian religion! And most instances of so-called satanic possession or pacts with the devil proved on closer inspection to be superstitious mummery. Of course, to deny the existence of Satan himself, to doubt his power—Terrier could not go so far as that; ecclesiastical bodies other than one small, ordinary monk were assigned the task of deciding about such matters touching the very foundations of theology. But on the other hand, it was clear as day that when a simple soul like that wet nurse maintained that she had spotted a devilish spirit, the devil himself could not possibly have a hand in it. The very fact that she thought she had spotted him was certain proof that there was nothing devilish to be found, for the devil would certainly never be stupid enough to let himself be unmasked by the wet nurse Jeanne Bussie. And with her nose no less! With the primitive organ of smell, the basest of the senses! As if hell smelled of sulfur and paradise of incense and myrrh! The worst sort of superstition, straight out of the darkest days of paganism, when people still lived like beasts, possessing no keenness of the eye, incapable of distinguishing colors, but presuming to be able to smell blood, to scent the difference between friend and foe, to be smelled out by cannibal giants and werewolves and the Furies, all the while offering their ghastly gods stinking, smoking burnt sacrifices. How repulsive! "The fool sees with his nose" rather than his eyes, they say, and apparently the light of God-given reason would have to shine yet another thousand years before the last remnants of such primitive beliefs were banished.

"Ah yes, and you poor little child! Innocent creature! Lying in your basket and slumbering away, with no notion of the ugly suspicions raised against you. That impudent woman dared to claim you don't smell the way human children are supposed to smell. Well, what do we have to say to that? Pooh-peedooh!"

And he rocked the basket gently on his knees, stroking the infant's head with his finger and repeating "poohpeedooh" from time to time, an expression he thought had a gentle, soothing effect on small children. "You're supposed to smell like caramel, what nonsense, poohpeedooh!"

After a while he pulled his finger back, held it under his nose and sniffed, but could smell nothing except the *choucroute* he had eaten at lunch.

He hesitated a moment, looked around him to make sure no one was watching, lifted the basket, lowered his fat nose into it. Expecting to inhale an odor, he sniffed all around the infant's head, so close to it that the thin reddish baby hair tickled his nostrils. He did not know exactly how babies' heads were supposed to smell. Certainly not like caramel, that much was clear, since caramel was melted sugar, and how could a baby that until now had drunk only milk smell like melted sugar? It might smell like milk, like wet nurse's milk. But it didn't smell like milk. It might smell like hair, like skin and hair and maybe a little bit of baby sweat. And Terrier sniffed with the intention of smelling skin, hair, and a little baby sweat. But he smelled nothing. For the life of him he couldn't. Apparently an infant has no odor, he thought, that must be it. An infant, assuming it is kept clean, simply doesn't smell, any more than it speaks, or walks, or writes. Such things come only with age. Strictly speaking, human beings first emit an odor when they reach puberty. That's how it is, that's all. Wasn't it Horace himself who wrote, "The youth is gamy as a buck, the maiden's fragrance blossoms as does the white narcissus ..."?—and the Romans knew all about that! The odor of humans is always a fleshly odor—that is, a sinful odor. How could an infant, which does not yet know sin even in its dreams, have an odor? How could it smell? Poohpee-dooh—not a chance of it!

He had placed the basket back on his knees and now rocked it gently. The babe still slept soundly. Its right fist, small and red, stuck out from under the cover and now and then twitched sweetly against his cheek. Terrier smiled and suddenly felt very cozy. For a moment he allowed himself the fantastic thought that he was the father of the child. He had not become a monk, but rather a normal citizen, an upstanding craftsman perhaps, had taken a wife, a warm wife fragrant with milk and wool, and had produced a son with her and he was rocking him here now on his own knees, his own child, poohpoohpoohpeedooh. . . . The thought of it made him feel good. There was something so normal and right about the idea. A father rocking his son on his knees, poohpeedooh, a vision as old as the world itself and yet always new and normal, as long as the world would exist, ah yes! Terrier felt his heart glow with sentimental coziness.

Then the child awoke. Its nose awoke first. The tiny nose moved, pushed upward, and sniffed. It sucked air in and snorted it back out in short puffs, like an imperfect sneeze. Then the nose wrinkled up, and the child opened its eyes. The eyes were of an uncertain color, between oyster gray and creamy opal white, covered with a kind of slimy film and apparently not very well adapted for sight. Terrier had the impression that they did not even perceive him. But not so the nose. While the child's dull eyes squinted into the void, the nose seemed to fix on a particular target, and Terrier had the very odd feeling that he himself, his person, Father Terrier, was that target. The tiny wings of flesh around the two tiny holes in the child's face swelled like a bud opening to bloom. Or rather, like the cups of that small meat-eating plant that was kept in the royal botanical gardens. And like the plant, they seemed to create an eerie suction. It seemed to Terrier as if the child saw him with its nostrils, as if it were staring intently at him, scrutinizing him, more piercingly than eyes could ever do, as if it were using its nose to devour something whole, something that came from him, from Terrier, and that he could not hold that something back or hide it. . . . The child with no smell was smelling at him shamelessly, that was it! It was establishing his scent! And all at once he felt as if he stank, of sweat and vinegar, of *choucroute* and unwashed clothes. He felt naked and ugly, as if someone were gaping at him while revealing nothing of himself. The child seemed to be smelling right through his skin, into his innards. His most tender emotions, his filthiest thoughts lay exposed to that greedy little nose, which wasn't even a proper nose, but only a pug of a nose, a tiny perforated organ, forever crinkling and puffing and quivering. Terrier shuddered. He felt sick to his stomach. He pulled back his own nose as if he smelled something foul that he wanted nothing to do with. Gone was the homey thought that this might be his own flesh and blood. Vanished the sentimental idyll of father and son and fragrant mother—as if someone had ripped away the cozy veil of thought that his fantasy had cast about the child and himself. A strange, cold creature lay there on his knees, a hostile animal, and were he not a man by nature prudent, God-fearing, and given to reason, in the rush of nausea he would have hurled it like a spider from him.

Terrier wrenched himself to his feet and set the basket on the table. He wanted to get rid of the thing, as quickly as possible, right away if possible, immediately if possible.

And then it began to wail. It squinted up its eyes, gaped its gullet wide, and gave a screech so repulsively

shrill that the blood in Terrier's veins congealed. He
shook the basket with an outstretched hand and
shouted "Poohpeedooh" to silence the child, but it
only bellowed more loudly and turned completely
blue in the face and looked as if it would burst from
bellowing.

Away with it! thought Terrier, away this very instant
with this . . . he was about to say "devil," but caught
himself and refrained . . . away with this monster,
with this insufferable child! But away where? He knew
a dozen wet nurses and orphanages in the neighborhood, but that was too near, too close for comfort, get
the thing farther away, so far away that you couldn't
hear it, so far away that it could not be dropped on
your doorstep again every hour or so; if possible it
must be taken to another parish, on the other side of
the river would be even better, and best of all *extra
muros*, in the Faubourg Saint-Antoine, that was it!
That was the place for this screaming brat, far off to
the east, beyond the Bastille, where at night the city
gates were locked.

And he hitched up his cassock and grabbed the
bellowing basket and ran off, ran through the tangle of
alleys to the rue du Faubourg Saint-Antoine, eastward
up the Seine, out of the city, far, far out the rue de
Charonne, almost to its very end, where at an address
near the cloister of Madeleine de Trenelle, he knew
there lived a certain Madame Gaillard, who took
children to board no matter of what age or sort, as
long as someone paid for them, and there he handed
over the child, still screaming, paid a year in advance,
and fled back into the city, and once at the cloister cast
his clothes from him as if they were foully soiled,
washed himself from head to foot, and crept into bed
in his cell, crossing himself repeatedly, praying long,
and finally with some relief falling asleep.

❧ *Four* ❧

MADAME GAILLARD'S life already lay behind her, though she was not yet thirty years old. To the world she looked as old as her years—and at the same time two, three, a hundred times older, like the mummy of a young girl. But on the inside she was long since dead. When she was a child, her father had struck her across the forehead with a poker, just above the base of the nose, and she had lost for good all sense of smell and every sense of human warmth and human coldness—indeed, every human passion. With that one blow, tenderness had become as foreign to her as enmity, joy as strange as despair. She felt nothing when later she slept with a man, and just as little when she bore her children. She did not grieve over those that died, nor rejoice over those that remained to her. When her husband beat her, she did not flinch, and she felt no sense of relief when he died of cholera in the Hôtel-Dieu. The only two sensations that she was aware of were a very slight depression at the approach of her monthly migraine and a very slight elevation of mood at its departure. Otherwise, this numbed woman felt nothing.

On the other hand . . . or perhaps precisely because

of her total lack of emotion . . . Madame Gaillard had a merciless sense of order and justice. She showed no preference for any one of the children entrusted to her nor discriminated against any one of them. She served up three meals a day and not the tiniest snack more. She diapered the little ones three times a day, but only until their second birthday. Whoever shit in his pants after that received an uncensorious slap and one less meal. Exactly one half of the boarding fees were spent for her wards, exactly one half she retained for herself. She did not attempt to increase her profits when prices went down; and in hard times she did not charge a single sol extra, even when it was a matter of life and death. Otherwise her business would have been of no value to her. She needed the money. She had figured it down to the penny. In her old age she wanted to buy an annuity, with just enough beyond that so that she could afford to die at home rather than perish miserably in the Hôtel-Dieu as her husband had. The death itself had left her cold. But she dreaded a communal, public death among hundreds of strangers. She wanted to afford a private death, and for that she needed her full cut of the boarding fees. True, there were winters when three or four of her two dozen little boarders died. Still, her record was considerably better than that of most other private foster mothers and surpassed by far the record of the great public and ecclesiastical orphanages, where the losses often came to nine out of ten. There were plenty of replacements. Paris produced over ten thousand new foundlings, bastards, and orphans a year. Several such losses were quite affordable.

For little Grenouille, Madame Gaillard's establishment was a blessing. He probably could not have survived anywhere else. But here, with this small-souled woman, he throve. He had a tough constitution. Whoever has survived his own birth in a garbage can is not so easily shoved back out of this world again. He could eat watery soup for days on end, he managed on the thinnest milk, digested the rottenest vegetables and spoiled meat. In the course of his childhood he survived the measles, dysentery, chicken pox, cholera, a twenty-foot fall into a well, and a scalding with boiling water poured over his chest. True, he bore scars and chafings and scabs from it all, and a slightly crippled foot left him with a limp, but he lived. He was as tough as a resistant bacterium and as content as a tick sitting quietly on a tree and living off a tiny drop of blood plundered years before. He required a minimum ration of food and clothing for his body. For his soul he required nothing. Security, attention, tenderness, love—or whatever all those things are called that children are said to require— were totally dispensable for the young Grenouille. Or rather, so it seems to us, he had totally dispensed with them just to go on living—from the very start. The cry that followed his birth, the cry with which he had brought himself to people's attention and his mother to the gallows, was not an instinctive cry for sympathy and love. That cry, emitted upon careful consideration, one might almost say upon mature consideration, was the newborn's decision *against* love and nevertheless *for* life. Under the circumstances, the latter was possible only without the former, and had the child demanded both, it would doubtless have abruptly come to a grisly end. Of course, it could have grabbed the other possibility open to it and held its peace and thus have chosen the path from birth to death without a detour by way of life, sparing itself and the world a great deal of mischief. But to have made such a modest exit would have demanded a modicum of native civility, and that Grenouille did not possess. He was an abomination from the start.

24

He decided in favor of life out of sheer spite and sheer malice.

Obviously he did not decide this as an adult would decide, who requires his more or less substantial experience and reason to choose among various options. But he did decide vegetatively, as a bean when once tossed aside must decide if it ought to germinate or had better let things be.

Or like that tick in the tree, for which life has nothing better to offer than perpetual hibernation. The ugly little tick, which by rolling its blue-gray body up into a ball offers the least possible surface to the world; which by making its skin smooth and dense emits nothing, lets not the tiniest bit of perspiration escape. The tick, which makes itself extra small and inconspicuous so that no one will see it and step on it. The lonely tick, which, wrapped up in itself, huddles in its tree, blind, deaf, and dumb, and simply sniffs, sniffs all year long, for miles around, for the blood of some passing animal that it could never reach on its own power. The tick could let itself drop. It could fall to the floor of the forest and creep a millimeter or two here or there on its six tiny legs and lie down to die under the leaves—it would be no great loss, God knows. But the tick, stubborn, sullen, and loathsome, huddles there and lives and waits. Waits, for that most improbable of chances that will bring blood, in animal form, directly beneath its tree. And only then does it abandon caution and drop, and scratch and bore and bite into that alien flesh. . . .

The young Grenouille was such a tick. He lived encapsulated in himself and waited for better times. He gave the world nothing but his dung—no smile, no cry, no glimmer in the eye, not even his own scent. Every other woman would have kicked this monstrous child out. But not Madame Gaillard. She could not smell that he did not smell, and she expected no stirrings from his soul, because her own was sealed tight.

The other children, however, sensed at once what Grenouille was about. From the first day, the new arrival gave them the creeps. They avoided the box in which he lay and edged closer together in their beds as if it had grown colder in the room. The younger ones would sometimes cry out in the night; they felt a draft sweep through the room. Others dreamed something was taking their breath away. One day the older ones conspired to suffocate him. They piled rags and blankets and straw over his face and weighed it all down with bricks. When Madame Gaillard dug him out the next morning, he was crumpled and squashed and blue, but not dead. They tried it a couple of times more, but in vain. Simple strangulation—using their bare hands or stopping up his mouth and nose— would have been a dependable method, but they did not dare try it. They didn't want to touch him. He disgusted them the way a fat spider that you can't bring yourself to crush in your own hand disgusts you.

As he grew older, they gave up their attempted murders. They probably realized that he could not be destroyed. Instead, they stayed out of his way, ran off, or at least avoided touching him. They did not hate him. They weren't jealous of him either, nor did they begrudge him the food he ate. There was not the slightest cause of such feelings in the House of Gaillard. It simply disturbed them that he was there. They could not stand the nonsmell of him. They were afraid of him.

⊱ *Five* ⊰

Looked at objectively, however, there was nothing at all about him to instill terror. As he grew older, he was not especially big, nor strong—ugly, true, but not so extremely ugly that people would necessarily have taken fright at him. He was not aggressive, nor under-handed, nor furtive, he did not provoke people. He preferred to keep out of their way. And he appeared to possess nothing even approaching a fearful intelligence. Not until age three did he finally begin to stand on two feet; he spoke his first word at four, it was the word "fishes," which in a moment of sudden excitement burst from him like an echo when a fishmonger coming up the rue de Charonne cried out his wares in the distance. The next words he parted with were "pelargonium," "goat stall," "savoy cabbage," and "Jacqueslorreur," this last being the name of a gardener's helper from the neighboring convent of the Filles de la Croix, who occasionally did rough, indeed very rough work for Madame Gaillard, and was most conspicuous for never once having washed in all his life. He was less concerned with verbs, adjectives, and expletives. Except for "yes" and "no"

27

—which, by the way, he used for the first time quite late—he used only nouns, and essentially only nouns for concrete objects, plants, animals, human beings—and only then if the objects, plants, animals, or human beings would subdue him with a sudden attack of odor.

One day as he sat on a cord of beechwood logs snapping and cracking in the March sun, he first uttered the word "wood." He had seen wood a hundred times before, had heard the word a hundred times before. He understood it, too, for he had often been sent to fetch wood in winter. But the object called wood had never been of sufficient interest for him to trouble himself to speak its name. It happened first on that March day as he sat on the cord of wood. The cord was stacked beneath overhanging eaves and formed a kind of bench along the south side of Madam Gaillard's shed. The top logs gave off a sweet burnt smell, and up from the depths of the cord came a mossy aroma; and in the warm sun, bits of resin odor crumbled from the pinewood planking of the shed.

Grenouille sat on the logs, his legs outstretched and his back leaned against the wall of the shed. He had closed his eyes and did not stir. He saw nothing, he heard nothing, he felt nothing. He only smelled the aroma of the wood rising up around him to be captured under the bonnet of the eaves. He drank in the aroma, he drowned in it, impregnating himself through his innermost pores, until he became wood himself; he lay on the cord of wood like a wooden puppet, like Pinocchio, as if dead, until after a long while, perhaps a half hour or more, he gagged up the word "wood." He vomited the word up, as if he were filled with wood to his ears, as if buried in wood to his neck, as if his stomach, his gorge, his nose were spilling over with wood. And that brought him to himself, rescued him only moments before the over-powering presence of the wood, its aroma, was about to suffocate him. He shook himself, slid down off the logs, and tottered away as if on wooden legs. Days later he was still completely fuddled by the intense olfactory experience, and whenever the memory of it rose up too powerfully within him he would mutter imploringly, over and over, "wood, wood."

And so he learned to speak. With words designating nonsmelling objects, with abstract ideas and the like, especially those of an ethical or moral nature, he had the greatest difficulty. He could not retain them, confused them with one another, and even as an adult used them unwillingly and often incorrectly: justice, conscience, God, joy, responsibility, humility, grati-tude, etc.—what these were meant to express re-mained a mystery to him.

On the other hand, everyday language soon would prove inadequate for designating all the olfactory notions that he had accumulated within himself. Soon he was no longer smelling mere wood, but kinds of wood: maple wood, oak wood, pinewood, elm wood, pearwood, old, young, rotting, moldering, mossy wood, down to single logs, chips, and splinters—and could clearly differentiate them as objects in a way that other people could not have done by sight. It was the same with other things. For instance, the white drink that Madame Gaillard served her wards each day, why should it be designated uniformly as milk, when to Grenouille's senses it smelled and tasted completely different every morning depending on how warm it was, which cow it had come from, what that cow had been eating, how much cream had been left in it and so on. . . . Or why should smoke possess only the name "smoke," when from minute to min-ute, second to second, the amalgam of hundreds of odors mixed iridescently into ever new and changing

29

unities as the smoke rose from the fire ... or why should earth, landscape, air—each filled at every step and every breath with yet another odor and thus animated with another identity—still be designated by just those three coarse words. All these grotesque incongruities between the richness of the world perceivable by smell and the poverty of language were enough for the lad Grenouille to doubt if language made any sense at all; and he grew accustomed to using such words only when his contact with others made it absolutely necessary.

At age six he had completely grasped his surroundings olfactorily. There was not an object in Madame Gaillard's house, no place along the northern reaches of the rue de Charonne, no person, no stone, tree, bush, or picket fence, no spot be it ever so small, that he did not know by smell, could not recognize again by holding its uniqueness firmly in his memory. He had gathered tens of thousands, hundreds of thousands of specific smells and kept them so clearly, so randomly, at his disposal, that he could not only recall them when he smelled them again, but could also actually smell them simply upon recollection. And what was more, he even knew how by sheer imagination to arrange new combinations of them, to the point where he created odors that did not exist in the real world. It was as if he were an autodidact possessed of a huge vocabulary of odors that enabled him to form at will great numbers of smelled sentences—and at an age when other children stammer words, so painfully drummed into them, to formulate their first very inadequate sentences describing the world. Perhaps the closest analogy to his talent is the musical wunderkind, who has heard his way inside melodies and harmonies to the alphabet of individual tones and now composes completely new melodies and harmonies all on his own. With the one difference, however, that the alphabet of odors is incomparably larger and more nuanced than that of tones; and with the additional difference that the creative activity of Grenouille the wunderkind took place only inside him and could be perceived by no one other than himself.

To the world he appeared to grow ever more secretive. What he loved most was to rove alone through the northern parts of the Faubourg Saint-Antoine, through vegetable gardens and vineyards, across meadows. Sometimes he did not come home in the evening, remained missing for days. The rod of punishment awaiting him he bore without a whimper of pain. Confining him to the house, denying him meals, sentencing him to hard labor—nothing could change his behavior. Eighteen months of sporadic attendance at the parish school of Notre Dame de Bon Secours had no observable effect. He learned to spell a bit and to write his own name, nothing more. His teacher considered him feebleminded.

Madame Gaillard, however, noticed that he had certain abilities and qualities that were highly unusual, if not to say supernatural: the childish fear of darkness and night seemed to be totally foreign to him. You could send him anytime on an errand to the cellar, where other children hardly dared go even with a lantern, or out to the shed to fetch wood on the blackest night. And he never took a light with him and still found his way around and immediately brought back what was demanded, without making one wrong move—not a stumble, not one thing knocked over. More remarkable still, Madame Gaillard thought she had discovered his apparent ability to see right through paper, cloth, wood, even through brick walls and locked doors. Without ever entering the dormitory, he knew how many of her wards—and which ones—were in there. He knew if there was a worm in

31

the cauliflower before the head was split open. And once, when she had hidden her money so well that she couldn't find it herself (she kept changing her hiding places), he pointed without a second's search to a spot behind a fireplace beam—and there it was! He could even see into the future, because he would infallibly predict the approach of a visitor long before the person arrived or of a thunderstorm when there was not the least cloud in the sky. Of course, he could not see any of these things with his eyes, but rather caught their scents with a nose that from day to day smelled such things more keenly and precisely: the worm in the cauliflower, the money behind a beam, and people on the other side of a wall or several blocks away. But Madame Gaillard would not have guessed that fact in her wildest dream, even if that blow with the poker had left her olfactory organ intact. She was convinced that, feebleminded or not, the lad had second sight. And since she also knew that people with second sight bring misfortune and death with them, he made her increasingly nervous. What made her more nervous still was the unbearable thought of living under the same roof with someone who had the gift of spotting hidden money behind walls and beams; and once she had discovered that Grenouille possessed this dreadful ability, she set about getting rid of him. And it just so happened that at about the same time—Grenouille had turned eight—the cloister of Saint-Merri, without mention of the reason, ceased to pay its yearly fee. Madame did not dun them. For appearances' sake, she waited an additional week, and when the money owed her still had not appeared, she took the lad by the hand and walked with him into the city.

She was acquainted with a tanner named Grimal, who lived near the river in the rue de la Mortellerie and had a notorious need for young laborers—not for regular apprentices and journeymen, but for cheap coolies. There were certain jobs in the trade—scraping the meat off rotting hides, mixing the poisonous tanning fluids and dyes, producing the caustic lyes—so perilous, that, if possible, a responsible tanning master did not waste his skilled workers on them, but instead used unemployed riffraff, tramps, or, indeed, stray children, about whom there would be no inquiry in dubious situations. Madame Gaillard knew of course that by all normal standards Grenouille would have no chance of survival in Grimal's tannery. But she was not a woman who bothered herself about such things. She had, after all, done her duty. Her custodianship was ended. What happened to her ward from here on was not her affair. If he made it through, well and good. If he died, that was well and good too—the main thing was that it all be done legally. And so she had Monsieur Grimal provide her with a written receipt for the boy she was handing over to him, gave him in return a receipt for her brokerage fee of fifteen francs, and set out again for home in the rue de Charonne. She felt not the slightest twinge of conscience. On the contrary, she thought her actions not merely legal but also just, for if a child for whom no one was paying were to stay on with her, it would necessarily be at the expense of the other children or, worse, at her own expense, endangering the future of the other children, or worse, her own future—that is, her own private and sheltered death, which was the only thing that she still desired from life.

Since we are to leave Madame Gaillard behind us at this point in our story and shall not meet her again, we shall take a few sentences to describe the end of her days. Although dead in her heart since childhood, Madame unfortunately lived to be very, very old. In 1782, just short of her seventieth birthday, she gave up her business, purchased her annuity as planned, sat in her little house, and waited for death. But death did not come. What came in its place was something not a soul in the world could have anticipated: a revolution, a rapid transformation of all social, moral, and transcendental affairs. At first this revolution had no effect on Madame Gaillard's personal fate. But then—she was almost eighty by now—all at once the man who held her annuity had to emigrate, was stripped of his holdings, and forced to auction off his possessions to a trouser manufacturer. For a while it looked as if even this change would have no fatal effect on Madame Gaillard, for the trouser manufacturer continued to pay her annuity punctually. But then came the day when she no longer received her money in the form of hard coin but as little slips of printed paper, and that marked the beginning of her economic demise.

Within two years, the annuity was no longer worth enough to pay for her firewood. Madame was forced to sell her house—at a ridiculously low price, since suddenly there were thousands of other people who also had to sell their houses. And once again she received in return only these stupid slips of paper, and once again within two years they were as good as worthless, and by 1797 (she was nearing ninety now) she had lost her entire fortune, scraped together from almost a century of hard work, and was living in a tiny furnished room in the rue des Coquilles. And only then—ten, twenty years too late—did death arrive, in the form of a protracted bout with a cancer that grabbed Madame by the throat, robbing her first of her appetite and then of her voice, so that she could raise not one word of protest as they carted her off to the Hôtel-Dieu. There they put her in a ward populated with hundreds of the mortally ill, the same ward in which her husband had died, laid her in a bed shared with total strangers, pressing body upon body

34

with five other women, and for three long weeks let her die in public view. She was then sewn into a sack, tossed onto a tumbrel at four in the morning with fifty other corpses, to the faint tinkle of a bell driven to the newly founded cemetery of Clamart, a mile beyond the city gates, and there laid in her final resting place, a mass grave beneath a thick layer of quicklime.

That was in the year 1799. Thank God Madame had suspected nothing of the fate awaiting her as she walked home that day in 1746, leaving Grenouille and our story behind. She might possibly have lost her faith in justice and with it the only meaning that she could make of life.

⪨ *Six* ⪩

FROM HIS first glance at Monsieur Grimal—no, from the first breath that sniffed in the odor enveloping Grimal—Grenouille knew that this man was capable of thrashing him to death for the least infraction. His life was worth precisely as much as the work he could accomplish and consisted only of whatever utility Grimal ascribed to it. And so, Grenouille came to heel, never once making an attempt to resist. With each new day, he would bottle up inside himself the energies of his defiance and contumacy and expend them solely to survive the impending ice age in his ticklike way. Tough, uncomplaining, inconspicuous, he tended the light of life's hopes as a very small, but carefully nourished flame. He was a paragon of docility, frugality, and diligence in his work, obeyed implicitly, and appeared satisfied with every meal offered. In the evening, he meekly let himself be locked up in a closet off to one side of the tannery floor, where tools were kept and the raw, salted hides were hung. There he slept on the hard, bare earthen floor. During the day he worked as long as there was light—eight hours in winter, fourteen, fifteen, sixteen

36

hours in summer. He scraped the meat from bestially stinking hides, watered them down, dehaired them, limed, bated, and fulled them, rubbed them down with pickling dung, chopped wood, stripped bark from birch and yew, climbed down into the tanning pits filled with caustic fumes, layered the hides and pelts just as the journeymen ordered him, spread them with smashed gallnuts, covered this ghastly funeral pyre with yew branches and earth. Years later, he would have to dig them up again and retrieve these mummified hide carcasses—now tanned leather—from their grave.

When he was not burying or digging up hides, he was hauling water. For months on end, he hauled water up from the river, always in two buckets, hundreds of bucketfuls a day, for tanning requires vast quantities of water, for soaking, for boiling, for dyeing. For months on end, the water hauling left him without a dry stitch on his body; by evening his clothes were dripping wet and his skin was cold and swollen like a soaked shammy.

After one year of an existence more animal than human, he contracted anthrax, a disease feared by tanners and usually fatal. Grimal had already written him off and was looking around for a replacement—not without regret, by the way, for he had never before had a more docile and productive worker than this Grenouille. But contrary to all expectation, Grenouille survived the illness. All he bore from it were scars from the large black carbuncles behind his ears and on his hands and cheeks, leaving him disfigured and even uglier than he had been before. It also left him immune to anthrax—an invaluable advantage—so that now he could strip the foulest hides with cut and bleeding hands and still run no danger of reinfection. This set him apart not only from the apprentices and journeymen, but also from his own potential successors. And because he could no longer be so easily replaced as before, the value of his work and thus the value of his life increased. Suddenly he no longer had to sleep on bare earth, but was allowed to build himself a plank bed in the closet, was given straw to scatter over it and a blanket of his own. He was no longer locked in at bedtime. His food was more adequate. Grimal no longer kept him as just any animal, but as a useful house pet.

When he was twelve, Grimal gave him half of Sunday off, and at thirteen he was even allowed to go out on weekend evenings for an hour after work and do whatever he liked. He had triumphed, for he was alive, and he possessed a small quantum of freedom sufficient for survival. The days of his hibernation were over. Grenouille the tick stirred again. He caught the scent of morning. He was seized with an urge to hunt. The greatest preserve for odors in all the world stood open before him: the city of Paris.

≈ *Seven* ≈

I<small>T WAS LIKE</small> living in utopia. The adjacent neighborhoods of Saint-Jacques-de-la-Boucherie and Saint-Eustache were a wonderland. In the narrow side streets off the rue Saint-Denis and the rue Saint-Martin, people lived so densely packed, each house so tightly pressed to the next, five, six stories high, that you could not see the sky, and the air at ground level formed damp canals where odors congealed. It was a mixture of human and animal smells, of water and stone and ashes and leather, of soap and fresh-baked bread and eggs boiled in vinegar, of noodles and smoothly polished brass, of sage and ale and tears, of grease and soggy straw and dry straw. Thousands upon thousands of odors formed an invisible gruel that filled the street ravines, only seldom evaporating above the rooftops and never from the ground below. The people who lived there no longer experienced this gruel as a special smell; it had arisen from them and they had been steeped in it over and over again; it was, after all, the very air they breathed and from which they lived, it was like clothes you have worn so long you no longer smell them or feel them against

your skin. Grenouille, however, smelled it all as if for
the first time. And he did not merely smell the
mixture of odors in the aggregate, but he dissected it
analytically into its smallest and most remote parts
and pieces. His discerning nose unraveled the knot
of vapor and stench into single strands of unitary
odors that could not be unthreaded further. Unwind-
ing and spinning out these threads gave him unspeak-
able joy.

He would often just stand there, leaning against a
wall or crouching in a dark corner, his eyes closed, his
mouth half open and nostrils flaring wide, quiet as a
feeding pike in a great, dark, slowly moving current.
And when at last a puff of air would toss a delicate
thread of scent his way, he would lunge at it and not
let go. Then he would smell at only this one odor,
holding it tight, pulling it into himself and preserving
it for all time. The odor might be an old acquaintance,
or a variation on one; it could be a brand-new one as
well, with hardly any similarity to anything he had
ever smelled, let alone seen, till that moment: the
odor of pressed silk, for example, the odor of a
wild-thyme tea, the odor of brocade embroidered
with silver thread, the odor of a cork from a bottle of
vintage wine, the odor of a tortoiseshell comb. Grenouille was out to find such odors still unknown to
him; he hunted them down with the passion and
patience of an angler and stored them up inside him.

When he had smelled his fill of the thick gruel of the
streets, he would go to airier terrain, where the odors
were thinner, mixing with the wind as they unfurled,
much as perfume does—to the market of Les Halles,
for instance, where the odors of the day lived on into
the evening, invisibly but ever so distinctly, as if the
vendors still swarmed among the crowd, as if the
baskets still stood there stuffed full of vegetables and
eggs, or the casks full of wine and vinegar, the sacks

with their spices and potatoes and flour, the crates of nails and screws, the meat tables, the tables full of cloth and dishes and shoe soles and all the hundreds of other things sold there during the day . . . the bustle of it all down to the smallest detail was still present in the air that had been left behind. Grenouille saw the whole market smelling, if it can be put that way. And he smelled it more precisely than many people could see it, for his perception was after the fact and thus of a higher order: an essence, a spirit of what had been, something undisturbed by the everyday accidents of the moment, like noise, glare, or the nauseating press of living human beings.

Or he would go to the spot where they had beheaded his mother, to the place de Grève, which stuck out to lick the river like a huge tongue. Here lay the ships, pulled up onto shore or moored to posts, and they smelled of coal and grain and hay and damp ropes.

And from the west, via this one passage cut through the city by the river, came a broad current of wind bringing with it the odors of the country, of the meadows around Neuilly, of the forests between Saint-Germain and Versailles, of far-off cities like Rouen or Caen and sometimes of the sea itself. The sea smelled like a sail whose billows had caught up water, salt, and a cold sun. It had a simple smell, the sea, but at the same time it smelled immense and unique, so much so that Grenouille hesitated to dissect the odors into fishy, salty, watery, seaweedy, fresh-airy, and so on. He preferred to leave the smell of the sea blended together, preserving it as a unit in his memory, relishing it whole. The smell of the sea pleased him so much that he wanted one day to take it in, pure and unadulterated, in such quantities that he could get drunk on it. And later, when he learned from stories how large the sea is and that you can sail upon it in ships for days on end without ever seeing land, nothing pleased him more than the image of himself sitting high up in the crow's nest of the foremost mast on such a ship, gliding on through the endless smell of the sea—which really was no smell, but a breath, an exhalation of breath, the end of all smells—dissolving with pleasure in that breath. But it was never to be, for Grenouille, who stood there on the riverbank at the place de Grève steadily breathing in and out the scraps of sea breeze that he could catch in his nose, would never in his life see the sea, the real sea, the immense ocean that lay to the west, and would never be able to mingle himself with its smell.

He had soon so thoroughly smelled out the quarter between Saint-Eustache and the Hôtel de Ville that he could find his way around in it by pitch-dark night. And so he expanded his hunting grounds, first westward to the Faubourg Saint-Honoré, then out along the rue Saint-Antoine to the Bastille, and finally across to the other bank of the river into the quarters of the Sorbonne and the Faubourg Saint-Germain where the rich people lived. Through the wrought-iron gates at their portals came the smells of coach leather and of the powder in the pages' wigs, and over the high walls passed the garden odors of broom and roses and freshly trimmed hedges. It was here as well that Grenouille first smelled perfume in the literal sense of the word: a simple lavender or rose water, with which the fountains of the gardens were filled on gala occasions; but also the more complex, more costly scents, of tincture of musk mixed with oils of neroli and tuberose, jonquil, jasmine, or cinnamon, that floated behind the carriages like rich ribbons on the evening breeze. He made note of these scents, registering them just as he would profane odors, with curiosity, but without particular admiration. Of course he realized that the purpose of perfumes was to create an intoxicating and alluring effect, and he recognized the value of the individual essences that comprised them. But on the whole they seemed to him rather coarse and ponderous, more slapdashed together than composed, and he knew that he could produce entirely different fragrances if he only had the basic ingredients at his disposal.

He knew many of these ingredients already from the flower and spice stalls at the market; others were new to him, and he filtered them out from the aromatic mixture and kept them unnamed in his memory: ambergris, civet, patchouli, sandalwood, bergamot, vetiver, opopanax, benzoin, hop blossom, castor . . .

He was not particular about it. He did not differentiate between what is commonly considered a good and a bad smell, not yet. He was greedy. The goal of the hunt was simply to possess everything the world could offer in the way of odors, and his only condition was that the odors be new ones. The smell of a sweating horse meant just as much to him as the tender green bouquet of a bursting rosebud, the acrid stench of a bug was no less worthy than the aroma rising from a larded veal roast in an aristocrat's kitchen. He devoured everything, everything, sucking it up into him. But there were no aesthetic principles governing the olfactory kitchen of his imagination, where he was forever synthesizing and concocting new aromatic combinations. He fashioned grotesqueries, only to destroy them again immediately, like a child playing with blocks—inventive and destructive, with no apparent norms for his creativity.

≫ *Eight* ≪

O<small>N</small> S<small>EPTEMBER</small> 1, 1753, the anniversary of the king's coronation, the city of Paris set off fireworks at the Pont-Royal. The display was not as spectacular as the fireworks celebrating the king's marriage, or as the legendary fireworks in honor of the dauphin's birth, but it was impressive nevertheless. They had mounted golden sunwheels on the masts of the ships. From the bridge itself so-called fire bulls spewed showers of burning stars into the river. And while from every side came the deafening roar of petards exploding and of firecrackers skipping across the cobblestones, rockets rose into the sky and painted white lilies against the black firmament. Thronging the bridge and the quays along both banks of the river, a crowd of many thousands accompanied the spectacle with ah's and oh's and even some "long live" 's—although the king had ascended his throne more than thirty-eight years before and the high point of his popularity was long since behind him. Fireworks can do that.

Grenouille stood silent in the shadow of the Pavillon de Flore, across from the Pont-Neuf on the right bank. He did not stir a finger to applaud, did not even

44

look up at the ascending rockets. He had come in hopes of getting a whiff of something new, but it soon became apparent that fireworks had nothing to offer in the way of odors. For all their extravagant variety as they glittered and gushed and crashed and whistled, they left behind a very monotonous mixture of smells: sulfur, oil, and saltpeter.

He was just about to leave this dreary exhibition and head homewards along the gallery of the Louvre when the wind brought him something, a tiny, hardly noticeable something, a crumb, an atom of scent; no, even less than that: it was more the premonition of a scent than the scent itself—and at the same time it was definitely a premonition of something he had never smelled before. He backed up against the wall, closed his eyes, and flared his nostrils. The scent was so exceptionally delicate and fine that he could not hold on to it; it continually eluded his perception, was masked by the powder smoke of the petards, blocked by the exudations of the crowd, fragmented and crushed by the thousands of other city odors. But then, suddenly, it was there again, a mere shred, the whiff of a magnificent premonition for only a second . . . and it vanished at once. Grenouille suffered agonies. For the first time, it was not just that his greedy nature was offended, but his very heart ached. He had the prescience of something extraordinary—this scent was the key for ordering all odors, one could understand nothing about odors if one did not understand this one scent, and his whole life would be bungled, if he, Grenouille, did not succeed in possessing it. He had to have it, not simply in order to possess it, but for his heart to be at peace.

He was almost sick with excitement. He had not yet even figured out what direction the scent was coming from. Sometimes there were intervals of several minutes before a shred was again wafted his way, and each time he was overcome by the horrible anxiety that he had lost it forever. He was finally rescued by a desperate conviction that the scent was coming from the other bank of the river, from somewhere to the southeast.

He moved away from the wall of the Pavillon de Flore, dived into the crowd, and made his way across the bridge. Every few strides he would stop and stand on tiptoe in order to take a sniff from above people's heads, at first smelling nothing for pure excitement; then finally there was something, he smelled the scent, stronger than before, knew that he was on the right track, dived in again, burrowed through the throng of gapers and pyrotechnicians unremittingly setting torch to their rocket fuses, lost the scent in the acrid smoke of the powder, panicked, shoved and jostled his way through and burrowed onward, and after countless minutes reached the far bank, the Hôtel de Mailly, the Quai Malaquest, the entrance to the rue de Seine. . . .

Here he stopped, gathering his forces, and smelled. He had it. He had hold of it tight. The odor came rolling down the rue de Seine like a ribbon, unmistakably clear, and yet as before very delicate and very fine. Grenouille felt his heart pounding, and he knew that it was not the exertion of running that had set it pounding, but rather his excited helplessness in the presence of this scent. He tried to recall something comparable, but had to discard all comparisons. This scent had a freshness, but not the freshness of limes or pomegranates, not the freshness of myrrh or cinnamon bark or curly mint or birch or camphor or pine needles, nor that of a May rain or a frosty wind or of well water . . . and at the same time it had warmth, but not as bergamot, cypress, or musk has, or jasmine or daffodils, not as rosewood has or iris. . . . This scent was a blend of both, of evanescence and substance, not a blend, but a unity, although slight and frail as well, and yet solid and sustaining, like a piece of thin, shimmering silk . . . and yet again not like silk, but like pastry soaked in honeysweet milk—and try as he would he couldn't fit those two together: milk and silk! This scent was inconceivable, indescribable, could not be categorized in any way—it really ought not to exist at all. And yet there it was as plain and splendid as day. Grenouille followed it, his fearful heart pounding, for he suspected that it was not he who followed the scent, but the scent that had captured him and was drawing him irresistibly to it.

He walked up the rue de Seine. No one was on the street. The houses stood empty and still. The people were down by the river watching the fireworks. No hectic odor of humans disturbed him, no biting stench of gunpowder. The street smelled of its usual smells: water, feces, rats, and vegetable matter. But above it hovered the ribbon, delicate and clear, leading Grenouille on. After a few steps, what little light the night afforded was swallowed by the tall buildings, and Grenouille walked on in darkness. He did not need to see. The scent led him firmly.

Fifty yards farther, he turned off to the right up the rue des Marais, a narrow alley hardly a span wide and darker still—if that was possible. Strangely enough, the scent was not much stronger. It was only purer, and in its augmented purity, it took on an even greater power of attraction. Grenouille walked with no will of his own. At one point, the scent pulled him strongly to the right, straight through what seemed to be a wall. A low entryway opened up, leading into a back courtyard. Grenouille moved along the passage like a somnambulist, moved across the courtyard, turned a corner, entered a second, smaller courtyard, and here finally there was light—a space of only a few square feet. A wooden roof hung out from the wall. Beneath it, a table, a candle stuck atop it. A girl was sitting at the table cleaning yellow plums. With her left hand, she took the fruit from a basket, stemmed and pitted it with a knife, and dropped it into a bucket. She might have been thirteen, fourteen years old. Grenouille stood still. He recognized at once the source of the scent that he had followed from half a mile away on the other bank of the river: not this squalid courtyard, not the plums. The source was the girl.

For a moment he was so confused that he actually thought he had never in all his life seen anything so beautiful as this girl—although he only caught her from behind in silhouette against the candlelight. He meant, of course, he had never smelled anything so beautiful. But since he knew the smell of humans, knew it a thousandfold, men, women, children, he could not conceive of how such an exquisite scent could be emitted by a human being. Normally human odor was nothing special, or it was ghastly. Children smelled insipid, men urinous, all sour sweat and cheese, women smelled of rancid fat and rotting fish. Totally uninteresting, repulsive—that was how humans smelled. . . . And so it happened that for the first time in his life, Grenouille did not trust his nose and had to call on his eyes for assistance if he was to believe what he smelled. This confusion of senses did not last long at all. Actually he required only a moment to convince himself optically—then to abandon himself all the more ruthlessly to olfactory perception. And now he *smelled* that this was a human being, smelled the sweat of her armpits, the oil in her hair, the fishy odor of her genitals, and smelled it all with the greatest pleasure. Her sweat smelled as fresh as the sea breeze, the tallow of her hair as sweet as nut oil, her genitals were as fragrant as the bouquet of water lilies, her skin as apricot blossoms . . . and the harmony of all these components yielded a perfume so rich, so balanced, so magical, that every perfume that Grenouille had smelled until now, every edifice of odors that he had so playfully created within himself, seemed at once to be utterly meaningless. A hundred thousand odors seemed worthless in the presence of this scent. This one scent was the higher principle, the pattern by which the others must be ordered. It was pure beauty.

Grenouille knew for certain that unless he possessed this scent, his life would have no meaning. He had to understand its smallest detail, to follow it to its last delicate tendril; the mere memory, however complex, was not enough. He wanted to press, to emboss this apotheosis of scent on his black, muddled soul, meticulously to explore it and from this point on, to think, to live, to smell only according to the innermost structures of its magic formula.

He slowly approached the girl, closer and closer, stepped under the overhanging roof, and halted one step behind her. She did not hear him.

She had red hair and wore a gray, sleeveless dress. Her arms were very white and her hands yellow with the juice of the halved plums. Grenouille stood bent over her and sucked in the undiluted fragrance of her as it rose from her nape, her hair, from the neckline of her dress. He let it flow into him like a gentle breeze. He had never felt so wonderful. But the girl felt the air turn cool.

She did not see Grenouille. But she was uneasy, sensed a strange chill, the kind one feels when suddenly overcome with some long discarded fear. She felt as if a cold draft had risen up behind her, as if someone had opened a door leading into a vast, cold cellar. And she laid the paring knife aside, pulled her arms to her chest, and turned around.

She was so frozen with terror at the sight of him

49

that he had plenty of time to put his hands to her throat. She did not attempt to cry out, did not budge, did not make the least motion to defend herself. He, in turn, did not look at her, did not see her delicate, freckled face, her red lips, her large sparkling green eyes, keeping his eyes closed tight as he strangled her, for he had only one concern—not to lose the least trace of her scent.

When she was dead he laid her on the ground among the plum pits, tore off her dress, and the stream of scent became a flood that inundated him with its fragrance. He thrust his face to her skin and swept his flared nostrils across her, from belly to breast, to neck, over her face and hair, and back to her belly, down to her genitals, to her thighs and white legs. He smelled her over from head to toe, he gathered up the last fragments of her scent under her chin, in her navel, and in the wrinkles inside her elbow.

And after he had smelled the last faded scent of her, he crouched beside her for a while, collecting himself, for he was brimful with her. He did not want to spill a drop of her scent. First he must seal up his innermost compartments. Then he stood up and blew out the candle.

Meanwhile people were starting home, singing and hurrahing their way up the rue de Seine. Grenouille smelled his way down the dark alley and out onto the rue des Petits Augustins, which lay parallel to the rue de Seine and led to the river. A little while later, the dead girl was discovered. A hue and cry arose. Torches were lit. The watch arrived. Grenouille had long since gained the other bank.

That night, his closet seemed to him a palace, and his plank bed a four-poster. Never before in his life had he known what happiness was. He knew at most some very rare states of numbed contentment. But now he was quivering with happiness and could not sleep for pure bliss. It was as if he had been born a second time; no, not a second time, the first time, for until now he had merely existed like an animal with a most nebulous self-awareness. But after today, he felt as if he finally knew who he really was: nothing less than a genius. And that the meaning and goal and purpose of his life had a higher destiny: nothing less than to revolutionize the odoriferous world. And that he alone in all the world possessed the means to carry it off: namely, his exquisite nose, his phenomenal memory, and, most important, the master scent taken from that girl in the rue des Marais. Contained within it was the magic formula for everything that could make a scent, a perfume, great: delicacy, power, stability, variety, and terrifying, irresistible beauty. He had found the compass for his future life. And like all gifted abominations, for whom some external event makes straight the way down into the chaotic vortex of their souls, Grenouille never again departed from what he believed was the direction fate had pointed him. It was clear to him now why he had clung to life so tenaciously, so savagely. He must become a creator of scents. And not just an average one. But, rather, the greatest perfumer of all time.

And during that same night, at first awake and then in his dreams, he inspected the vast rubble of his memory. He examined the millions and millions of building blocks of odor and arranged them systematically: good with good, bad with bad, fine with fine, coarse with coarse, fetid with fetid, ambrosial with ambrosial. In the course of the next week, this system grew ever more refined, the catalog of odors ever more comprehensive and differentiated, the hierarchy ever clearer. And soon he could begin to erect the first carefully planned structures of odor: houses, walls, stairways, towers, cellars, rooms, secret chambers . . . an inner fortress built of the most magnificent odors, that each day grew larger, that each day grew more beautiful and more perfectly framed.

A murder had been the start of this splendor—if he was at all aware of the fact, it was a matter of total indifference to him. Already he could no longer recall how the girl from the rue des Marais had looked, not her face, not her body. He had preserved the best part of her and made it his own: the principle of her scent.

❧ *Nine* ❧

THERE WERE a baker's dozen of perfumers in Paris in those days. Six of them resided on the right bank, six on the left, and one exactly in the middle, that is, on the Pont-au-Change, which connected the right bank with the Ile de la Cité. This bridge was so crammed with four-story buildings that you could not glimpse the river when crossing it and instead imagined yourself on solid ground on a perfectly normal street—and a very elegant one at that. Indeed, the Pont-au-Change was considered one of the finest business addresses in the city. The most renowned shops were to be found here; here were the goldsmiths, the cabinetmakers, the best wigmakers and pursemakers, the manufacturers of the finest lingerie and stockings, the picture framers, the merchants for riding boots, the embroiderers of epaulets, the molders of gold buttons, and the bankers. And here as well stood the business and residence of the perfumer and glover Giuseppe Baldini. Above his display window was stretched a sumptuous green-lacquered baldachin, next to which hung Baldini's coat of arms, all in gold: a golden flacon, from which grew a bouquet of

53

golden flowers. And before the door lay a red carpet, also bearing the Baldini coat of arms embroidered in gold. When you opened the door, Persian chimes rang out, and two silver herons began spewing violet-scented toilet water from their beaks into a gold-plated vessel, which in turn was shaped like the flacon in the Baldini coat of arms.

Behind the counter of light boxwood, however, stood Baldini himself, old and stiff as a pillar, in a silver-powdered wig and a blue coat adorned with gold frogs. A cloud of the frangipani with which he sprayed himself every morning enveloped him almost visibly, removing him to a hazy distance. So immobile was he, he looked like part of his own inventory. Only if the chimes rang and the herons spewed—both of which occurred rather seldom—did he suddenly come to life, his body folding up into a small, scrambling figure that scurried out from behind the counter with numerous bows and scrapes, so quickly that the cloud of frangipani could hardly keep up with him, and bade his customer take a seat while he exhibited the most exquisite perfumes and cosmetics.

Baldini had thousands of them. His stock ranged from *essences absolues*—floral oils, tinctures, extracts, secretions, balms, resins, and other drugs in dry, liquid, or waxy form—through diverse pomades, pastes, powders, soaps, creams, sachets, bandolines, brilliantines, mustache waxes, wart removers, and beauty spots, all the way to bath oils, lotions, smelling salts, toilet vinegars, and countless genuine perfumes. But Baldini was not content with these products of classic beauty care. It was his ambition to assemble in his shop everything that had a scent or in some fashion contributed to the production of scent. And so in addition to incense pastilles, incense candles, and cords, there were also sundry spices, from anise seeds to zapota seeds, syrups, cordials, and fruit brandies, wines from Cyprus, Málaga, and Corinth, honeys, coffees, teas, candied and dried fruits, figs, bonbons, chocolates, chestnuts, and even pickled capers, cucumbers, and onions, and marinated tuna. Plus perfumed sealing waxes, stationery, lover's ink scented with attar of roses, writing kits of Spanish leather, penholders of white sandalwood, caskets and chests of cedarwood, potpourris and bowls for flower petals, brass incense holders, crystal flacons and cruses with stoppers of cut amber, scented gloves, handkerchiefs, sewing cushions filled with mace, and musk-sprinkled wallpaper that could fill a room with scent for more than a century.

Naturally there was not room for all these wares in the splendid but small shop that opened onto the street (or onto the bridge), and so for lack of a cellar, storage rooms occupied not just the attic, but the whole second and third floors, as well as almost every room facing the river on the ground floor. The result was that an indescribable chaos of odors reigned in the House of Baldini. However exquisite the quality of individual items—for Baldini bought wares of only highest quality—the blend of odors was almost unbearable, as if each musician in a thousand-member orchestra were playing a different melody at fortissimo. Baldini and his assistants were themselves inured to this chaos, like aging orchestra conductors (all of whom are hard of hearing, of course); and even his wife, who lived on the fourth floor, bitterly defending it against further encroachments by the storage area, hardly noticed the many odors herself anymore. Not so the customer entering Baldini's shop for the first time. The prevailing mishmash of odors hit him like a punch in the face. Depending on his constitution, it might exalt or daze him, but in any case caused such a confusion of senses that he often no longer knew what he had come for. Errand boys forgot their orders.

Belligerent gentlemen grew queasy. And many ladies took a spell, half-hysteric, half-claustrophobic, fainted away, and could be revived only with the most pungent smelling salts of clove oil, ammonia, and camphor.

Under such conditions, it was really not at all astonishing that the Persian chimes at the door of Giuseppe Baldini's shop rang and the silver herons spewed less and less frequently.

❧*Ten*❧

C HÉNIER!" BALDINI cried from behind the counter where for hours he had stood rigid as a pillar, staring at the door. "Put on your wig!" And out from among the kegs of olive oil and dangling Bayonne hams appeared Chénier—Baldini's assistant, somewhat younger than the latter, but already an old man himself—and moved toward the elegant front of the shop. He pulled his wig from his coat pocket and shoved it on his head. "Are you going out, Monsieur Baldini?"

"No," said Baldini. "I shall retire to my study for a few hours, and I do not wish to be disturbed under any circumstances."

"Ah, I see! You are creating a new perfume."

BALDINI: Correct. With which to impregnate a Spanish
             hide for Count Verhamont. He wants something
             like . . . like . . . I think he said it's called Amor
             and Psyche, and comes he says from that . . .
             that bungler in the rue Saint-André-des-Arts,
             that . . . that . . .
CHÉNIER: Pélissier.

BALDINI: Yes. Indeed. That's the bungler's name. Amor and Psyche, by Pélissier.—Do you know it?

CHÉNIER: Yes, yes. I do indeed. You can smell it everywhere these days. Smell it on every street corner. But if you ask me—nothing special! It most certainly can't be compared in any way with what you will create, Monsieur Baldini.

BALDINI: Naturally not.

CHÉNIER: It's a terribly common scent, this Amor and Psyche.

BALDINI: Vulgar?

CHÉNIER: Totally vulgar, like everything from Pélissier. I believe it contains lime oil.

BALDINI: Really? What else?

CHÉNIER: Essence of orange blossom perhaps. And maybe tincture of rosemary. But I can't say for sure.

BALDINI: It's of no consequence at all to me in any case.

CHÉNIER: Naturally not.

BALDINI: I could care less what that bungler Pélissier slops into his perfumes. I certainly would not take my inspiration from him, I assure you.

CHÉNIER: You're absolutely right, monsieur.

BALDINI: As you know, I take my inspiration from no one. As you know, I create my own perfumes.

CHÉNIER: I do know, monsieur.

BALDINI: I alone give birth to them.

CHÉNIER: I know.

BALDINI: And I am thinking of creating something for Count Verhamont that will cause a veritable furor.

CHÉNIER: I am sure it will, Monsieur Baldini.

BALDINI: Take charge of the shop. I need peace and quiet. Don't let anyone near me, Chénier.

And with that, he shuffled away—not at all like a statue, but as befitted his age, bent over, but so far that he looked almost as if he had been beaten—and slowly climbed the stairs to his study on the second floor.

Chénier took his place behind the counter, positioning himself exactly as his master had stood before, and stared fixedly at the door. He knew what would happen in the next few hours: absolutely nothing in the shop, and up in Baldini's study, the usual catastrophe. Baldini would take off his blue coat drenched in frangipani, sit down at his desk, and wait for inspiration. The inspiration would not come. He would then hurry over to the cupboard with its hundreds of vials and start mixing them haphazardly. The mixture would be a failure. He would curse, fling open the window, and pour the stuff into the river. He would try something else, that too would be a failure, he would then rave and rant and throw a howling fit there in the stifling, odor-filled room. At about seven o'clock he would come back down, miserable, trembling and whining, and say: "Chénier, I've lost my nose, I cannot give birth to this perfume, I cannot deliver the Spanish hide to the count, all is lost, I am dead inside, I want to die, Chénier, please, help me die!" And Chénier would suggest that someone be sent to Pélissier's for a bottle of Amor and Psyche, and Baldini would acquiesce, but only on condition that not a soul should learn of his shame. Chénier would swear himself to silence, and tonight they would perfume Count Verhamont's leather with the other man's product. That was how it would be, no doubt of it, and Chénier only wished that the whole circus were already over. Baldini was no longer a great perfumer. At one time, to be sure, in his youth, thirty, forty years ago, he had composed Rose of the South and Baldini's Gallant Bouquet, the two truly great perfumes to which he owed his fortune. But now he was old and exhausted and did not know current fashions and modern tastes, and whenever he did manage to concoct a new perfume of his own, it was some totally old-fashioned, unmarketable stuff that within a year they had to dilute ten to one and peddle as an additive for fountains. What a shame, Chénier thought as he checked the sit of his wig in the mirror—a shame about old Baldini; a shame about his beautiful shop, because he's sure to ruin it; and a shame about me, because by the time he has ruined it, I'll be too old to take it over. . . .

❧ *Eleven* ❦

GIUSEPPE BALDINI had indeed taken off his redolent coat, but only out of long-standing habit. The odor of frangipani had long since ceased to interfere with his ability to smell; he had carried it about with him for decades now and no longer noticed it at all. And although he had closed the doors to his study and asked for peace and quiet, he had not sat down at his desk to ponder and wait for inspiration, for he knew far better than Chénier that inspiration would not strike—after all, it never had before. He was old and exhausted, that much was true, and was no longer a great perfumer; but he knew that he had never in his life been one. He had inherited Rose of the South from his father, and the formula for Baldini's Gallant Bouquet had been bought from a traveling Genoese spice salesman. The rest of his perfumes were old familiar blends. He had never invented anything. He was not an inventor. He was a careful producer of traditional scents; he was like a cook who runs a great kitchen with a routine and good recipes, but has never created a dish of his own. He staged this whole

61

hocus-pocus with a study and experiments and inspiration and hush-hush secrecy only because that was part of the professional image of a perfumer and glover. A perfumer was fifty percent alchemist who created miracles—that's what people wanted. Fine! That his art was a craft like any other, only he knew, and was proud of the fact. He didn't want to be an inventor. He was very suspicious of inventions, for they always meant that some rule would have to be broken. And he had no intention of inventing some new perfume for Count Verhamont. Nor was he about to let Chénier talk him into obtaining Amor and Psyche from Pélissier this evening. He already had some. There it stood on his desk by the window, in a little glass flacon with a cut-glass stopper. He had bought it a couple of days before. Naturally not in person. He couldn't go to Pelissier and buy perfume in person! But through a go-between, who had used yet another go-between. . . . Caution was necessary. Because Baldini did not simply want to use the perfume to scent the Spanish hide—the small quantity he had bought was not sufficient for that in any case. He had something much nastier in mind: he wanted to copy it.

That was, moreover, not forbidden. It was merely highly improper. To create a clandestine imitation of a competitor's perfume and sell it under one's own name was terribly improper. But more improper still was to get caught at it, and that was why Chénier must know nothing about it, for Chénier was a gossip.

How awful, that an honest man should feel compelled to travel such crooked paths! How awful, that the most precious thing a man possesses, his own honor, should be sullied by such shabby dealings! But what was he to do? Count Verhamont was, after all, a customer he dared not lose. He had hardly a single customer left now. He would soon have to start chasing after customers as he had in his twenties at the start of his career, when he had wandered the streets with a boxful of wares dangling at his belly. God knew, he, Giuseppe Baldini—owner of the largest perfume establishment in Paris, with the best possible address—only managed to stay out of the red by making house calls, valise in hand. And that did not suit him at all, for he was well over sixty and hated waiting in cold antechambers and parading *eau des millefleurs* and four thieves' vinegar before old marquises or foisting a migraine salve off on them. Besides which, there was such disgusting competition in those antechambers. There was that upstart Brouet from the rue Dauphine, who claimed to have the greatest line of pomades in Europe; or Calteau from the rue Mauconseil, who had managed to become purveyor to the household of the duchesse d'Artois; or this totally unpredictable Antoine Pélissier from the rue Saint-André-des-Arts, who every season launched a new scent that the whole world went crazy over.

Perfumes like Pélissier's could make a shambles of the whole market. If the rage one year was Hungary water and Baldini had accordingly stocked up on lavender, bergamot, and rosemary to cover the demand—here came Pélissier with his Air de Musc, an ultra-heavy musk scent. Suddenly everyone had to reek like an animal, and Baldini had to rework his rosemary into hair oil and sew the lavender into sachets. If, however, he then bought adequate supplies of musk, civet, and castor for the next year, Pélissier would take a notion to create a perfume called Forest Blossom, which would be an immediate success. And when, after long nights of experiment or costly bribes, Baldini had finally found out the ingredients in Forest

Blossom—Pélissier would trump him again with Turkish Nights or Lisbon Spice or Bouquet de la Cour or some such damn thing. The man was indeed a danger to the whole trade with his reckless creativity. It made you wish for a return to the old rigid guild laws. Made you wish for draconian measures against this nonconformist, against this inflationist of scent. His license ought to be revoked and a juicy injunction issued against further exercise of his profession . . . and, just on principle, the fellow ought to be taught a lesson! Because this Pélissier wasn't even a trained perfumer and glover. His father had been nothing but a vinegar maker, and Pélissier was a vinegar maker too, nothing else. But as a vinegar maker he was entitled to handle spirits, and only because of that had the skunk been able to crash the gates and wreak havoc in the park of the true perfumers. What did people need with a new perfume every season? Was that necessary? The public had been very content before with violet cologne and simple floral bouquets that you changed a soupçon every ten years or so. For thousands of years people had made do with incense and myrrh, a few balms, oils, and dried aromatic herbs. And even once they had learned to use retorts and alembics for distilling herbs, flowers, and woods and stealing the aromatic base of their vapors in the form of volatile oils, to crush seeds and pits and fruit rinds in oak presses, and to extract the scent from petals with carefully filtered oils—even then, the number of perfumes had been modest. In those days a figure like Pélissier would have been an impossibility, for back then just for the production of a simple pomade you needed abilities of which this vinegar mixer could not even dream. You had to be able not merely to distill, but also to act as maker of salves, apothecary, alchemist, and craftsman, merchant, humanist, and gardener all in one. You had to be able to distinguish sheep suet from calves' suet, a victoria violet from a parma violet. You had to be fluent in Latin. You had to know when heliotrope is harvested and when pelargonium blooms, and that the jasmine blossom loses its scent at sunrise. Obviously Pélissier had not the vaguest notion of such matters. He had probably never left Paris, never in all his life seen jasmine in bloom. Not to mention having a whit of the Herculean elbow grease needed to wring a dollop of *concrétion* or a few drops of *essence absolue* from a hundred thousand jasmine blossoms. Probably he knew such things—knew jasmine—only as a bottle of dark brown liquid concentrate that stood in his locked cabinet alongside the many other bottles from which he mixed his fashionable perfumes. No, in the good old days of true craftsmen, a man like this coxcomb Pélissier would never have got his foot in the door. He lacked everything: character, education, serenity, and a sense for the hierarchy within a guild. He owed his few successes at perfumery solely to the discovery made some two hundred years before by that genius Mauritius Frangipani—an Italian, let it be noted!—that odors are soluble in rectified spirit. By mixing his aromatic powder with alcohol and so transferring its odor to a volatile liquid, Frangipani had liberated scent from matter, had etherialized scent, had discovered scent as pure scent; in short, he had created perfume. What a feat! What an epoch-making achievement! Comparable really only to the greatest accomplishments of humankind, like the invention of writing by the Assyrians, Euclidean geometry, the ideas of Plato, or the metamorphosis of grapes into wine by the Greeks. A truly Promethean act!

And yet, just as all great accomplishments of the

spirit cast both shadow and light, offering humankind
vexation and misery along with their benefits, so, too,
Frangipani's marvelous invention had its unfortunate
results. For now that people knew how to bind the
essence of flowers and herbs, woods, resins, and
animal secretions within tinctures and fill them into
bottles, the art of perfumery was slipping bit by bit
from the hands of the masters of the craft and
becoming accessible to mountebanks, at least a moun-
tebank with a passably discerning nose, like this
skunk Pélissier. Without ever bothering to learn how
the marvelous contents of these bottles had come to
be, they could simply follow their olfactory whims
and concoct whatever popped into their heads or
struck the public's momentary fancy.

So much was certain: at age thirty-five, this bastard
Pélissier already possessed a larger fortune than he,
Baldini, had finally accumulated after three genera-
tions of constant hard work. And Pélissier's grew
daily, while his, Baldini's, daily shrank. That sort of
thing would not have been even remotely possible
before! That a reputable craftsman and established
commerçant should have to struggle to exist—that
had begun to happen only in the last few decades! And
only since this hectic mania for novelty had broken
out in every quarter, this desperate desire for action,
this craze of experimentation, this rodomontade in
commerce, in trade, and in the sciences!

Or this insanity about speed. What was the need for
all these new roads being dug up everywhere, and
these new bridges? What purpose did they serve?
What was the advantage of being in Lyon within a
week? Who set any store by that? Whom did it profit?
Or crossing the Atlantic, racing to America in a
month—as if people hadn't got along without that
continent for thousands of years. What had civilized

man lost that he was looking for out there in jungles inhabited by Indians or Negroes. People even traveled to Lapland, up there in the north, with its eternal ice and savages who gorged themselves on raw fish. And now they hoped to discover yet another continent that was said to lie in the South Pacific, wherever that might be. And why all this insanity? Because the others were doing the same, the Spaniards, the damned English, the impertinent Dutch, whom you then had to go out and fight, which you couldn't in the least afford. One of those battleships easily cost a good 300,000 livres, and a single cannon shot would sink it in five minutes, for good and all, paid for with our taxes. The minister of finance had recently demanded one-tenth of all income, and that was simply ruinous, even if you didn't pay Monsieur his tithe. The very attitude was perverse.

Man's misfortune stems from the fact that he does not want to stay in the room where he belongs. Pascal said that. And Pascal was a great man, a Frangipani of the intellect, a real craftsman, so to speak, and no one wants one of those anymore. People read incendiary books now by Huguenots or Englishmen. Or they write tracts or so-called scientific masterpieces that put anything and everything in question. Nothing is supposed to be right anymore, suddenly everything ought to be different. The latest is that little animals never before seen are swimming about in a glass of water; they say syphilis is a completely normal disease and no longer the punishment of God. God didn't make the world in seven days, it's said, but over millions of years, if it was He at all. Savages are human beings like us; we raise our children wrong; and the earth is no longer round like it was, but flat on the top and bottom like a melon—as if that made a damn bit of difference! In every field, people question and bore and scrutinize and pry and dabble with experiments. It's no longer enough for a man to say that something is so or how it is so—everything now has to be proven besides, preferably with witnesses and numbers and one or another of these ridiculous experiments. These Diderots and d'Alemberts and Voltaires and Rousseaus or whatever names these scribblers have—there are even clerics among them and gentlemen of noble birth!—they've finally managed to infect the whole society with their perfidious fidgets, with their sheer delight in discontent and their unwillingness to be satisfied with anything in this world, in short, with the boundless chaos that reigns inside their own heads!

Wherever you looked, hectic excitement. People reading books, even women. Priests dawdling in coffeehouses. And if the police intervened and stuck one of the chief scoundrels in prison, publishers howled and submitted petitions, ladies and gentlemen of the highest rank used their influence, and within a couple of weeks he was set free or allowed out of the country, from where he went right on with his unconscionable pamphleteering. In the salons people chattered about nothing but the orbits of comets and expeditions, about leverage and Newton, about building canals, the circulation of the blood, and the diameter of the earth.

The king himself had had them demonstrate some sort of newfangled nonsense, a kind of artificial thunderstorm they called electricity. With the whole court looking on, some fellow rubbed a bottle, and it gave off a spark, and His Majesty, so it was said, appeared deeply impressed. Unthinkable! that his great-grandfather, the truly great Louis, under whose beneficent reign Baldini had been lucky enough to have lived for many years, would have allowed such a

ridiculous demonstration in his presence. But that
was the temper of the times, and it would all come to
a bad end.

When, without the least embarrassment, people
could brazenly call into question the authority of
God's Church; when they could speak of the
monarchy—equally a creature of God's grace—and
the sacred person of the king himself as if they were
both simply interchangeable items in a catalog of
various forms of government to be selected on a
whim; when they had the ultimate audacity—and
have it they did—to describe God Himself, the Al-
mighty, Very God of Very God, as dispensable and to
maintain in all earnestness that order, morals, and
happiness on this earth could be conceived of without
Him, purely as matters of man's inherent morality
and reason . . . God, good God!—then you needn't
wonder that everything was turned upside down, that
morals had degenerated, and that humankind had
brought down upon itself the judgment of Him whom
it denied. It would come to a bad end. The great
comet of 1681—they had mocked it, calling it a mere
clump of stars, while in truth it was an omen sent by
God in warning, for it had portended, as was clear by
now, a century of decline and disintegration, ending
in the spiritual, political, and religious quagmire
that man had created for himself, into which he
would one day sink and where only glossy, stinking swamp flowers flourished, like Pélissier himself!

Baldini stood at the window, an old man, and gazed
malevolently at the sun angled above the river. Barges
emerged beneath him and slid slowly to the west,
toward the Pont-Neuf and the quay below the galler-
ies of the Louvre. No one poled barges against the
current here, for that they used the channel on the

other side of the island. Here everything flowed away
from you—the empty and the heavily laden ships, the
rowboats, and the flat-bottomed punts of the fisher-
men, the dirty brown and the golden-curled water—
everything flowed away, slowly, broadly, and inevitably. And if Baldini looked directly below him, straight
down the wall, it seemed to him as if the flowing water
were sucking the foundations of the bridge with it,
and he grew dizzy.

He had made a mistake buying a house on the
bridge, and a second when he selected one on the
western side. Because constantly before his eyes now
was a river flowing from him; and it was as if he
himself and his house and the wealth he had accumulated over many decades were flowing away like the
river, while he was too old and too weak to oppose the
powerful current. Sometimes when he had business
on the left bank, in the quarter of the Sorbonne or
around Saint-Sulpice, he would not walk across the
island and the Pont-Saint-Michel, but would take
the longer way across the Pont-Neuf, for it was a
bridge without buildings. And then he would stand
at the eastern parapet and gaze up the river, just
for once to see everything flowing toward him;
and for a few moments he basked in the notion
that his life had been turned around, that his
business was prospering, his family thriving, that
women threw themselves at him, that his own life,
instead of dwindling away, was growing and growing.

But then, if he lifted his gaze the least bit, he could
see his own house, tall and spindly and fragile, several
hundred yards away on the Pont-au-Change, and he
saw the window of his study on the second floor and
saw himself standing there at the window, saw himself
looking out at the river and watching the water flow

away, just as now. And then the beautiful dream would vanish, and Baldini would turn away from where he had stood on the Pont-Neuf, more despondent than before—as despondent as he was now, turning away from the window and taking his seat at his desk.

⨳ *Twelve* ⨲

BEFORE HIM stood the flacon with Pélissier's perfume. Glistening golden brown in the sunlight, the liquid was clear, not clouded in the least. It looked totally innocent, like a light tea—and yet contained, in addition to four-fifths alcohol, one-fifth of a mysterious mixture that could set a whole city trembling with excitement. The mixture, moreover, might consist of three or thirty different ingredients, prepared from among countless possibilities in very precise proportions to one another. It was the soul of the perfume—if one could speak of a perfume made by this ice-cold profiteer Pélissier as having a soul—and the task now was to discover its composition.

Baldini blew his nose carefully and pulled down the blind at the window, since direct sunlight was harmful to every artificial scent or refined concentration of odors. He pulled a fresh white lace handkerchief out of a desk drawer and unfolded it. Then, holding his head far back and pinching his nostrils together, he opened the flacon with a gentle turn of the stopper. He did not want, for God's sake, to get a premature olfactory sensation directly from the bottle. Perfume must be smelled in its efflorescent, gaseous state, never as a concentrate. He sprinkled a few drops onto the handkerchief, waved it in the air to drive off the alcohol, and then held it to his nose. In three short, jerky tugs, he snatched up the scent as if it were a powder, immediately blew it out again, fanned himself, took another sniff in waltz time, and finally drew one long, deep breath, which he then exhaled slowly with several pauses, as if letting it slide down a long, gently sloping staircase. He tossed the handkerchief onto his desk and fell back into his armchair.

The perfume was disgustingly good. That miserable Pélissier was unfortunately a virtuoso. A master, to heaven's shame, even if he had never learned one thing a thousand times over! Baldini wished he had created it himself, this Amor and Psyche. There was nothing common about it. An absolute classic—full and harmonious. And for all that, fascinatingly new. It was fresh, but not frenetic. It was floral, without being unctuous. It possessed depth, a splendid, abiding, voluptuous, rich brown depth—and yet was not in the least excessive or bombastic.

Baldini stood up almost in reverence and held the handkerchief under his nose once again. "Wonderful, wonderful . . ." he murmured, sniffing greedily. "It has a cheerful character, it's charming, it's like a melody, puts you in a good mood at once. . . . What nonsense, a good mood!" And he flung the handkerchief back onto his desk in anger, turned away, and walked to the farthest corner of the room, as if ashamed of his enthusiasm.

Ridiculous! Letting himself be swept up in such eulogies—"like a melody, cheerful, wonderful, good mood." How idiotic. Childishly idiotic. A moment's impression. An old weakness. A matter of temperament. Most likely his Italian blood. Judge not as long as you're smelling! That is rule number one, Baldini, you muttonhead! Smell when you're smelling and judge after you have smelled! Amor and Psyche is not half bad as a perfume. A thoroughly successful product. A cleverly managed bit of concocting. If not to say conjuring. And you could expect nothing but conjuring from a man like Pélissier. Of course a fellow like Pélissier would not manufacture some hackneyed perfume. The scoundrel conjured with complete mastery of his art, confusing your sense of smell with its perfect harmony. In the classical arts of scent, the man was a wolf in sheep's clothing. In short, he was a monster with talent. And what was worse, a perverter of the true faith.

But you, Baldini, are not going to be fooled. You were surprised for a moment by your first impression of this concoction. But do you know how it will smell an hour from now when its volatile ingredients have fled and the central structure emerges? Or how it will smell this evening when all that is still perceptible are the heavy, dark components that now lie in odorous twilight beneath a veil of flowers? Wait and see, Baldini!

The second rule is: perfume lives in time; it has its youth, its maturity, and its old age. And only if it gives off a scent equally pleasant at all three different stages of its life, can it be called successful. How often have we not discovered that a mixture that smelled delightfully fresh when first tested, after a brief interval was more like rotten fruit, and finally reeked of nothing but the pure civet we had used too much of. Utmost caution with the civet! One drop too much brings catastrophe. An old source of error. Who knows—perhaps Pélissier got carried away with the civet. Perhaps by this evening all that's left of his ambitious Amor and Psyche will be just a whiff of cat piss. We shall see.

We shall smell it. Just as a sharp ax can split a log

into tiny splinters, our nose will fragment every detail of this perfume. And then it will be only too apparent that this ostensibly magical scent was created by the most ordinary, familiar methods. We, Baldini, perfumer, shall catch Pélissier, the vinegar man, at his tricks. We shall rip the mask from his ugly face and show the innovator just what the old craft is capable of. We'll scrupulously imitate his mixture, his fashionable perfume. It will be born anew in our hands, so perfectly copied that the humbug himself won't be able to tell it from his own. No! That's not enough! We shall improve on it! We'll show up his mistakes and rinse them away, and then rub his nose in it. You're a bungler, Pélissier! An old stinker is what you are! An upstart in the craft of perfumery, and nothing more.

And now to work, Baldini! Sharpen your nose and smell without sentimentality! Dissect the scent by the rules of the art! You must have the formula by this evening!

And he made a dive for his desk, grabbing paper, ink, and a fresh handkerchief, laid it all out properly, and began his analysis. The procedure was this: to dip the handkerchief in perfume, pass it rapidly under his nose, and extract from the fleeting cloud of scent one or another of its ingredients without being significantly distracted by the complex blending of its other parts; then, holding the handkerchief at the end of his outstretched arm, to jot down the name of the ingredient he had discovered, and repeat the process at once, letting the handkerchief flit by his nose, snatching at the next fragment of scent, and so on. . . .

❧ *Thirteen* ❧

HE WORKED WITHOUT pause for two hours—with increasingly hectic movements, increasingly slipshod scribblings of his pen on the paper, and increasingly large doses of perfume sprinkled onto his handkerchief and held to his nose.

He could hardly smell anything now, the volatile substances he was inhaling had long since drugged him; he could no longer recognize what he thought had been established beyond doubt at the start of his analysis. He knew that it was pointless to continue smelling. He would never ascertain the ingredients of this newfangled perfume, certainly not today, nor tomorrow either, when his nose would have recovered, God willing. He had never learned fractionary smelling. Dissecting scents, fragmenting a unity, whether well or not-so-well blended, into its simple components was a wretched, loathsome business. It did not interest him. He did not want to continue.

But his hand automatically kept on making the dainty motion, practiced a thousand times over, of dunking the handkerchief, shaking it out, and whisking it rapidly past his face, and with each whisk he

76

automatically snapped up a portion of scent-drenched air, only to let it out again with the proper exhalations and pauses. Until finally his own nose liberated him from the torture, swelling in allergic reaction till it was stopped up as tight as if plugged with wax. He could not smell a thing now, could hardly breathe. It was as if a bad cold had soldered his nose shut; little tears gathered in the corners of his eyes. Thank God in heaven! Now he could quit in good conscience. He had done his duty, to the best of his abilities, according to all the rules of the art, and was, as so often before, defeated. *Ultra posse nemo obligatur.* Closing time. Tomorrow morning he would send off to Pélissier's for a large bottle of Amor and Psyche and use it to scent the Spanish hide for Count Verhamont, as per order. And after that he would take his valise, full of old-fashioned soaps, scent bags, pomades, and sachets and make his rounds among the salons of doddering countesses. And one day the last doddering countess would be dead, and with her his last customer. By then he would himself be doddering and would have to sell his business, to Pélissier or another one of these upstart merchants—perhaps he would get a few thousand livres for it. And he would pack one or two bags and go off to Italy with his old wife, if she was not dead herself by then. And if he survived the trip, he would buy a little house in the country near Messina where things were cheap. And there in bitterest poverty he, Giuseppe Baldini, once the greatest perfumer of Paris, would die—whenever God willed it. And that was well and good.

He stoppered the flacon, laid down his pen, and wiped the drenched handkerchief across his forehead one last time. He could sense the cooling effect of the evaporating alcohol, but nothing else. Then the sun went down.

Baldini stood up. He opened the jalousie and his

body was bathed to the knees in the sunset, caught fire like a burnt-out torch glimmering low. He saw the deep red rim of the sun behind the Louvre and the softer fire across the slate roofs of the city. On the river shining like gold below him, the ships had disappeared. And a wind must have come up, for gusts were serrating the surface, and it glittered now here, now there, moving ever closer, as if a giant hand were scattering millions of louis d'or over the water. For a moment it seemed the direction of the river had changed: it was flowing toward Baldini, a shimmering flood of pure gold.

Baldini's eyes were moist and sad. He stood there motionless for a long time gazing at the splendid scene. Then, suddenly, he flung both window casements wide and pitched the flacon with Pélissier's perfume away in a high arc. He saw it splash and rend the glittering carpet of water for an instant.

Fresh air streamed into the room. Baldini gulped for breath and noticed that the swelling in his nose was subsiding. Then he closed the window. At almost the same moment, night fell, very suddenly. The view of a glistening golden city and river turned into a rigid, ashen gray silhouette. Inside the room, all at once it was dark. Baldini resumed the same position as before and stared out of the window. "I shall not send anyone to Pélissier's in the morning," he said, grasping the back of his armchair with both hands. "I shall not do it. And I shall not make my tour of the salons either. Instead, I shall go to the notary tomorrow morning and sell my house and my business. That is what I shall do. *E basta!*"

The expression on his face was that of a cheeky young boy, and he suddenly felt very happy. He was once again the old, the young Baldini, as bold and determined as ever to contend with fate—even if contending meant a retreat in this case. And what if it

did! There was nothing else to do. These were stupid
times, and they left him no choice. God gives good
times and bad times, but He does not wish us to
bemoan and bewail the bad times, but to prove
ourselves men. And He had given His sign. That
golden, blood-red mirage of the city had been a
warning: act now, Baldini, before it is too late! Your
house still stands firm, your storage rooms are still
full, you will still be able to get a good price for your
slumping business. The decisions are still in your
hands. To grow old living modestly in Messina had
not been his goal in life, true—but it was more
honorable and pleasing to God than to perish in
splendor in Paris. Let the Brouets, Calteaus, and
Pélissiers have their triumph. Giuseppe Baldini was
clearing out. But he did it unbent and of his own free
will!

He was quite proud of himself now. And his mind
was finally at peace. For the first time in years, there
was an easing in his back of the subordinate's cramp
that had tensed his neck and given an increasingly
obsequious hunch to his shoulders. And he stood up
straight without strain, relaxed and free and pleased
with himself. His breath passed lightly through his
nose. He could clearly smell the scent of Amor and
Psyche that reigned in the room, but he did not let it
affect him anymore. Baldini had changed his life and
felt wonderful. He would go up to his wife now and
inform her of his decision, and then he would make a
pilgrimage to Notre-Dame and light a candle thank-
ing God for His gracious prompting and for having
endowed him, Giuseppe Baldini, with such unbelievable strength of character.

With almost youthful élan, he plopped his wig onto
his bald head, slipped into his blue coat, grabbed the
candlestick from the desk, and left his study. He had
just lit the tallow candle in the stairwell to light his

PERFUME

way up to his living quarters when he heard a doorbell
ring on the ground floor. It was not the Persian chimes
at the shop door, but the shrill ring of the servants'
entrance, a repulsive sound that had always annoyed
him. He had often made up his mind to have the thing
removed and replaced with a more pleasant bell, but
then the cost would always seem excessive. The
thought suddenly occurred to him—and he giggled as
it did—that it made no difference now, he would be
selling the obtrusive doorbell along with the house.
Let his successor deal with the vexation!

The bell rang shrilly again. He cocked his ear for
sounds below. Apparently Chénier had already left
the shop. And the servant girl seemed not about to
answer it either. So Baldini went downstairs to open
the door himself.

He pulled back the bolt, swung the heavy door
open—and saw nothing. The darkness completely
swallowed the light of his candle. Then, very gradually, he began to make out a figure, a child or a
half-grown boy carrying something over his arm.

"What do you want?"

"I'm from Maître Grimal, I'm delivering the goatskins," said the figure and stepped closer and held out
to him a stack of hides hanging from his cocked arm.
By the light of his candle, Baldini could now see the
boy's face and his nervous, searching eyes. He carried
himself hunched over. He looked as if he were hiding
behind his own outstretched arm, waiting to be struck
a blow. It was Grenouille.

❧ *Fourteen* ❧

THE GOATSKINS for the Spanish leather! Baldini
remembered now. He had ordered the hides from
Grimal a few days before, the finest, softest goatskin
to be used as a blotter for Count Verhamont's desk,
fifteen francs apiece. But he really did not need them
anymore and could spare the expense. On the other
hand, if he were simply to send the boy back . . . ?
Who knew—it could make a bad impression, people
might begin to talk, rumors might start: Baldini is
getting undependable, Baldini isn't getting any orders, Baldini can't pay his bills . . . and that would
not be good; no, no, because something like that was
likely to lower the selling price of his business. It
would be better to accept these useless goatskins. No
one needed to know ahead of time that Giuseppe
Baldini had changed his life.

"Come in!"

He let the boy inside, and they walked across to the
shop, Baldini leading with the candle, Grenouille
behind him with the hides. It was the first time
Grenouille had ever been in a perfumery, a place in

81

which odors are not accessories but stand unabashedly at the center of interest. Naturally he knew every single perfumery and apothecary in the city, had stood for nights on end at their shop windows, his nose pressed to the cracks of their doors. He knew every single odor handled here and had often merged them in his innermost thoughts to create the most splendid perfumes. So there was nothing new awaiting him. And yet, just as a musically gifted child burns to see an orchestra up close or to climb into the church choir where the organ keyboard lies hidden, Grenouille burned to see a perfumery from the inside; and when he had heard that leather was to be delivered to Baldini, he had done all he could to make sure that he would be the one to deliver it.

And here he stood in Baldini's shop, on the one spot in Paris with the greatest number of professional scents assembled in one small space. He could not see much in the fleeting light of the candle, only brief glimpses of the shadows thrown by the counter with its scales, the two herons above the vessel, an armchair for the customers, the dark cupboards along the walls, the brief flash of bronze utensils and white labels on bottles and crucibles; nor could he smell anything beyond what he could already smell from the street. But he at once felt the seriousness that reigned in these rooms, you might almost call it a holy seriousness, if the word "holy" had held any meaning whatever for Grenouille; for he could feel the cold seriousness, the craftsmanlike sobriety, the staid business sense that adhered to every piece of furniture, every utensil, to tubs, bottles, and pots. And as he walked behind Baldini, in Baldini's shadow—for Baldini did not take the trouble to light his way—he was overcome by the idea that he belonged here and nowhere else, that he would stay here, that from here he would shake the world from its foundations.

The idea was, of course, one of perfectly grotesque immodesty. There was nothing, absolutely nothing, that could justify a stray tanner's helper of dubious origin, without connections or protection, without the least social standing, to hope that he would get so much as a toehold in the most renowned perfume shop in Paris—all the less so, since we know that the decision had been made to dissolve the business. But what had formed in Grenouille's immodest thoughts was not, after all, a matter of hope, but of certainty. He knew that the only reason he would leave this shop would be to fetch his clothes from Grimal's, and then never again. The tick had scented blood. It had been dormant for years, encapsulated, and had waited. Now it let itself drop, for better or for worse, entirely without hope. And that was why he was so certain.

They had crossed through the shop. Baldini opened the back room that faced the river and served partly as a storeroom, partly as a workshop and laboratory where soaps were cooked, pomades stirred, and toilet waters blended in big-bellied bottles. "There!" he said, pointing to a large table in front of the window, "lay them there!"

Grenouille stepped out from Baldini's shadow, laid the leather on the table, but quickly jumped back again, placing himself between Baldini and the door. Baldini stood there for a while. He held the candle to one side to prevent the wax from dripping on the table and stroked the smooth surface of the skins with the back of his fingers. Then he pulled back the top one and ran his hand across the velvety reverse side, rough and yet soft at the same time. They were very good goatskins. Just made for Spanish leather. As they dried they would hardly shrink, and when correctly pared they would become supple again; he could feel that at once just by pressing one between his thumb and index finger. They could be impregnated with scent for five to ten years. They were very, very good hides—perhaps he could make gloves from them, three pairs for himself and three for his wife, for the trip to Messina.

He pulled back his hand. He was touched by the way this worktable looked: everything lay ready, the glass basin for the perfume bath, the glass plate for drying, the mortars for mixing the tincture, pestle and spatula, brush and parer and shears. It was as if these things were only sleeping because it was dark and would come to life in the morning. Should he perhaps take the table with him to Messina? And a few of the tools, only the most important ones . . . ? You could sit and work very nicely at this table. The boards were oak, and legs as well, and it was cross-braced, so that nothing about it could wiggle or wobble, acids couldn't mar it, or oils or slips of a knife—but it would cost a fortune to take it with him to Messina! Even by ship! And therefore it would be sold, the table would be sold tomorrow, and everything that lay on it, under it, and beside it would be sold as well! Because he, Baldini, might have a sentimental heart, but he also had strength of character, and so he would follow through on his decision, as difficult as that was to do; he would give it all up with tears in his eyes, but he would do it nonetheless, because he knew he was right—he had been given a sign.

He turned to go. There at the door stood this little deformed person he had almost forgotten about. "They're fine," Baldini said. "Tell your master that the skins are fine. I'll come by in the next few days and pay for them."

"Yes, sir," said Grenouille, but stood where he was, blocking the way for Baldini, who was ready to leave the workshop. Baldini was somewhat startled, but so unsuspecting that he took the boy's behavior not for insolence but for shyness.

"What is it?" he asked. "Is there something else I can do for you? Well? Speak up!"

Grenouille stood there cowering and gazing at Baldini with a look of apparent timidity, but which in reality came from a cunning intensity.

"I want to work for you, Maître Baldini. Work for you, here in your business."

It was not spoken as a request, but as a demand; nor was it really spoken, but squeezed out, hissed out in reptile fashion. And once again, Baldini misread Grenouille's outrageous self-confidence as boyish awkwardness. He gave him a friendly smile. "You're a tanner's apprentice, my lad," he said. "I have no use for a tanner's apprentice. I have a journeyman already, and I don't need an apprentice."

"You want to make these goatskins smell good, Maître Baldini? You want to make this leather I've brought you smell good, don't you?" Grenouille hissed, as if he had paid not the least attention to Baldini's answer.

"Yes indeed," said Baldini.

"With Amor and Psyche by Pélissier?" Grenouille asked, cowering even more than before.

At that, a wave of mild terror swept through Baldini's body. Not because he asked himself how this lad knew all about it so exactly, but simply because the boy had said the name of the wretched perfume that had defeated his efforts at decoding today.

"How did you ever get the absurd idea that I would use someone else's perfume to . . ."

"You reek of it!" Grenouille hissed. "You have it on your forehead, and in your right coat pocket is a handkerchief soaked with it. It's not very good, this Amor and Psyche, it's bad, there's too much bergamot and too much rosemary and not enough attar of roses."

"Aha!" Baldini said, totally surprised that the con-

PERFUME

versation had veered from the general to the specific.
"What else?"

"Orange blossom, lime, clove, musk, jasmine, alcohol, and something that I don't know the name of,
there, you see, right there! In that bottle!" And he
pointed a finger into the darkness. Baldini held the
candlestick up in that direction, his gaze following the
boy's index finger toward a cupboard and falling upon
a bottle filled with a grayish yellow balm.

"Storax?" he asked.

Grenouille nodded. "Yes. That's in it too. Storax."
And then he squirmed as if doubling up with a cramp
and muttered the word at least a dozen times to
himself: "Storaxstoraxstoraxstorax . . ."

Baldini held his candle up to this lump of humankind wheezing "storax" and thought: Either he is
possessed, or a thieving impostor, or truly gifted. For
it was perfectly possible that the list of ingredients, if
mixed in the right proportions, could result in the
perfume Amor and Psyche—it was, in fact, probable.
Attar of roses, clove, and storax—it was those three
ingredients that he had searched for so desperately
this afternoon. Joining them with the other parts of
the composition—which he believed he had recognized as well—would unite the segments into a pretty,
rounded pastry. It was now only a question of the
exact proportions in which you had to join them. To
find that out, he, Baldini, would have to run experiments for several days, a horrible task, almost worse
than the basic identification of the parts, for it meant
you had to measure and weigh and record and all the
while pay damn close attention, because the least bit
of inattention—a tremble of the pipette, a mistake in
counting drops—could ruin the whole thing. And
every botched attempt was dreadfully expensive.
Every ruined mixture was worth a small fortune. . . .

86

He wanted to test this mannikin, wanted to ask
him about the exact formula for Amor and Psyche. If
he knew it, to the drop and dram, then he was
obviously an impostor who had somehow pinched the
recipe from Pélissier in order to gain access and get a
position with him, Baldini. But if he came close, then
he was a genius of scent and as such provoked
Baldini's professional interest. Not that Baldini
would jeopardize his firm decision to give up his
business! This perfume by Pélissier was itself not the
important thing to him. Even if the fellow could
deliver it to him by the gallon, Baldini would not
dream of scenting Count Verhamont's Spanish hides
with it, but . . . But he had not been a perfumer his
life long, had not concerned himself his life long with
the blending of scents, to have lost all professional
passions from one moment to the next. Right now he
was interested in finding out the formula for this
damned perfume, and beyond that, in studying the
gifts of this mysterious boy, who had parsed a scent
right off his forehead. He wanted to know what was
behind that. He was quite simply curious.

"You have, it appears, a fine nose, young man," he
said, once Grenouille had ceased his wheezings; and
he stepped back into the workshop, carefully setting
the candlestick on the worktable, "without doubt, a
fine nose, but . . ."

"I have the best nose in Paris, Maître Baldini,"
Grenouille interrupted with a rasp. "I know all the
odors in the world, all of them, only I don't know the
names of some of them, but I can learn the names.
The odors that have names, there aren't many of
those, there are only a few thousand. I'll learn them
all, I'll never forget the name of that balm, storax, the
balm is called storax, it's called storax . . ."

"Silence!" shouted Baldini. "Do not interrupt me

when I'm speaking! You are impertinent and insolent. No one knows a thousand odors by name. Even I don't know a thousand of them by name, at best a few hundred, for there aren't more than a few hundred in our business, all the rest aren't odors, they are simply stenches."

During the rather lengthy interruption that had burst from him, Grenouille had almost unfolded his body, had in fact been so excited for the moment that he had flailed both arms in circles to suggest the "all, all of them" that he knew. But at Baldini's reply he collapsed back into himself, like a black toad lurking there motionless on the threshold.

"I have, of course, been aware," Baldini continued, "for some time now that Amor and Psyche consisted of storax, attar of roses, and cloves, plus bergamot and extract of rosemary et cetera. All that is needed to find that out is, as I said, a passably fine nose, and it may well be that God has given you a passably fine nose, as He has many, many other people as well—particularly at your age. A perfumer, however"—and here Baldini raised his index finger and puffed out his chest—"a perfumer, however, needs more than a passably fine nose. He needs an incorruptible, hard-working organ that has been trained to smell for many decades, enabling him to decipher even the most complicated odors by composition and proportion, as well as to create new, unknown mixtures of scent. Such a nose"—and here he tapped his with his finger—"is not something one *has*, young man! It is something one acquires, by perseverance and diligence. Or could you perhaps give me the exact formula for Amor and Psyche on the spot? Well? Could you?"

Grenouille did not answer.

"Could you perhaps give me a rough guess?" Baldini said, bending forward a bit to get a better look at the toad at his door. "Just a rough one, an estimation? Well, speak up, best nose in Paris!"

But Grenouille was silent.

"You see?" said Baldini, equally both satisfied and disappointed; and he straightened up. "You can't do it. Of course you can't. You're one of those people who know whether there is chervil or parsley in the soup at mealtime. That's fine, there's something to be said for that. But that doesn't make you a cook, not by a long shot. Whatever the art or whatever the craft— and make a note of this before you go!—talent means next to nothing, while experience, acquired in humility and with hard work, means everything."

He was reaching for the candlestick on the table, when from the doorway came Grenouille's pinched snarl: "I don't know what a formula is, maître. I don't know that, but otherwise I know everything!"

"A formula is the alpha and omega of every perfume," replied Baldini sternly, for he wanted to end this conversation—now. "It contains scrupulously exact instructions for the proportions needed to mix individual ingredients so that the result is the unmistakable scent one desires. That is a formula. It is the recipe—if that is a word you understand better."

"Formula, formula," rasped Grenouille and grew somewhat larger in the doorway. "I don't need a formula. I have the recipe in my nose. Can I mix it for you, maître, can I mix it, can I?"

"How's that?" cried Baldini in a rather loud voice and held the candle up to the gnome's face. "How would you mix it?"

For the first time, Grenouille did not flinch. "Why, they're all here, all the ones you need, all the scents, they're all here, in this room," he said, pointing again into the darkness. "There's attar of roses! There's orange blossom! That's clove! That's rosemary, there . . . !"

"Certainly they're here!" roared Baldini. "They are all here. But I'm telling you, you blockhead, that is of no use if one does not have the formula!"

". . . There's jasmine! Alcohol there! Bergamot there! Storax there!" Grenouille went on crowing, and at each name he pointed to a different spot in the room, although it was so dark that at best you could surmise the shadows of the cupboards filled with bottles.

"You can see in the dark, can you?" Baldini went on. "You not only have the best nose, but also the keenest eyes in Paris, do you? Now if you have passably good ears, then open them up, because I'm telling you: you are a little swindler. You probably picked up your information at Pélissier's, did some spying, is that it? And now you think you can pull the wool over my eyes, right?"

Grenouille was now standing up, completely unfolded to full size, so to speak, in the doorway, his legs slightly apart, his arms slightly spread, so that he looked like a black spider that had latched onto the threshold and frame. "Give me ten minutes," he said in close to a normal, fluent pattern of speech, "and I will produce for you the perfume Amor and Psyche. Right now, right here in this room. Maître, give me just five minutes!"

"Do you suppose I'd let you slop around here in my laboratory? With essences that are worth a fortune? You?"

"Yes," said Grenouille.

"Bah!" Baldini shouted, exhaling all at once every bit of air he had in him. Then he took a deep breath and a long look at Grenouille the spider, and thought it over. Basically it makes no difference, he thought, because it will all be over tomorrow anyway. I know for a fact that he can't do what he claims he can, can't possibly do it. Why, that would make him greater than the great Frangipani. But why shouldn't I let him demonstrate before my eyes what I know to be true? It is possible that someday in Messina—people do grow very strange in old age and their minds fix on the craziest ideas—I'll get the notion that I had failed to recognize an olfactory genius, a creature upon whom the grace of God had been poured out in superabundance, a wunderkind. . . . It's totally out of the question. Everything my reason tells me says it is out of the question—but miracles do happen, that is certain. So what if, when I lie dying in Messina someday, the thought comes to me there on my deathbed: On that evening, back in Paris, I shut my eyes to a miracle . . . ? That would not be very pleasant, Baldini. Let the fool waste a few drops of attar of roses and musk tincture; you would have wasted them yourself if Pélissier's perfume had still interested you. And what are a few drops—though expensive ones, very, very expensive!—compared to certain knowledge and a peaceful old age?

"Now pay attention!" he said with an affectedly stern voice. "Pay attention! I . . . what is your name, anyway?"

"Grenouille," said Grenouille. "Jean-Baptiste Grenouille."

"Aha," said Baldini. "All right then, now pay attention, Jean-Baptiste Grenouille! I have thought it over. You shall have the opportunity, now, this very moment, to prove your assertion. Your grandiose failure will also be an opportunity for you to learn the virtue of humility, which—although one may pardon the total lack of its development at your tender age—will be an absolute prerequisite for later advancement as a member of your guild and for your standing as a man, a man of honor, a dutiful subject, and a good Christian. I am prepared to teach you this lesson at my own expense. For certain reasons, I am feeling generous this evening, and, who knows, perhaps the recollection of this scene will amuse me one day. But do not suppose that you can dupe me! Giuseppe Baldini's nose is old, but it is still sharp, sharp enough immediately to recognize the slightest difference between your mixture and this product here." And at that he pulled the handkerchief drenched in Amor and Psyche from his pocket and waved it under Grenouille's nose. "Come closer, best nose in Paris! Come here to the table and show me what you can do. But be careful not to drop anything or knock anything over. Don't touch anything yet. Let me provide some light first. We want to have lots of illumination for this little experiment, don't we?"

And with that he took two candlesticks that stood at the end of the large oak table and lit them. He placed all three next to one another along the back, pushed the goatskins to one side, cleared the middle of the table. Then, with a few composed yet rapid motions, he fetched from a small stand the utensils needed for the task—the big-bellied mixing bottle, the glass funnel, the pipette, the small and large measuring glasses —and placed them in proper order on the oaken surface.

Grenouille had meanwhile freed himself from the doorframe. Even while Baldini was making his pompous speech, the stiffness and cunning intensity had fallen away from him. He had heard only the approval, only the "yes," with the inner jubilation of a child that has sulked its way to some permission granted and thumbs its nose at the limitations, conditions, and moral admonitions tied to it. Standing there at his ease and letting the rest of Baldini's oration flow by, he was for the first time more human than animal, because he knew that he had already conquered the man who had yielded to him.

While Baldini was still fussing with his candlesticks

at the table, Grenouille had already slipped off into the darkness of the laboratory with its cupboards full of precious essences, oils, and tinctures, and following his sure-scenting nose, grabbed each of the necessary bottles from the shelves. There were nine altogether: essence of orange blossom, lime oil, attars of rose and clove, extracts of jasmine, bergamot, and rosemary, musk tincture, and storax balm, all quickly plucked down and set at the ready on the edge of the table. The last item he lugged over was a demijohn full of high-proof rectified spirit. Then he placed himself behind Baldini—who was still arranging his mixing utensils with deliberate pedantry, moving this glass back a bit, that one over more to one side, so that everything would be in its old accustomed order and displayed to its best advantage in the candlelight—and waited, quivering with impatience, for the old man to get out of the way and make room for him.

"There!" Baldini said at last, stepping aside. "I've lined up everything you'll require for—let us graciously call it—your 'experiment.' Don't break anything, don't spill anything. Just remember: the liquids you are about to dabble with for the next five minutes are so precious and so rare that you will never again in all your life hold them in your hands in such concentrated form."

"How much of it shall I make for you, maître?" Grenouille asked.

"Make what . . . ?" said Baldini, who had not yet finished his speech.

"How much of the perfume?" rasped Grenouille. "How much of it do you want? Shall I fill this big bottle here to the rim?" And he pointed to a mixing bottle that held a gallon at the very least.

"No, you shall not!" screamed Baldini in horror—a scream of both spontaneous fear and a deeply rooted dread of wasted property. Embarrassed at what his scream had revealed, he followed it up by roaring, "And don't interrupt me when I am speaking, either!" Then in a calm voice tinged with irony, he continued, "Why would we need a gallon of a perfume that neither of us thinks much of? Half a beakerful will do, really. But since such small quantities are difficult to measure, I'll allow you to start with a third of a mixing bottle."

"Good," said Grenouille. "I'm going to fill a third of this bottle with Amor and Psyche. But, Maître Baldini, I will do it in my own way. I don't know if it will be how a craftsman would do it. I don't know how that's done. But I will do it my own way."

"As you please," said Baldini, who knew that in this business there was no "your way" or "my way," but one and only one way, which consisted of knowing the formula and, using the appropriate calculations for the quantity one desired, creating a precisely measured concentrate of the various essences, which then had to be volatilized into a true perfume by mixing it in a precise ratio with alcohol—usually varying between one-to-ten and one-to-twenty. There was no other way, that he knew. And therefore what he was now called upon to witness—first with derisive hauteur, then with dismay, and finally with helpless astonishment—seemed to him nothing less than a miracle. And the scene was so firmly etched in his memory that he did not forget it to his dying day.

❧ *Fifteen* ❧

THE LITTLE MAN named Grenouille first uncorked the demijohn of alcohol. Heaving the heavy vessel up gave him difficulty. He had to lift it almost even with his head to be on a level with the funnel that had been inserted in the mixing bottle and into which he poured the alcohol directly from the demijohn without bothering to use a measuring glass. Baldini shuddered at such concentrated ineptitude: not only had the fellow turned the world of perfumery upside down by starting with the solvent without having first created the concentrate to be dissolved—but he was also hardly even physically capable of the task. He was shaking with exertion, and Baldini was waiting at any moment for the heavy demijohn to come crashing down and smash everything on the table to pieces. The candles, he thought, for God's sake, the candles! There's going to be an explosion, he'll burn my house down . . . ! And he was about to lunge for the demijohn and grab it out of the madman's hands when Grenouille set it down himself, getting it back on the floor all in one piece, and stoppered it. A clear, light liquid swayed in the bottle—not a drop spilled. For a few moments Grenouille panted for breath, but with a look of contentment on his face as if the hardest part of the job were behind him. And indeed, what happened now proceeded with such speed that Baldini could hardly follow it with his eyes, let alone keep track of the order in which it occurred or make even partial sense of the procedure.

Grenouille grabbed apparently at random from the row of essences in their flacons, pulled out the glass stoppers, held the contents under his nose for an instant, splashed a bit of one bottle, dribbled a drop or two of another, poured a dash of a third into the funnel, and so on. Pipette, test tube, measuring glass, spoons and rods—all the utensils that allow the perfumer to control the complicated process of mixing—Grenouille did not so much as touch a single one of them. It was as if he were just playing, splashing and swishing like a child busy cooking up some ghastly brew of water, grass, and mud, which he then asserts to be soup. Yes, like a child, thought Baldini; all at once he looks like a child, despite his ungainly hands, despite his scarred, pockmarked face and his bulbous old-man's nose. I took him to be older than he is; but now he seems much younger to me; he looks as if he were three or four; looks just like one of those unapproachable, incomprehensible, willful little prehuman creatures, who in their ostensible innocence think only of themselves, who want to subordinate the whole world to their despotic will, and would do it, too, if one let them pursue their megalomaniacal ways and did not apply the strictest pedagogical principles to guide them to a disciplined, self-controlled, fully human existence. There was just such a fanatical child trapped inside this young man, standing at the table with eyes aglow, having forgotten everything around him, apparently no longer aware that there was anything else in the laboratory but himself and these bottles that he tipped into the funnel with nimble awkwardness to mix up an insane brew that he would confidently swear—and would truly believe!—to be the exquisite perfume Amor and Psyche. Baldini shuddered as he watched the fellow bustling about in the candlelight, so shockingly absurd and so shockingly self-confident. In the old days—so he thought, and for a moment he felt as sad and miserable and furious as he had that afternoon while gazing out onto the city glowing ruddy in the twilight—in the old days people like that simply did not exist; he was an entirely new specimen of the race, one that could arise only in exhausted, dissipated times like these. . . . But he was about to be taught his lesson, the impertinent boy. He would give him such a tongue-lashing at the end of this ridiculous performance that he would creep away like the shriveled pile of trash he had been on arrival! Vermin! One dared not get involved with anyone at all these days, the world was simply teeming with absurd vermin!

Baldini was so busy with his personal exasperation and disgust at the age that he did not really comprehend what was intended when Grenouille suddenly stoppered up all the flacons, pulled the funnel out of the mixing bottle, grabbed the neck of the bottle with his right hand, capped it with the palm of his left, and shook it vigorously. Only when the bottle had been spun through the air several times, its precious contents sloshing back and forth like lemonade between belly and neck, did Baldini let loose a shout of rage and horror. "Stop it!" he screeched. "That's enough! Stop it this moment! *Basta!* Put that bottle back on the table and don't touch anything else, do you understand, nothing else! I must have been crazy to listen to your asinine gibberish. The way you handle these things, your crudity, your primitive lack of judgment, demonstrate to me that you are a bungler, a barbaric bungler, and a beastly, cheeky, snot-nosed brat besides. You wouldn't make a good lemonade mixer, not even a good licorice-water vendor, let alone a perfumer! Just be glad, be grateful and content that your master lets you slop around in tanning fluids! Do not dare it ever again, do you hear me? Do not dare ever again to set a foot across the threshold of a perfumer's shop!"

Thus spoke Baldini. And even as he spoke, the air around him was saturated with the odor of Amor and Psyche. Odors have a power of persuasion stronger than that of words, appearances, emotions, or will. The persuasive power of an odor cannot be fended off, it enters into us like breath into our lungs, it fills us up, imbues us totally. There is no remedy for it.

Grenouille had set down the bottle, removing his perfume-moistened hand from its neck and wiping it on his shirttail. One, two steps back—and the clumsy way he hunched his body together under Baldini's tirade sent enough waves rolling out into the room to spread the newly created scent in all directions. Nothing more was needed. True, Baldini ranted on, railed and cursed, but with every breath his outward show of rage found less and less inner nourishment. He sensed he had been proved wrong, which was why his peroration could only soar to empty pathos. And when he fell silent, had been silent for a good while, he had no need of Grenouille's remark: "It's all done." He knew that already.

But nevertheless, although in the meantime air heavy with Amor and Psyche was undulating all about him, he stepped up to the old oak table to make his test. He pulled a fresh snowy white lace handkerchief from his coat pocket, the left one, unfolded it and sprinkled it with a few drops that he extracted from the mixing bottle with the long pipette. He waved the handkerchief with outstretched arm to aerate it and then pulled it past his nose with the delicate, well-practiced motion, soaking up its scent. Letting it out again in little puffs, he sat down on a stool. Where before his face had been bright red with erupting anger, all at once he had grown pale. "Incredible," he murmured softly to himself, "by God—incredible." And he pressed the handkerchief to his nose again and again and sniffed and shook his head and muttered, "Incredible." It was Amor and Psyche, beyond the shadow of a doubt Amor and Psyche, that despicable, ingenious blend of scents, so exactly copied that not even Pélissier himself would have been able to distinguish it from his own product. "Incredible . . ."

Small and ashen, the great Baldini sat on his stool, looking ridiculous with handkerchief in hand, pressing it to his nose like an old maid with the sniffles. By now he was totally speechless. He didn't even say "incredible" anymore, but nodding gently and staring at the contents of the mixing bottle, could only let out a monotone "Hmm, hmm, hmm . . . hmm, hmm, hmm . . . hmm, hmm, hmm." After a while, Grenouille approached, stepping up to the table soundlessly as a shadow.

"It's not a good perfume," he said. "It's been put together very bad, this perfume has."

"Hmm, hmm, hmm," said Baldini, and Grenouille continued, "If you'll let me, maître, I'll make it better. Give me a minute and I'll make a proper perfume out of it!"

"Hmm, hmm, hmm," said Baldini and nodded. Not in consent, but because he was in such a helplessly apathetic condition that he would have said "hmm, hmm, hmm," and nodded to anything. And he went on nodding and murmuring "hmm, hmm, hmm," and made no effort to interfere as Grenouille began to mix away a second time, pouring the alcohol from the demijohn into the mixing bottle a second time (right on top of the perfume already in it), tipping the contents of flacons a second time in apparently random order and quantity into the funnel. Only at the end of the procedure—Grenouille did not shake the bottle this time, but swirled it about gently like a brandy glass, perhaps in deference to Baldini's delicacy, perhaps because the contents seemed more precious to him this time—only then, as the liquid whirled about in the bottle, did Baldini awaken from his numbed state and stand up, the handkerchief still pressed to his nose, of course, as if he were arming himself against yet another attack upon his most private self.

"It's all done, maître," Grenouille said. "Now it's a really good scent."

"Yes, yes, fine, fine," Baldini replied and waved him off with his free hand.

"Don't you want to test it?" Grenouille gurgled on. "Don't you want to, maître? Aren't you going to test it?"

"Later. I'm not in the mood to test it at the moment . . . have other things on my mind. Go now! Come on!"

And he picked up one of the candlesticks and passed through the door into the shop. Grenouille followed him. They entered the narrow hallway that led to the servants' entrance. The old man shuffled up to the doorway, pulled back the bolt, and opened the door. He stepped aside to let the lad out.

"Can't I come to work for you, maître, can't I?" Grenouille asked, standing on the threshold, hunched over again, the lurking look returning to his eye.

"I don't know," said Baldini. "I shall think about it. Go."

And then Grenouille had vanished, gone in a split second, swallowed up by the darkness. Baldini stood there and stared into the night. In his right hand he held the candlestick, in his left the handkerchief, like someone with a nosebleed, but in fact he was simply frightened. He quickly bolted the door. Then he took the protective handkerchief from his face, shoved it into his pocket, and walked back through the shop to his laboratory.

The scent was so heavenly fine that tears welled into Baldini's eyes. He did not have to test it, he simply stood at the table in front of the mixing bottle and breathed. The perfume was glorious. It was to Amor and Psyche as a symphony is to the scratching of a lonely violin. And it was more. Baldini closed his eyes and watched as the most sublime memories were awakened within him. He saw himself as a young man walking through the evening gardens of Naples; he saw himself lying in the arms of a woman with dark curly hair and saw the silhouette of a bouquet of roses on the windowsill as the night wind passed by; he heard the random song of birds and the distant music from a harbor tavern; he heard whisperings at his ear, he heard I-love-you and felt his hair ruffle with bliss, now! now at this very moment! He forced open his eyes and groaned with pleasure. This perfume was not like any perfume known before. It was not a scent that made things smell better, not some sachet, some toiletry. It was something completely new, capable of creating a whole world, a magical, rich world, and in an instant you forgot all the loathsomeness around you and felt so rich, so at ease, so free, so fine. . . .

The hairs that had ruffled up on Baldini's arm fell back again, and a befuddling peace took possession of his soul. He picked up the leather, the goat leather lying at the table's edge, and a knife, and trimmed away. Then he laid the pieces in the glass basin and poured the new perfume over them. He fixed a pane of glass over the basin, divided the rest of the perfume between two small bottles, applied labels to them, and wrote the words Nuit Napolitaine on them. Then he extinguished the candles and left.

Once upstairs, he said nothing to his wife while they ate. Above all, he said nothing about the solemn decision he had arrived at that afternoon. And his wife said nothing either, for she noticed that he was in good spirits, and that was enough for her. Nor did he walk over to Notre-Dame to thank God for his strength of character. Indeed, that night he forgot, for the first time ever, to say his evening prayers.

❧ *Sixteen* ❦

THE NEXT MORNING he went straight to Grimal.
First he paid for his goat leather, paid in full, without
a grumble or the least bit of haggling. And then he
invited Grimal to the Tour d'Argent for a bottle of
white wine and negotiations concerning the purchase
of Grenouille, his apprentice. It goes without saying
that he did not reveal to him the why's and where-
fore's of this purchase. He told some story about how
he had a large order for scented leather and to fill it he
needed unskilled help. He required a lad of few needs,
who would do simple tasks, cutting leather and so
forth. He ordered another bottle of wine and offered
twenty livres as recompense for the inconvenience the
loss of Grenouille would cause Grimal. Twenty livres
was an enormous sum. Grimal immediately took him
up on it. They walked to the tannery, where, strangely
enough, Grenouille was waiting with his bundle already packed. Baldini paid the twenty livres and took
him along at once, well aware that he had just made
the best deal of his life.

Grimal, who for his part was convinced that he had
just made the best deal of his life, returned to the Tour

d'Argent, there drank two more bottles of wine, moved over to the Lion d'Or on the other bank around noon, and got so rip-roaring drunk there that when he decided to go back to the Tour d'Argent late that night, he got the rue Geoffroi L'Anier confused with the rue des Nonaindières, and instead of coming out directly onto the Pont-Marie as he had intended, he was brought by ill fortune to the Quai des Ormes, where he splashed lengthwise and face first into the water like a soft mattress. He was dead in an instant. The river, however, needed considerable time to drag him out from the shallows, past the barges moored there, into the stronger main current, and not until the early morning hours did Grimal the tanner—or, better, his soaked carcass—float briskly downriver toward the west.

As he passed the Pont-au-Change, soundlessly, without bumping against the bridge piers, sixty feet directly overhead Jean-Baptiste Grenouille was going to bed. A bunk had been set up for him in a back corner of Baldini's laboratory, and he was now about to take possession of it—while his former employer floated down the cold Seine, all four limbs extended. Grenouille rolled himself up into a little ball like a tick. As he fell off to sleep, he sank deeper and deeper into himself, leading the triumphant entry into his innermost fortress, where he dreamed of an odoriferous victory banquet, a gigantic orgy with clouds of incense and fogs of myrrh, held in his own honor.

❧ *Seventeen* ❧

WITH THE acquisition of Grenouille, the House of Giuseppe Baldini began its ascent to national, indeed European renown. The Persian chimes never stopped ringing, the herons never stopped spewing in the shop on the Pont-au-Change.

The very first evening, Grenouille had to prepare a large demijohn full of Nuit Napolitaine, of which over eighty flacons were sold in the course of the next day. The fame of the scent spread like wildfire. Chénier's eyes grew glassy from the moneys paid and his back ached from all the deep bows he had to make, for only persons of high, indeed highest, rank—or at least the servants of persons of high and highest rank—appeared. One day the door was flung back so hard it rattled, in stepped the footman of Count d'Argenson and shouted, as only footmen can shout, that he wanted five bottles of this new scent. Chénier was still shaking with awe fifteen minutes later, for Count d'Argenson was commissary and war minister to His Majesty and the most powerful man in Paris.

While Chénier was subjected to the onslaught of customers in the shop, Baldini had shut himself up in his laboratory with his new apprentice. He justified this state of affairs to Chénier with a fantastic theory that he called "division of labor and increased productivity." For years, he explained, he had patiently watched while Pélissier and his ilk—despisers of the ancient craft, all—had enticed his customers away and made a shambles of his business. His forbearance was now at an end. He was accepting their challenge and striking back at these cheeky parvenus, and, what was more, with their own weapons. Every season, every month, if necessary every week, he would play trumps, a new perfume. And what perfumes they would be! He would draw fully upon his creative talents. And for that it was necessary that he—assisted only by an unskilled helper—would be solely and exclusively responsible for the production of scents, while Chénier would devote himself exclusively to their sale. By using such modern methods, they would open a new chapter in the history of perfumery, sweeping aside their competitors and growing incomparably rich—yes, he had consciously and explicitly said "they," because he intended to allow his old and trusted journeyman to share a given percentage of these incomparable riches.

Only a few days before, Chénier would have regarded such talk as a sign of his master's incipient senility. "Ready for the Charité," he would have thought. "It won't be long now before he lays down the pestle for good." But now he was not thinking at all. He didn't get around to it, he simply had too much to do. He had so much to do that come evening he was so exhausted he could hardly empty out the cashbox and siphon off his cut. Not in his wildest dreams would he have doubted that things were not on the up and up, though Baldini emerged from his laboratory almost daily with some new scent.

And what scents they were! Not just perfumes of

high, indeed highest, quality, but also crèmes and powders, soaps, hair tonics, toilet waters, oils. . . . Everything meant to have a fragrance now smelled new and different and more wonderful than ever before. And as if bewitched, the public pounced upon everything, absolutely everything—even the new-fangled scented hair ribbons that Baldini created one day on a curious whim. And price was no object. Everything that Baldini produced was a success. And the successes were so overwhelming that Chénier accepted them as natural phenomena and did not seek out their cause. That perhaps the new apprentice, that awkward gnome, who was housed like a dog in the laboratory and whom one saw sometimes when the master stepped out, standing in the background wiping off glasses and cleaning mortars—that this cipher of a man might be implicated in the fabulous blossoming of their business, Chénier would not have believed had he been told it.

Naturally, the gnome had everything to do with it. Everything Baldini brought into the shop and left for Chénier to sell was only a fraction of what Grenouille was mixing up behind closed doors. Baldini couldn't smell fast enough to keep up with him. At times he was truly tormented by having to choose among the glories that Grenouille produced. This sorcerer's apprentice could have provided recipes for all the perfumers of France without once repeating himself, without once producing something of inferior or even average quality. As a matter of fact, he could *not* have provided them with recipes, i.e., formulas, for at first Grenouille still composed his scents in the totally chaotic and unprofessional manner familiar to Baldini, mixing his ingredients impromptu and in apparent wild confusion. Unable to control the crazy business, but hoping at least to get some notion of it, Baldini demanded one day that Grenouille use scales, measuring glasses, and the pipette when preparing his mixtures, even though he considered them unnecessary; further, he was to get used to regarding the alcohol not as another fragrance, but as a solvent to be added at the end; and, for God's sake, he would simply have to go about things more slowly, at an easier and slower pace, as befitted a craftsman.

Grenouille did it. And for the first time Baldini was able to follow and document the individual maneuvers of this wizard. Paper and pen in hand, constantly urging a slower pace, he sat next to Grenouille and jotted down how many drams of this, how many level measures of that, how many drops of some other ingredient wandered into the mixing bottles. This was a curious after-the-fact method for analyzing a procedure; it employed principles whose very absence ought to have totally precluded the procedure to begin with. But by employing this method, Baldini finally managed to obtain such synthetic formulas. *How* it was that Grenouille could mix his perfumes without the formulas was still a puzzle, or better, a miracle, to Baldini, but at least he had captured this miracle in a formula, satisfying in part his thirst for rules and order and preventing the total collapse of his perfumer's universe.

In due time he ferreted out the recipes for all the perfumes Grenouille had thus far invented, and finally he forbade him to create new scents unless he, Baldini, was present with pen and paper to observe the process with Argus eyes and to document it step by step. In his fastidious, prickly hand, he copied his notes, soon consisting of dozens of formulas, into two different little books—one he locked in his fireproof safe and the other he always carried with him, even sleeping with it at night. That reassured him. For now, should he wish, he could himself perform Grenouille's miracles, which had on first encounter so profoundly shaken him. He believed that by collecting these written formulas, he could exorcise the terrible creative chaos erupting from his apprentice. Also the fact that he no longer merely stood there staring stupidly, but was able to participate in the creative process by observing and recording it, had a soothing effect on Baldini and strengthened his self-confidence. After a while he even came to believe that he made a not insignificant contribution to the success of these sublime scents. And when he had once entered them in his little books and entrusted them to his safe and his bosom, he no longer doubted that they were now his and his alone.

But Grenouille, too, profited from the disciplined procedures Baldini had forced upon him. He was not dependent on them himself. He never had to look up an old formula to reconstruct a perfume weeks or months later, for he never forgot an odor. But by using the obligatory measuring glasses and scales, he learned the language of perfumery, and he sensed instinctively that the knowledge of this language could be of service to him. After a few weeks Grenouille had mastered not only the names of all the odors in Baldini's laboratory, but he was also able to record the formulas for his perfumes on his own and, vice versa, to convert other people's formulas and instructions into perfumes and other scented products. And not merely that! Once he had learned to express his fragrant ideas in drops and drams, he no longer even needed the intermediate step of experimentation. When Baldini assigned him a new scent, whether for a handkerchief cologne, a sachet, or a face paint, Grenouille no longer reached for flacons and powders, but instead simply sat himself down at the table and wrote the formula straight out. He had learned to extend the journey from his mental notion of a scent to the finished perfume by way of writing down the formula. For him it was a detour. In the world's eyes—that is, in Baldini's—it was progress. Grenouille's miracles remained the same. But the recipes he now supplied along with them removed the terror, and that was for the best. The more Grenouille mastered the tricks and tools of the trade, the better he was able to express himself in the conventional language of perfumery—and the less his master feared and suspected him. While still regarding him as a person with exceptional olfactory gifts, Baldini no longer considered him a second Frangipani or, worse, some weird wizard—and that was fine with Grenouille. The regulations of the craft functioned as a welcome disguise. He virtually lulled Baldini to sleep with his exemplary procedures, weighing ingredients, swirling the mixing bottles, sprinkling the test handkerchief. He could shake it out almost as delicately, pass it beneath his nose almost as elegantly as his master. And from time to time, at well-spaced intervals, he would make mistakes that could not fail to capture Baldini's notice: forgetting to filter, setting the scales wrong, fixing the percentage of ambergris tincture in the formula ridiculously high. And took his scoldings for the mistakes, correcting them then most conscientiously. Thus he managed to lull Baldini into the illusion that ultimately this was all perfectly normal. He was not out to cheat the old man after all. He truly wanted to learn from him. Not how to mix perfumes, not how to compose a scent correctly, not that of course! In that sphere, there was no one in the world who could have taught him anything, nor would the ingredients available in Baldini's shop have even begun to suffice for his notions about how to realize a truly great perfume. The scents he could create at Baldini's were playthings compared with those he carried within him and that he intended to create one day. But for that, he knew, two indispensable prerequisites must be met. The first was the cloak of middle-class respectability, the status of a journeyman at the least, under the protection of which he could indulge his true passions and follow his true goals unimpeded. The second was the knowledge of the craft itself, the way in which scents were produced, isolated, concentrated, preserved, and thus first made available for higher ends. For Grenouille did indeed possess the best nose in the world, both analytical and visionary, but he did not yet have the ability to make those scents realities.

❧ Eighteen ❧

And so he gladly let himself be instructed in the arts of making soap from lard, sewing gloves of chamois, mixing powders from wheat flour and almond bran and pulverized violet roots. Rolled scented candles made of charcoal, saltpeter, and sandalwood chips. Pressed Oriental pastilles of myrrh, benzoin, and powdered amber. Kneaded frankincense, shellac, vetiver, and cinnamon into balls of incense. Sifted and spatulated *poudre impériale* out of crushed rose petals, lavender flowers, cascarilla bark. Stirred face paints, whites and vein blues, and molded greasy sticks of carmine for the lips. Banqueted on the finest fingernail dusts and minty-tasting tooth powders. Mixed liquids for curling periwigs and wart drops for corns, bleaches to remove freckles from the complexion and nightshade extract for the eyes, Spanish fly for the gentlemen and hygienic vinegars for the ladies. . . . Grenouille learned to produce all such *eaux* and powders, toilet and beauty preparations, plus teas and herbal blends, liqueurs, marinades, and such—in short, he learned, with no particular inter-

112

est but without complaint and with success, everything that Baldini knew to teach him from his great store of traditional lore.

He was an especially eager pupil, however, whenever Baldini instructed him in the production of tinctures, extracts, and essences. He was indefatigable when it came to crushing bitter almond seeds in the screw press or mashing musk pods or mincing dollops of gray, greasy ambergris with a chopping knife or grating violet roots and digesting the shavings in the finest alcohol. He learned how to use a separatory funnel that could draw off the purest oil of crushed lemon rinds from the milky dregs. He learned to dry herbs and flowers on grates placed in warm, shady spots and to preserve what was once rustling foliage in wax-sealed crocks and caskets. He learned the art of rinsing pomades and producing, filtering, concentrating, clarifying, and rectifying infusions.

To be sure, Baldini's laboratory was not a proper place for fabricating floral or herbal oils on a grand scale. It would have been hard to find sufficient quantities of fresh plants in Paris for that. But from time to time, when they could get cheap, fresh rosemary, sage, mint, or anise seeds at the market, or a shipment of valerian roots, caraway seeds, nutmegs, or dried clove blossoms had come in, then the alchemist in Baldini would stir, and he would bring out the large alembic, a copper distilling vessel, atop it a head for condensing liquids—a so-called moor's head alembic, he proudly announced—which he had used forty years before for distilling lavender out on the open southern exposures of Liguria's slopes and on the heights of the Lubéron. And while Grenouille chopped up what was to be distilled, Baldini hectically bustled about heating a brick-lined hearth—because speed was the alpha and omega of this procedure—and placed on it a copper kettle, the bottom well covered with water. He threw in the minced plants, quickly closed off the double-walled moor's head, and connected two hoses to allow water to pass in and out. This clever mechanism for cooling the water, he explained, was something he had added on later, since out in the field, of course, one had simply used bellowed air for cooling. And then he blew on the fire.

Slowly the kettle came to a boil. And after a while, the distillate started to flow out of the moor's head's third tap into a Florentine flask that Baldini had set below it—at first hesitantly, drop by drop, then in a threadlike stream. It looked rather unimpressive to begin with, like some thin, murky soup. Bit by bit, however—especially after the first flask had been replaced with a second and set aside to settle—the brew separated into two different liquids: below, the floral or herbal fluid; above, a thick floating layer of oil. If one carefully poured off the fluid—which had only the lightest aroma—through the lower spout of the Florentine flask, the pure oil was left behind—the essence, the heavily scented principle of the plant.

Grenouille was fascinated by the process. If ever anything in his life had kindled his enthusiasm— granted, not a visible enthusiasm but a hidden one, an excitement burning with a cold flame—then it was this procedure for using fire, water, steam, and a cunning apparatus to snatch the scented soul from matter. That scented soul, that ethereal oil, was in fact the best thing about matter, the only reason for his interest in it. The rest of the stupid stuff—the blossoms, leaves, rind, fruit, color, beauty, vitality, and all those other useless qualities—were of no concern to him. They were mere husk and ballast, to be disposed of.

From time to time, when the distillate had grown watery and clear, they took the alembic from the fire, opened it, and shook out the cooked muck. It looked as flabby and pale as soggy straw, like the bleached bones of little birds, like vegetables that had been boiled too long, insipid and stringy, pulpy, hardly still recognizable for what it was, disgustingly cadaverous, and almost totally robbed of its own odor. They threw it out the window into the river. Then they fed the alembic with new, fresh plants, poured in more water, and set it back on the hearth. And once again the kettle began to simmer, and again the lifeblood of the plants dripped into the Florentine flask. This often went on all night long. Baldini watched the hearth, Grenouille kept an eye on the flasks; there was nothing else to do while waiting for the next batch.

They sat on footstools by the fire, under the spell of the rotund flacon—both spellbound, if for very different reasons. Baldini enjoyed the blaze of the fire and the flickering red of the flames and the copper, he loved the crackling of the burning wood, the gurgle of the alembic, for it was like the old days. You could lose yourself in it! He fetched a bottle of wine from the shop, for the heat made him thirsty, and drinking wine was like the old days too. And then he began to tell stories, from the old days, endless stories. About the War of the Spanish Succession, when his own participation against the Austrians had had a decisive influence on the outcome; about the Camisards, together with whom he had haunted the Cévennes; about the daughter of a Huguenot in the Esterel, who, intoxicated by the scent of lavender, had complied with his wishes; about a forest fire that he had damn near started and which would then have probably set the entire Provence ablaze, as sure as there was a heaven and hell, for a biting mistral had been blow-

115

ing; and over and over he told about distilling out in the open fields, at night, by moonlight, accompanied by wine and the screech of cicadas, and about a lavender oil that he had created, one so refined and powerful that you could have weighed it out in silver; about his apprentice years in Genoa, about his journeyman years in the city of Grasse, where there were as many perfumers as shoemakers, some of them so rich they lived like princes, in magnificent houses with shaded gardens and terraces and wainscoted dining rooms where they feasted with porcelain and golden cutlery, and so on. . . .

Such were the stories Baldini told while he drank his wine and his cheeks grew ruddy from the wine and the blazing fire and from his own enthusiastic storytelling. Grenouille, however, who sat back more in the shadows, did not listen to him at all. He did not care about old tales, he was interested in one thing only: this new process. He stared uninterruptedly at the tube at the top of the alembic out of which the distillate ran in a thin stream. And as he stared at it, he imagined that he himself was such an alembic, simmering away inside just like this one, out of which there likewise gushed a distillate, but a better, a newer, an unfamiliar distillate of those exquisite plants that he tended within him, that blossomed there, their bouquet unknown to anyone but himself, and that with their unique scent he could turn the world into a fragrant Garden of Eden, where life would be relatively bearable for him, olfactorily speaking. To be a giant alembic, flooding the whole world with a distillate of his own making, that was the daydream to which Grenouille gave himself up.

But while Baldini, inflamed by the wine, continued to tell ever more extravagant tales of the old days and got more and more tangled up in his uninhibited enthusiasms, Grenouille soon abandoned his bizarre fantasy. For the moment he banished from his thoughts the notion of a giant alembic, and instead he pondered how he might make use of his newly gained knowledge for more immediate goals.

❧ *Nineteen* ❧

IT WASN'T LONG before he had become a specialist in the field of distillation. He discovered—and his nose was of more use in the discovery than Baldini's rules and regulations—that the heat of the fire played a significant role in the quality of the distillate. Every plant, every flower, every sort of wood, and every oil-yielding seed demanded a special procedure. Sometimes you had to build up the hottest head of steam, sometimes you just left it at a moderate boil, and some flowers yielded their best only if you let them steep over the lowest possible flame.

It was much the same with their preparation. Mint and lavender could be distilled by the bunch. Other things needed to be carefully culled, plucked, chopped, grated, crushed, or even made into pulp before they were placed in the copper kettle. Many things simply could not be distilled at all—which irritated Grenouille no end.

Having observed what a sure hand Grenouille had with the apparatus, Baldini had given him free rein with the alembic, and Grenouille had taken full advantage of that freedom. While still mixing per-

fumes and producing other scented and herbal products during the day, he occupied himself at night
exclusively with the art of distillation. His plan was to
create entirely new basic odors, and with them to
produce at least some of the scents that he bore within
him. At first he had some small successes. He succeeded in producing oils from nettles and from cress
seeds, toilet water from the fresh bark of elderberry
and from yew sprigs. These distillates were only
barely similar to the odor of their ingredients, but
they were at least interesting enough to be processed
further. But there were also substances with which the
procedure was a complete failure. Grenouille tried for
instance to distill the odor of glass, the clayey, cool
odor of smooth glass, something a normal human
being cannot perceive at all. He got himself both
window glass and bottle glass and tried working with
it in large pieces, in fragments, in slivers, as dust—all
without the least success. He distilled brass, porcelain, and leather, grain and gravel. He distilled plain
dirt. Blood and wood and fresh fish. His own hair. By
the end he was distilling plain water, water from the
Seine, the distinctive odor of which seemed to him
worth preserving. He believed that with the help of an
alembic he could rob these materials of their characteristic odors, just as could be done with thyme,
lavender, and caraway seeds. He did not know that
distillation is nothing more than a process for separat-
ing complex substances into volatile and less volatile
components and that it is only useful in the art of
perfumery because the volatile essential oils of certain
plants can be extracted from the rest, which have little
or no scent. For substances lacking these essential
oils, the distilling process is, of course, wholly pointless. For us moderns, educated in the natural sciences,
that is immediately apparent. For Grenouille, however, this knowledge was won painfully after a long

chain of disappointing experiments. For months on end he sat at his alembic night after night and tried every way he could think to distill radically new scents, scents that had never existed on earth before in a concentrated form. But except for a few ridiculous plant oils, nothing came of it. From the immeasurably deep and fecund well of his imagination, he had pumped not a single drop of a real and fragrant essence, had been unable to realize a single atom of his olfactory preoccupations.

When it finally became clear to him that he had failed, he halted his experiments and fell mortally ill.

❧ *Twenty* ❧

HE CAME DOWN with a high fever, which for the first few days was accompanied by heavy sweats, but which later, as if the pores of his skin were no longer enough, produced countless pustules. Grenouille's body was strewn with reddish blisters. Many of them popped open, releasing their watery contents, only to fill up again. Others grew into true boils, swelling up thick and red and then erupting like craters, spewing viscous pus and blood streaked with yellow. In time, with his hundreds of ulcerous wounds, Grenouille looked like some martyr stoned from the inside out.

Naturally, Baldini was worried. It would have been very unpleasant for him to lose his precious apprentice just at the moment when he was planning to expand his business beyond the borders of the capital and out across the whole country. For increasingly, orders for those innovative scents that Paris was so crazy about were indeed coming not only from the provinces but also from foreign courts. And Baldini was playing with the idea of taking care of these orders by opening a branch in the Faubourg Saint-Antoine, virtually a small factory, where the fastest-moving scents could be mixed in quantity and bottled in quantity in smart little flacons, packed by smart little girls, and sent off to Holland, England, and Greater Germany. Such an enterprise was not exactly legal for a master perfumer residing in Paris, but Baldini had recently gained the protection of people in high places; his exquisite scents had done that for him—not just with the commissary, but also with such important personages as the gentleman holding the franchise for the Paris customs office or with a member of the Conseil Royal des Finances and promoter of flourishing commercial undertakings like Monsieur Feydeau de Brou. The latter had even held out the prospect of a royal patent, truly the best thing that one could hope for, a kind of carte blanche for circumventing all civil and professional restrictions; it meant the end of all business worries and the guarantee of secure, permanent, unassailable prosperity.

And Baldini was carrying yet another plan under his heart, his favorite plan, a sort of counterplan to the factory in the Faubourg Saint-Antoine, where his wares, though not mass produced, would be made available to anyone. But for a selected number of well-placed, highly placed clients, he wanted to create —or rather, have created—personal perfumes that would fit only their wearer, like tailored clothes, would be used only by the wearer, and would bear his or her illustrious name. He could imagine a Parfum de la Marquise de Cernay, a Parfum de la Maréchale de Villar, a Parfum du Duc d'Aiguillon, and so on. He dreamed of a Parfum de Madame la Marquise de Pompadour, even of a Parfum de Sa Majesté le Roi, in a flacon of costliest cut agate with a holder of chased gold and, hidden on the inside of the base, the engraved words: "Giuseppe Baldini, Parfumeur." The king's name and his own, both on the same object. To such glorious heights had Baldini's ideas risen! And now Grenouille had fallen ill. Even though Grimal, might he rest in peace, had sworn there had never been anything wrong with him, that he could stand up to anything, had even put the black plague behind him. And here he had gone and fallen ill, mortally ill. What if he were to die? Dreadful! For with him would die the splendid plans for the factory, for the smart little girls, for the patent, and for the king's perfume.

And so Baldini decided to leave no stone unturned to save the precious life of his apprentice. He ordered him moved from his bunk in the laboratory to a clean bed on the top floor. He had the bed made up with damask. He helped bear the patient up the narrow stairway with his own hands, despite his unutterable disgust at the pustules and festering boils. He ordered his wife to heat chicken broth and wine. He sent for the most renowned physician in the neighborhood, a certain Procope, who demanded payment in advance —twenty francs!—before he would even bother to pay a call.

The doctor came, lifted up the sheet with dainty fingers, took one look at Grenouille's body, which truly looked as if it had been riddled with hundreds of bullets, and left the room without ever having opened the bag that his attendant always carried about with him. The case, so began his report to Baldini, was quite clear. What they had was a case of syphilitic smallpox complicated by festering measles *in stadio ultimo.* No treatment was called for, since a lancet for bleeding could not be properly inserted into the deteriorating body, which was more like a corpse than a living organism. And although the characteristic pestilential stench associated with the illness was not yet noticeable—an amazing detail and a minor curiosity from a strictly scientific point of view—there could not be the least doubt of the patient's demise within the next forty-eight hours, as surely as his name was Doctor Procope. Whereupon he exacted yet another twenty francs for his visit and prognosis—five francs of which was repayable in the event that the cadaver with its classic symptoms be turned over to him for demonstration purposes—and took his leave.

Baldini was beside himself. He wailed and lamented in despair. He bit his fingers, raging at his fate. Once again, just before reaching his goal, his grand, very grand plans had been thwarted. At one point it had been Pélissier and his cohorts with their wealth of ingenuity. Now it was this boy with his inexhaustible store of new scents, this scruffy brat who was worth more than his weight in gold, who had decided now of all times to come down with syphilitic smallpox and festering measles *in stadio ultimo.* Now of all times! Why not two years from now? Why not one? By then he could have been plundered like a silver mine, like a golden ass. He could have gone ahead and died next year. But no! He was dying now, God damn it all, within forty-eight hours!

For a brief moment, Baldini considered the idea of a pilgrimage to Notre-Dame, where he would light a candle and plead with the Mother of God for Grenouille's recovery. But he let the idea go, for matters were too pressing. He ran to get paper and ink, then shooed his wife out of the sickroom. He was going to keep watch himself. Then he sat down in a chair next to the bed, his notepaper on his knees, the pen wet with ink in his hand, and attempted to take Grenouille's perfumatory confession. For God's sake, he dare not slip away without a word, taking along the treasures he bore inside him. Would he not in these last hours leave a testament behind in faithful hands, so that posterity would not be deprived of the finest scents of all time? He, Baldini, would faithfully administer that testament, the canon of formulas for the

124

most sublime scents ever smelled, would bring them all to full bloom. He would attach undying fame to Grenouille's name, he would—yes, he swore it by everything holy—lay the best of these scents at the feet of the king, in an agate flacon with gold chasing and the engraved dedication, "From Jean-Baptiste Grenouille, Parfumeur, Paris." So spoke—or better, whispered—Baldini into Grenouille's ear, unremittingly beseeching, pleading, wheedling.

But all in vain. Grenouille yielded nothing except watery secretions and bloody pus. He lay there mute in his damask and parted with those disgusting fluids, but not with his treasures, his knowledge, not a single formula for a scent. Baldini would have loved to throttle him, to club him to death, to beat those precious secrets out of that moribund body, had there been any chance of success . . . and had it not so blatantly contradicted his understanding of a Christian's love for his neighbor.

And so he went on purring and crooning in his sweetest tones, and coddled his patient, and—though only after a great and dreadful struggle with himself—dabbed with cooling presses the patient's sweat-drenched brow and the seething volcanoes of his wounds, and spooned wine into his mouth hoping to bring words to his tongue—all night long and all in vain. In the gray of dawn he gave up. He fell exhausted into an armchair at the far end of the room and stared—no longer in rage, really, but merely yielding to silent resignation—at Grenouille's small dying body there in the bed, whom he could neither save nor rob, nor from whom he could salvage anything else for himself, whose death he could only witness numbly, like a captain watching his ship sink, taking all his wealth with it into the depths.

And then all at once the lips of the dying boy opened, and in a voice whose clarity and firmness betrayed next to nothing of his immediate demise, he spoke. "Tell me, maître, are there other ways to extract the scent from things besides pressing or distilling?"

Baldini, believing the voice had come either from his own imagination or from the next world, answered mechanically, "Yes, there are."

"What are they?" came the question from the bed. And Baldini opened his tired eyes wide. Grenouille lay there motionless among his pillows. Had the corpse spoken?

"What are they?" came the renewed question, and this time Baldini noticed Grenouille's lips move. It's over now, he thought. This is the end, this is the madness of fever or the throes of death. And he stood up, went over to the bed, and bent down to the sick man. His eyes were open and he gazed up at Baldini with the same strange, lurking look that he had fixed on him at their first meeting.

"What are they?" he asked.

Baldini felt a pang in his heart—he could not deny a dying man his last wish—and he answered, "There are three other ways, my son: *enfleurage à chaud, enfleurage à froid,* and *enfleurage à l'huile.* They are superior to distillation in several ways, and they are used for extraction of the finest of all scents: jasmine, rose, and orange blossom."

"Where?" asked Grenouille.

"In the south," answered Baldini. "Above all, in the town of Grasse."

"Good," said Grenouille.

And with that he closed his eyes. Baldini raised himself up slowly. He was very depressed. He gathered up his notepaper, on which he had not written a single line, and blew out the candle. Day was dawning already. He was dead tired. One ought to have sent for a priest, he thought. Then he made a hasty sign of the cross with his right hand and left the room.

Grenouille was, however, anything but dead. He was only sleeping very soundly, deep in dreams, sucking fluids back into himself. The blisters were already beginning to dry out on his skin, the craters of pus had begun to drain, the wounds to close. Within a week he was well again.

❧ *Twenty-one* ❧

H E WOULD HAVE loved then and there to have left for the south, where he could learn the new techniques the old man had told him about. But that was of course out of the question. He was after all only an apprentice, which was to say, a nobody. Strictly speaking, as Baldini explained to him—this was after he had overcome his initial joy at Grenouille's resurrection—strictly speaking, he was less than a nobody, since a proper apprentice needed to be of faultless, i.e., legitimate, birth, to have relatives of like standing, and to have a certificate of indenture, all of which he lacked. Should he, Baldini, nevertheless decide one day to help him obtain his journeyman's papers, that would happen only on the basis of Grenouille's uncommon talents, his faultless behavior from then on, and his, Baldini's, own infinite kindness, which, though it often had worked to his own disadvantage, he would forever be incapable of denying.

To be sure, it was a good while before he fulfilled his promised kindness—just a little under three years.

During that period and with Grenouille's help, Baldini realized his high-flying dreams. He built his factory in the Faubourg Saint-Antoine, succeeded in his scheme for exclusive perfumes at court, received a royal patent. His fine fragrances were sold as far off as St. Petersburg, as Palermo, as Copenhagen. A musk-impregnated item was much sought after even in Constantinople, where God knows they already had enough scents of their own. Baldini's perfumes could be smelled both in elegant offices in the City of London and at the court in Parma, both in the royal castle at Warsaw and in the little *Schloss* of the Graf von und zu Lippe-Detmold. Having reconciled himself to living out his old age in bitterest poverty near Messina, Baldini was now at age seventy indisputably Europe's greatest perfumer and one of the richest citizens of Paris.

Early in 1756—he had in the meantime acquired the adjoining building on the Pont-au-Change, using it solely as a residence, since the old building was literally stuffed full to the attic with scents and spices—he informed Grenouille that he was now willing to release him, but only on three conditions: first, he would not be allowed to produce in the future any of the perfumes now under Baldini's roof, nor sell their formulas to third parties; second, he must leave Paris and not enter it again for as long as Baldini lived; and third, he was to keep the first two conditions absolutely secret. He was to swear to this by all the saints, by the poor soul of his mother, and on his own honor.

Grenouille, who neither had any honor nor believed in any saints or in the poor soul of his mother, swore it. He would have sworn to anything. He would have accepted any condition Baldini might propose, because he wanted those silly journeyman's papers

129

that would make it possible for him to live an inconspicuous life, to travel undisturbed, and to find a job.
Everything else was unimportant to him. What kinds
of conditions were those anyway! Not enter Paris
again? What did he need Paris for! He knew it down
to its last stinking cranny, he took it with him
wherever he went, he had owned Paris for years now.
—Not produce any of Baldini's top-selling perfumes,
not pass on their formulas? As if he could not invent a
thousand others, just as good and better, if and when
he wanted to! But he didn't want to at all. He did not
in the least intend to go into competition with Baldini
or any other bourgeois perfumer. He was not out to
make his fortune with his art; he didn't even want to
live from it if he could find another way to make a
living. He wanted to empty himself of his innermost
being, of nothing less than his innermost being, which
he considered more wonderful than anything else the
world had to offer. And thus Baldini's conditions were
no conditions at all for Grenouille.

He set out in spring, early one May morning.
Baldini had given him a little rucksack, a second shirt,
two pairs of stockings, a large sausage, a horse blanket, and twenty-five francs. That was far more than he
was obligated to do, Baldini said, considering that
Grenouille had not paid a sol in fees for the profound
education he had received. He was obligated to pay
two francs in severance, nothing more. But he could
no more deny his own kindly nature than he could the
deep sympathy for Jean-Baptiste that had accumulated in his heart over the years. He wished him good
luck in his wanderings and once more warned him
emphatically not to forget his oath. With that, he
accompanied him to the servants' entrance where he
had once taken him in, and let him go.

He did not give him his hand—his sympathy did
not reach quite that far. He had never shaken hands

with him. He had always avoided so much as touching him, out of some kind of sanctimonious loathing, as if there were some danger that he could be infected or contaminated. He merely said a brief *adieu*. And Grenouille nodded and ducked away and was gone. The street was empty.

≽ *Twenty-two* ≼

BALDINI WATCHED him go, shuffling across the bridge to the island, small, bent, bearing his rucksack like a hunchback, looking from the rear like an old man. On the far side, where the street made a dogleg at the Palais de Parlement, he lost sight of him and felt extraordinarily relieved.

He had never liked the fellow, he could finally admit it now. He had never felt comfortable the whole time he had housed him under his roof and plundered him. He felt much as would a man of spotless character who does some forbidden deed for the first time, who uses underhanded tricks when playing a game. True, the risk that people might catch up with him was small, and the prospects for success had been great; but even so, his nervousness and bad conscience were equally great. In fact, not a day had passed in all those years when he had not been haunted by the notion that in some way or other he would have to pay for having got involved with this man. If only it turns out all right!—that had been his continual anxious prayer—if only I succeed in reaping the profits of this risky adventure without having

to pay the piper! If only I succeed! What I'm doing is
not right, but God will wink His eye, I'm sure He will.
He has punished me hard enough many times in my
life, without any cause, so that it would only be just if
He would deal graciously with me this time. What
wrong have I actually done, if there has been a wrong?
At the worst I am operating somewhat outside guild
regulations by exploiting the wonderful gifts of an
unskilled worker and passing off his talent as my own.
At the worst I have wandered a bit off the traditional
path of guild virtue. At the very worst, I am doing
today what I myself have condemned in the past. Is
that a crime? Other people cheat their whole life long.
I have only fudged a bit for a couple of years. And
only because of purest chance I was given a once-in-a-
lifetime opportunity. Perhaps it wasn't chance at all,
but God Himself, who sent this wizard into my house,
to make up for the days of humiliation by Pélissier
and his cohorts. Perhaps Divine Providence was not
directing Himself at me at all, but *against* Pélissier!
That's perfectly possible! How else would God have
been able to punish Pélissier other than by raising me
up? My luck, in that case, would be the means by
which divine justice has achieved its end, and thus I
not only ought to accept it, but I must, without shame
and without the least regret. . . .

Such had often been Baldini's thoughts during
those years—mornings, when he would descend the
narrow stairway to his shop, evenings, when he would
climb back up carrying the contents of the cashbox to
count the heavy gold and silver coins, and at night,
when he lay next to the snoring bag of bones that was
his wife, unable to sleep for fear of his good fortune.

But now such sinister thoughts had come to an end.
His uncanny guest was gone and would never return
again. Yet the riches remained and were secure far
into the future. Baldini laid a hand to his chest and

felt, beneath the cloth of his coat, that little book beside his beating heart. Six hundred formulas were recorded there, more than a whole generation of perfumers would ever be able to implement. If he were to lose everything today, he could, with just this wonderful little book, be a rich man once again within a year. Truly he could not ask for more!

From the gables of the houses across the way, the morning sun fell golden and warm on his face. Baldini was still looking to the south, down the street in the direction of the Palais de Parlement—it was simply too delightful not to see anything more of Grenouille! —and, washed over by a sense of gratitude, he decided to make that pilgrimage to Notre-Dame today, to cast a gold coin in the alms box, to light three candles, and on his knees to thank his Lord for having heaped such good fortune on him and having spared him from retribution.

But then that same afternoon, just as he was about to head for the church, something absurd happened: a rumor surfaced that the English had declared war on France. That was of itself hardly disquieting. But since Baldini had planned to send a shipment of perfume to London that very day, he postponed his visit to Notre-Dame and instead went into the city to make inquiries and from there to go out to his factory in the Faubourg Saint-Antoine and cancel the shipment to London for the present. That night in bed, just before falling asleep, he had a brilliant idea: in light of the hostilities about to break out over the colonies in the New World, he would launch a perfume under the name of Prestige du Québec, a heroic, resinous scent, whose success—this much was certain —would more than repay him for the loss of business with England. With that sweet thought in his silly old head, relieved and bedded now on its pillow, beneath which the pressure of the little book of formulas was pleasantly palpable, Maître Baldini fell asleep and awoke no more in this life.

For that night a minor catastrophe occurred, which, with appropriate delays, resulted in a royal decree requiring that little by little all the buildings on all the bridges of Paris be torn down. For with no apparent reason, the west side of the Pont-au-Change, between the third and fourth piers, collapsed. Two buildings were hurtled into the river, so completely and suddenly that none of their occupants could be rescued. Fortunately, it was a matter of only two persons, to wit: Giuseppe Baldini and his wife, Teresa. The servants had gone out, either with or without permission. Chénier, who first returned home in the small hours slightly drunk—or rather, intended to return home, since there was no home left—suffered a nervous breakdown. He had sacrificed thirty long years of his life in hopes of being named heir in Baldini's will, for the old man had neither children nor relatives. And now, at one blow, the entire inheritance was gone, everything, house, business, raw materials, laboratory, Baldini himself—indeed even the will, which perhaps might have offered him a chance of becoming owner of the factory.

Nothing was found, not the bodies, not the safe, not the little books with their six hundred formulas. Only one thing remained of Giuseppe Baldini, Europe's greatest perfumer: a very motley odor—of musk, cinnamon, vinegar, lavender, and a thousand other things—that took several weeks to float high above the Seine from Paris to Le Havre.

PART
❧2❧

❧Twenty-three ❦

WHEN THE House of Giuseppe Baldini collapsed, Grenouille was already on the road to Orléans. He had left the enveloping haze of the city behind him; and with every step he took away from it, the air about him grew clearer, purer, and cleaner. It became thinner as well. Gone was the roiling of hundreds, thousands of changing odors at every pace; instead, the few odors there were—of the sandy road, meadows, the earth, plants, water—extended across the countryside in long currents, swelling slowly, abating slowly, with hardly an abrupt break.

For Grenouille, this simplicity seemed a deliverance. The leisurely odors coaxed his nose. For the first time in his life he did not have to prepare himself to catch the scent of something new, unexpected, hostile —or to lose a pleasant smell—with every breath. For the first time he could almost breathe freely, did not constantly have to be on the olfactory lookout. We say "almost," for of course nothing ever passed truly freely through Grenouille's nose. Even when there was not the least reason for it, he was always alert to, always wary of everything that came from outside and

139

had to be let inside. His whole life long, even in those few moments when he had experienced some inkling of satisfaction, contentment, and perhaps even happiness, he had preferred exhaling to inhaling—just as he had begun life not with a hopeful gasp for air but with a bloodcurdling scream. But except for that one proviso, which for him was simply a constitutional limitation, the farther Grenouille got from Paris, the better he felt, the more easily he breathed, the lighter his step, until he even managed sporadically to carry himself erect, so that when seen from a distance he looked almost like an ordinary itinerant journeyman, like a perfectly normal human being.

Most liberating for him was the fact that other people were so far away. More people lived more densely packed in Paris than in any other city in the world. Six, seven hundred thousand people lived in Paris. Its streets and squares teemed with them, and the houses were crammed full of them from cellars to attics. There was hardly a corner of Paris that was not paralyzed with people, not a stone, not a patch of earth that did not reek of humans.

As he began to withdraw from them, it became clear to Grenouille for the first time that for eighteen years their compacted human effluvium had oppressed him like air heavy with an imminent thunderstorm. Until now he had thought that it was the world in general he wanted to squirm away from. But it was not the world, it was the people in it. You could live, so it seemed, in this world, in this world devoid of humanity.

On the third day of his journey he found himself under the influence of the olfactory gravity of Orléans. Long before any visible sign indicated that he was in the vicinity of a city, Grenouille sensed a condensation of human stuff in the air and, reversing his original plan, decided to avoid Orléans. He did not

want to have his newfound respiratory freedom ruined so soon by the sultry climate of humans. He
circled the city in a giant arc, came upon the Loire at
Châteauneuf, and crossed it at Sully. His sausage
lasted that far. He bought himself a new one and,
leaving the river behind, pushed on to the interior.

He now avoided not just cities, but villages as well.
He was almost intoxicated by air that grew ever more
rarefied, ever more devoid of humankind. He would
approach a settlement or some isolated farm only to
get new supplies, buying his bread and disappearing
again into the woods. After a few weeks even those
few travelers he met on out-of-the-way paths proved
too much for him; he could no longer bear the
concentrated odor that appeared punctually with
farmers out to mow the first hay on the meadows. He
nervously skirted every herd of sheep—not because
of the sheep, but to get away from the odor of the
shepherds. He headed straight across country and put
up with mile-long detours whenever he caught the
scent of a troop of riders still several hours distant.
Not because, like other itinerant journeymen and
vagabonds, he feared being stopped and asked for his
papers and then perhaps pressed into military service
—he didn't even know there was a war on—but solely
because he was disgusted by the human smell of the
horsemen. And so it happened quite naturally and as
the result of no particular decision that his plan to
take the fastest road to Grasse gradually faded; the
plan unraveled in freedom, so to speak, as did all his
other plans and intentions. Grenouille no longer
wanted to go somewhere, but only to go away, away
from human beings.

Finally, he traveled only by night. During the day
he crept into thickets, slept under bushes, in under-
brush, in the most inaccessible spots, rolled up in a
ball like an animal, his earthen-colored horse blanket

pulled up over his body and head, his nose wedged in the crook of an elbow so that not the faintest foreign odor could disturb his dreams. He awoke at sunset, sniffed in all directions, and only when he could smell that the last farmer had left his fields and the most daring wanderer had sought shelter from the descending darkness, only when night and its presumed dangers had swept the countryside clean of people, did Grenouille creep out of hiding and set out again on his journey. He did not need light to see by. Even before, when he was traveling by day, he had often closed his eyes for hours on end and merely followed his nose. The gaudy landscape, the dazzling abrupt definition of sight hurt his eyes. He was delighted only by moonlight. Moonlight knew no colors and traced the contours of the terrain only very softly. It covered the land with a dirty gray, strangling life all night long. This world molded in lead, where nothing moved but the wind that fell sometimes like a shadow over the gray forests, and where nothing lived but the scent of the naked earth, was the only world that he accepted, for it was much like the world of his soul.

He headed south. Approximately south—for he did not steer by magnetic compass, but only by the compass of his nose, which sent him skirting every city, every village, every settlement. For weeks he met not a single person. And he might have been able to cradle himself in the soothing belief that he was alone in a world bathed in darkness or the cold light of the moon, had his delicate compass not taught him better.

Humans existed by night as well. And there were humans in the most remote regions. They had only pulled back like rats into their lairs to sleep. The earth was not cleansed of them, for even in sleep they exuded their odor, which then forced its way out between the cracks of their dwellings and into the open air, poisoning a natural world only apparently left to its own devices. The more Grenouille had become accustomed to purer air, the more sensitive he was to human odor, which suddenly, quite unexpectedly, would come floating by in the night, ghastly as the stench of manure, betraying the presence of some shepherd's hut or charcoal burner's cottage or thieves' den. And then he would flee farther, increasingly sensitive to the increasingly infrequent smell of humankind. Thus his nose led him to ever more remote regions of the country, ever farther from human beings, driving him on ever more insistently toward the magnetic pole of the greatest possible solitude.

✄ *Twenty-four* ✄

T HAT POLE, the point of the kingdom most distant
from humankind, was located in the Massif Central of the Auvergne, about five days' journey south
of Clermont, on the peak of a six-thousand-foot-
high volcano named Plomb du Cantal.

The mountain consisted of a giant cone of blue-gray
rock and was surrounded by an endless, barren high-
land studded with a few trees charred by fire and
overgrown with gray moss and gray brush, out of
which here and there brown boulders jutted up like
rotten teeth. Even by light of day, the region was so
dismal and dreary that the poorest shepherd in this
poverty-stricken province would not have driven his
animals here. And by night, by the bleaching light of
the moon, it was such a godforsaken wilderness that it
seemed not of this world. Even Lebrun, the bandit of
the Auvergne, though pursued from all sides, had
preferred to fight his way through to the Cévennes and
there be captured, drawn, and quartered rather than
to hide out on the Plomb du Cantal, where certainly
no one would have sought or found him, but where

likewise he would certainly have died a solitary, living death that had seemed to him worse still. For miles around the mountain, there lived not one human being, nor even a respectable mammal—at best a few bats and a couple of beetles and adders. No one had scaled the peak for decades.

Grenouille reached the mountain one August night in the year 1756. As dawn broke, he was standing on the peak. He did not yet know that his journey was at an end. He thought that this was only a stopping place on the way to ever purer air, and he turned full circle and let his nose move across the vast panorama of the volcanic wilderness: to the east, where the broad high plain of Saint-Flour and the marshes of the Riou River lay; to the north, to the region from which he had come and where he had wandered for days through pitted limestone mountains; to the west, from where the soft wind of morning brought him nothing but the smells of stone and tough grass; finally to the south, where the foothills of the Plomb stretched for miles to the dark gorges of the Truyère. Everywhere, in every direction, humanity lay equally remote from him, and a step in any direction would have meant closer proximity to human beings. The compass spun about. It no longer provided orientation. Grenouille was at his goal. And at the same time he was taken captive.

As the sun rose, he was still standing on the same spot, his nose held up to the air. With a desperate effort he tried to get a whiff of the direction from which threatening humanity came, and of the opposite direction to which he could flee still farther. He assumed that in whatever direction he turned he ought to detect some latent scrap of human odor. But there was nothing. Here there was only peace, olfactory peace, if it can be put that way. Spread all about, as if softly rustling, lay nothing but the drifting, homogeneous odor of dead stones, of gray lichen, and of withered grasses—nothing else.

Grenouille needed a very long time to believe what he was not smelling. He was not prepared for his good luck. His mistrust fought against his good sense for quite a while. He even used his eyes to aid him as the sun rose, and he scanned the horizon for the least sign of human presence, for the roof of a hut, the smoke of a fire, a fence, a bridge, a herd. He held his hands to his ears and listened, for a scythe being whetted, for the bark of a dog or the cry of a child. That whole day he stood fast in the blazing heat on the peak of the Plomb du Cantal and waited in vain for the slightest evidence. Only as the sun set did his mistrust gradually fade before an ever increasing sense of euphoria. He had escaped the abhorrent taint! He was truly completely alone! He was the only human being in the world!

He erupted with thundering jubilation. Like a shipwrecked sailor ecstatically greeting the sight of an inhabited island after weeks of aimless drifting, Grenouille celebrated his arrival at the mountain of solitude. He shouted for joy. He cast aside his rucksack, blanket, walking stick, and stamped his feet on the ground, threw his arms to the sky, danced in circles, roared his own name to the four winds, clenched his fists, shaking them triumphantly at the great, wide country lying below him and at the setting sun—triumphantly, as if he personally had chased it from the sky. He carried on like a madman until late into the night.

✣ *Twenty-five* ✣

H<small>E SPENT THE</small> next few days settling in on the mountain—for he had made up his mind that he would not be leaving this blessed region all that soon. First he sniffed around for water and in a crevasse a little below the top found it running across the rock in a thin film. It was not much, but if he patiently licked at it for an hour, he could quench his daily need for liquids. He also found nourishment in the form of small salamanders and ring snakes; he pinched off their heads, then devoured them whole. He also ate dry lichen and grass and mossberries. Such a diet, although totally unacceptable by bourgeois standards, did not disgust him in the least. In the past weeks and months he had no longer fed himself with food processed by human hands—bread, sausage, cheese —but instead, whenever he felt hungry, had wolfed down anything vaguely edible that had crossed his path. He was anything but a gourmet. He had no use for sensual gratification, unless that gratification consisted of pure, incorporeal odors. He had no use for creature comforts either and would have been quite

147

content to set up camp on bare stone. But he found something better.

Near his watering spot he discovered a natural tunnel leading back into the mountain by many twists and turns, until after a hundred feet or so it came to an end in a rock slide. The back of the tunnel was so narrow that Grenouille's shoulders touched the rock and so low that he could walk only hunched down. But he could sit, and if he curled up, could even lie down. That completely satisfied his requirements for comfort. For the spot had incalculable advantages: at the end of the tunnel it was pitch-black night even during the day, it was deathly quiet, and the air he breathed was moist, salty, cool. Grenouille could smell at once that no living creature had ever entered the place. As he took possession of it, he was overcome by a sense of something like sacred awe. He carefully spread his horse blanket on the ground as if dressing an altar and lay down on it. He felt blessedly wonderful. He was lying a hundred and fifty feet below the earth, inside the loneliest mountain in France—as if in his own grave. Never in his life had he felt so secure, certainly not in his mother's belly. The world could go up in flames out there, but he would not even notice it here. He began to cry softly. He did not know whom to thank for such good fortune.

In the days that followed he went into the open only to lick at his watering spot, quickly to relieve himself of his urine and excrement, and to hunt lizards and snakes. They were easy to bag at night when they retreated under flat stones or into little holes where he could trace them with his nose.

He climbed back up to the peak a few more times during the first weeks to sniff out the horizon. But soon that had become more a wearisome habit than a necessity, for he had not once scented the least threat.

And so he finally gave up these excursions and was concerned only with getting back into his crypt as quickly as possible once he had taken care of the most basic chores necessary for simple survival. For here, inside the crypt, was where he truly lived. Which is to say, for well over twenty hours a day in total darkness and in total silence and in total immobility, he sat on his horse blanket at the end of the stony corridor, his back resting on the rock slide, his shoulders wedged between the rocks, and enjoyed himself.

We are familiar with people who seek out solitude: penitents, failures, saints, or prophets. They retreat to deserts, preferably, where they live on locusts and honey. Others, however, live in caves or cells on remote islands; some—more spectacularly—squat in cages mounted high atop poles swaying in the breeze. They do this to be nearer to God. Their solitude is a self-mortification by which they do penance. They act in the belief that they are living a life pleasing to God. Or they wait months, years, for their solitude to be broken by some divine message that they hope then speedily to broadcast among mankind.

Grenouille's case was nothing of the sort. There was not the least notion of God in his head. He was not doing penance nor waiting for some supernatural inspiration. He had withdrawn solely for his own personal pleasure, only to be near to himself. No longer distracted by anything external, he basked in his own existence and found it splendid. He lay in his stony crypt like his own corpse, hardly breathing, his heart hardly beating—and yet lived as intensively and dissolutely as ever a rake had lived in the wide world outside.

≫ *Twenty-six* ≪

THE SETTING FOR these debaucheries was—how could it be otherwise—the innermost empire where he had buried the husks of every odor encountered since birth. To enhance the mood, he first conjured up those that were earliest and most remote: the hostile, steaming vapors of Madame Gaillard's bedroom; the bone-dry, leathery bouquet of her hands; the vinegary breath of Father Terrier; the hysterical, hot maternal sweat of Bussie the wet nurse; the carrion stench of the Cimetière des Innocents; the homicidal odor of his mother. And he wallowed in disgust and loathing, and his hair stood on end at the delicious horror.

Sometimes, if this repulsive aperitif did not quite get him into stride, he would allow himself a brief, odoriferous detour to Grimal's for a whiff of the stench of raw, meaty skins and tanning broths, or he imagined the collective effluvium of six hundred thousand Parisians in the sultry, oppressive heat of late summer.

And then all at once, the pent-up hate would erupt with orgasmic force—that was, after all, the point of the exercise. Like a thunderstorm he rolled across these odors that had dared offend his patrician nose. He thrashed at them as hail thrashes a grainfield; like a hurricane, he scattered the rabble and drowned them in a grand purifying deluge of distilled water. And how just was his anger. How great his revenge. Ah! What a sublime moment! Grenouille, the little man, quivered with excitement, his body writhed with voluptuous delight and arched so high that he slammed his head against the roof of the tunnel, only to sink back slowly and lie there lolling in satiation. It really was too pleasant, this volcanic act that extinguished all obnoxious odors, really too pleasant. . . . This was almost his favorite routine in the whole repertoire of his innermost universal theater, for it imparted to him the wonderful sense of righteous exhaustion that comes after only truly grand heroic deeds.

Now he could rest awhile in good conscience. He stretched out—to the extent his body fit within the narrow stony quarters. Deep inside, however, on the cleanly swept mats of his soul, he stretched out comfortably to the fullest and dozed away, letting delicate scents play about his nose: a spicy gust, for instance, as if borne here from springtime meadows; a mild May wind wafting through the first green leaves of beech; a sea breeze, with the bitterness of salted almonds. It was late afternoon when he arose— something like late afternoon, for naturally there was no afternoon or forenoon or evening or morning, there was neither light nor darkness, nor were there spring meadows nor green beech leaves . . . there were no real things at all in Grenouille's innermost universe, only the odors of things. (Which is why the *façon de parler* speaks of that universe as a landscape; an adequate expression, to be sure, but the only possible one, since our language is of no use when it comes to describing the smellable world.) It was, then, late afternoon: that is, a condition and a moment within Grenouille's soul such as reigns over the south when the siesta is done and the paralysis of midday slowly recedes and life's urge begins again after such constraint. The heat kindled by rage—the enemy of sublime scents—had fled, the pack of demons was annihilated. The fields within him lay soft and burnished beneath the lascivious peace of his awakening —and they waited for the will of their lord to come upon them.

And Grenouille rose up—as noted—and shook the sleep from his limbs. He stood up, the great innermost Grenouille. Like a giant he planted himself, in all his glory and grandeur, splendid to look upon—damn shame that no one saw him!—and looked about him, proud and majestic.

Yes! This was his empire! The incomparable Empire of Grenouille! Created and ruled over by him, the incomparable Grenouille, laid waste by him if he so chose and then raised up again, made boundless by him and defended with a flaming sword against every intruder. Here there was naught but his will, the will of the great, splendid, incomparable Grenouille. And now that the evil stench of the past had been swept away, he desired that his empire be fragrant. And with mighty strides he passed across the fallow fields and sowed fragrance of all kinds, wastefully here, sparingly there, in plantations of endless dimension and in small, intimate parcels, strewing seeds by the fistful or tucking them in one by one in selected spots. To the farthermost regions of his empire, Grenouille the Great, the frantic gardener, hurried, and soon there was not a cranny left into which he had not thrown a seed of fragrance.

And when he saw that it was good and that the whole earth was saturated with his divine Grenouille seeds, then Grenouille the Great let descend a shower of rectified spirit, soft and steady, and everywhere and overall the seed began to germinate and sprout, bringing forth shoots to gladden his heart. On the plantations it rolled in luxurious waves, and in the hidden gardens the stems stood full with sap. The blossoms all but exploded from their buds.

Then Grenouille the Great commanded the rain to stop. And it was so. And he sent the gentle sun of his smile upon the land; whereupon, to a bud, the hosts of blossoms unfolded their glory, from one end of his empire unto the other, creating a single rainbowed carpet woven from myriad precious capsules of fragrance. And Grenouille the Great saw that it was good, very, very good. And he caused the wind of his breath to blow across the land. And the blossoms, thus caressed, spilled over with scent and intermingled their teeming scents into one constantly changing scent that in all its variety was nevertheless merged into the odor of universal homage to Him, Grenouille the Great, the Incomparable, the Magnificent, who, enthroned upon his gold-scented cloud, sniffed his breath back in again, and the sweet savor of the sacrifice was pleasing unto him. And he deigned to bless his creation several times over, from whom came thanksgiving with songs of praise and rejoicing and yet further outpourings of glorious fragrance. Meanwhile evening was come, and the scents spilled over still and united with the blue of night to form ever more fantastic airs. A veritable gala of scent awaited, with one gigantic burst of fragrant diamond-studded fireworks.

Grenouille the Great, however, had tired a little and yawned and spoke: "Behold, I have done a great thing, and I am well pleased. But as with all the works once finished, it begins to bore me. I shall withdraw, and to crown this strenuous day I shall allow myself yet one more small delectation in the chambers of my heart."

So spoke Grenouille the Great and, while the peasantry of scent danced and celebrated beneath him, he glided with wide-stretched wings down from his golden clouds, across the nocturnal fields of his soul, and home to his heart.

⋗ Twenty-seven ⋖

AH, RETURNING home was pleasant! The double role
of avenger and creator of worlds was not a little
taxing, and then to be celebrated afterwards for hours
on end by one's own offspring was not the perfect way
to relax either. Weary of the duties of divine creator
and official host, Grenouille the Great longed for
some small domestic bliss.

His heart was a purple castle. It lay in a rock-strewn
desert, concealed by dunes, surrounded by a marshy
oasis, and set behind stone walls. It could be reached
only from the air. It had a thousand private rooms
and a thousand underground chambers and a thousand elegant salons, among them one with a purple
sofa when Grenouille—no longer Grenouille the
Great, but only the quite private Grenouille, or simply dear little Jean-Baptiste—would recover from the
labors of the day.

The castle's private rooms, however, were shelved
from floor to ceiling, and on those shelves were all the
odors that Grenouille had collected in the course of
his life, several million of them. And in the castle's
cellars the best scents of his life were stored in casks.

155

When properly aged, they were drawn off into bottles that lay in miles of damp, cool corridors and were arranged by vintage and estate. There were so many that they could not all be drunk in a single lifetime.

Once dear little Jean-Baptiste had finally returned *chez soi,* lying on his simple, cozy sofa in his purple salon—his boots finally pulled off, so to speak—he clapped his hands and called his servants, who were invisible, intangible, inaudible, and above all inodorous, and thus totally imaginary servants, and ordered them to go to the private rooms and get this or that volume from the great library of odors and to the cellars to fetch something for him to drink. The imaginary servants hurried off, and Grenouille's stomach cramped in tormented expectation. He suddenly felt like a drunkard who is afraid that the shot of brandy he has ordered at the bar will, for some reason or other, be denied him. What if the cellar or the library were suddenly empty, if the wine in the casks had gone sour? Why were they keeping him waiting? Why did they not come? He needed the stuff now, he needed it desperately, he was addicted, he would die on the spot if he did not get it.

Calm yourself, Jean-Baptiste! Calm yourself, my friend! They're coming, they're coming, they're bringing what you crave. The servants are winging their way here with it. They are carrying the book of odors on an invisible tray, and in their white-gloved, invisible hands they are carrying those precious bottles, they set them down, ever so carefully, they bow, and they disappear.

And then, left alone, at last—once again!—left alone, Jean-Baptiste reaches for the odors he craves, opens the first bottle, pours a glass full to the rim, puts it to his lips, and drinks. Drinks the glass of cool scent down in one draft, and it is luscious. It is so refreshingly good that dear Jean-Baptiste's eyes fill with tears of bliss, and he immediately pours himself a second glass: a scent from the year 1752, sniffed up in spring, before sunrise on the Pont-Royal, his nose directed to the west, from where a light breeze bore the blended odors of sea and forest and a touch of the tarry smell of the barges tied up at the bank. It was the scent from the end of his first night spent roaming about Paris without Grimal's permission. It was the fresh odor of the approaching day, of the first daybreak that he had ever known in freedom. That odor had been the pledge of freedom. It had been the pledge of a different life. The odor of that morning was for Grenouille the odor of hope. He guarded it carefully. And he drank of it daily.

Once he had emptied the second glass, all his nervousness, all his doubt and insecurity, fell away from him, and he was filled with glorious contentment. He pressed his back against the soft cushions of his sofa, opened a book, and began to read from his memoirs. He read about the odors of his childhood, of his schooldays, about the odors of the broad streets and hidden nooks of the city, about human odors. And a pleasant shudder washed over him, for the odors he now called up were indeed those that he despised, that he had exterminated. With sickened interest, Grenouille read from the book of revolting odors, and when his disgust outweighed his interest, he simply slammed the book shut, laid it aside, and picked up another.

All the while he drank without pause from his noble scents. After the bottle of hope, he uncorked one from the year 1744, filled with the warm scent of the wood outside Madame Gaillard's house. And after that he drank a bottle of the scent of a summer evening, imbued with perfume and heavy with blossoms, gleaned from the edge of a park in Saint-Germain-des-Prés, dated 1753.

He was now scent-logged. His arms and legs grew heavier and heavier as they pressed into the cushions. His mind was wonderfully fogged. But it was not yet the end of his debauch. His eyes could read no more, true, the book had long since fallen from his hand—but he did not want to call an end to the evening without having emptied one last bottle, the most splendid of all: the scent of the girl from the rue des Marais. . . .

He drank it reverently and he sat upright on the sofa to do so—although that was difficult and the purple salon whirled and swayed with every move. Like a schoolboy, his knees pressed together, his feet side by side, his left hand resting on his left thigh, that was how little Grenouille drank the most precious scent from the cellars of his heart, glass after glass, and grew sadder and sadder as he drank. He knew that he was drinking too much. He knew that he could not handle so much good scent. And yet he drank till the bottle was empty. He walked along the dark passage from the street into the rear courtyard. He made for the glow of light. The girl was sitting there pitting yellow plums. Far in the distance, the rockets and petards of the fireworks were booming. . . .

He put the glass down and sat there for a while yet, several minutes, stiff with sentimentality and guzzling, until the last aftertaste had vanished from his palate. He stared vacantly ahead. His head was suddenly as empty as the bottle. Then he toppled sideways onto the purple sofa, and from one moment to the next sank into a numbed sleep.

At the same time, the other Grenouille fell asleep on his horse blanket. And his sleep was just as fathomless as that of the innermost Grenouille, for the Herculean deeds and excesses of the one had more than exhausted the other—they were, after all, one and the same person.

When he awoke, however, he did not awaken in the purple salon of his purple castle behind the seven walls, nor upon the vernal fields of scent within his soul, but most decidedly in his stony dungeon at the end of a tunnel, on hard ground, in the dark. And he was nauseated with hunger and thirst, and as chilled and miserable as a drunkard after a night of carousing. He crept on all fours out of his tunnel.

Outside it would be some time of day or another, usually toward the beginning or end of night; but even at midnight, the brightness of the starlight pricked his eyes like needles. The air seemed dusty to him, acrid, searing his lungs; the landscape was brittle; he bumped against the stones. And even the most delicate odors came sharp and caustic into a nose unaccustomed to the world. Grenouille the tick had grown as touchy as a hermit crab that has left its shell to wander naked through the sea.

He went to his watering spot, licked the moisture from the wall, for an hour, for two; it was pure torture. Time would not end, time in which the real world scorched his skin. He ripped a few scraps of moss from the stones, choked them down, squatted, shitting as he ate—it must all be done quickly, quickly, quickly. And as if he were a hunted creature, a little soft-fleshed animal, and the hawks were already circling in the sky overhead, he ran back to his cave, to the end of the tunnel where his horse blanket was spread. There he was safe at last.

He leaned back against the stony debris, stretched out his legs, and waited. He had to hold his body very still, very still, like some vessel about to slosh over from too much motion. Gradually he managed to gain control of his breathing. His excited heart beat more steadily; the pounding of the waves inside him subsided slowly. And suddenly solitude fell across his heart like a dusky reflection. He closed his eyes. The dark doors within him opened, and he entered. The next performance in the theater of Grenouille's soul was beginning.

❧ Twenty-eight ❧

AND SO IT WENT, day in day out, week in week out, month in month out. So it went for seven long years.

Meanwhile war raged in the world outside, a world war. Men fought in Silesia and Saxony, in Hanover and the Low Countries, in Bohemia and Pomerania. The king's troops died in Hesse and Westphalia, on the Balearic Islands, in India, on the Mississippi and in Canada, if they had not already succumbed to typhoid on the journey. The war robbed a million people of their lives, France of its colonial empire, and all the warring nations of so much money that they finally decided, with heavy hearts, to end it.

One winter during this period, Grenouille almost froze to death, without ever noticing it. For five days he lay in his purple salon, and when he awoke in his tunnel he was so cold he could not move. He closed his eyes again and would have slept himself to death. But then the weather turned around, there was a thaw, and he was saved.

Once the snow was so deep that he did not have the

161

strength to burrow down to the lichen. He fed himself on the stiff carcasses of frozen bats.

Once a dead raven lay at the mouth of the cave. He ate it. These were the only events in the outside world of which he took notice for seven years. Otherwise he lived only within his mountain, only within the self-made empire of his soul. And he would have remained there until his death (since he lacked for nothing), if catastrophe had not struck, driving him from his mountain, vomiting him back out into the world.

❧ *Twenty-nine* ❧

T HE CATASTROPHE was not an earthquake, nor a
forest fire, nor an avalanche, nor a cave-in. It was
not an external catastrophe at all, but an internal one,
and as such particularly distressing, because it
blocked Grenouille's favorite means of escape. It
happened in his sleep. Or better, in his dreams. Or
better still, in a dream while he slept in the heart of
his fantasies.

He lay on his sofa in the purple salon and slept, the
empty bottles all about him. He had drunk an enormous amount, with two whole bottles of the scent of
the red-haired girl for a nightcap. Apparently it had
been too much; for his sleep, though deep as death
itself, was not dreamless this time, but threaded with
ghostly wisps of dreams. These wisps were clearly
recognizable as scraps of odors. At first they merely
floated in thin threads past Grenouille's nose, but
then they grew thicker, more cloudlike. And now it
seemed as if he were standing in the middle of a moor
from which fog was rising. The fog slowly climbed
higher. Soon Grenouille was completely wrapped in
fog, saturated with fog, and it seemed he could not get

163

his breath for the foggy vapor. If he did not want to suffocate, he would have to breathe the fog in. And the fog was, as noted, an odor. And Grenouille knew what kind of odor. The fog was his own odor. His, Grenouille's, own body odor was the fog.

And the awful thing was that Grenouille, although he knew that this odor was *his* odor, could not smell it. Virtually drowning in himself, he could not for the life of him smell himself!

As this became clear to him, he gave a scream as dreadful and loud as if he were being burned alive. The scream smashed through the walls of the purple salon, through the walls of the castle, and sped away from his heart across the ditches and swamps and deserts, hurtled across the nocturnal landscape of his soul like a fire storm, howled its way out of his mouth, down the winding tunnel, out into the world, and far across the high plains of Saint-Flour—as if the mountain itself were screaming. And Grenouille awoke at his own scream. In waking, he thrashed about as if he had to drive off the odorless fog trying to suffocate him. He was deathly afraid, his whole body shook with the raw fear of death. Had his scream not ripped open the fog, he would have drowned in himself—a gruesome death. He shuddered as he recalled it. And as he sat there shivering and trying to gather his confused, terrified thoughts, he knew one thing for sure: he would change his life, if only because he did not want to dream such a frightening dream a second time. He would not survive it a second time.

He threw his horse blanket over his shoulders and crept out into the open. It was already morning outside, a late February morning. The sun was shining. The earth smelled of moist stones, moss, and water. On the wind there already lay a light bouquet of anemones. He squatted on the ground before his cave. The sunlight warmed him. He breathed in the fresh air. Whenever he thought of the fog that he had escaped, a shudder would pass over him. And he shuddered, too, from the pleasure of the warmth he felt on his back. It was good, really, that this external world still existed, if only as a place of refuge. Nor could he bear the awful thought of how it would have been not to find a world at the entrance to the tunnel! No light, no odor, no nothing—only that ghastly fog inside, outside, everywhere . . .

Gradually the shock subsided. Gradually the grip of anxiety loosened, and Grenouille began to feel safer. Toward noon he was his old cold-blooded self. He laid the index and middle fingers of his left hand under his nose and breathed along the backs of his fingers. He smelled the moist spring air spiced with anemones. He did not smell anything of his fingers. He turned his hand over and sniffed at the palm. He sensed the warmth of his hand, but smelled nothing. Then he rolled up the ragged sleeve of his shirt, buried his nose in the crook of his elbow. He knew that this was the spot where all humans smell like themselves. But he could smell nothing. He could not smell anything in his armpits, nor on his feet, not around his genitals when he bent down to them as far as he possibly could. It was grotesque: he, Grenouille, who could smell other people miles away, was incapable of smelling his own genitals not a handspan away! Nevertheless, he did not panic, but considered it all coolly and spoke to himself as follows: "It is not that I do not smell, for everything smells. It is, rather, that I cannot smell that I smell, because I have smelled myself day in day out since my birth, and my nose is therefore dulled against my own smell. If I could separate my own smell, or at least a part of it, from me and then return to it after being weaned from it for a while, then I would most certainly be able to smell it—and therefore me."

He laid the horse blanket aside and took off his clothes, or at least what remained of them—rags and tatters were what he took off. For seven years he had not removed them from his body. They had to be fully saturated with his own odor. He tossed them into a pile at the cave entrance and walked away. Then, for the first time in seven years, he once again climbed to the top of the mountain. There he stood on the same spot where he had stood on the day of his arrival, held his nose to the west, and let the wind whistle around his naked body. His intention was thoroughly to air himself, to be pumped so full of the west wind—and that meant with the odor of the sea and wet meadows —that this odor would counterbalance his own body odor, creating a gradient of odors between himself and his clothes, which he would then be in a position to smell. And to prevent his nose from taking in the least bit of his own odor, he bent his body forward, stretching his neck out as far as he could against the wind, with his arms stretched behind him. He looked like a swimmer just before he dives into the water.

He held this totally ridiculous pose for several hours, and even by such pale sunlight, his skin, maggot white from lack of sun, was turned a lobster red. Toward evening he climbed back down to the cave. From far off he could see his clothes lying in a pile. The last few yards, he held his nose closed and opened it again only when he had lowered it right down onto the pile. He made the sniffing test he had learned from Baldini, snatching up the air and then letting it out again in spurts. And to catch the odor, he used both hands to form a bell around his clothes, with his nose stuck into it as the clapper. He did everything possible to extract his own odor from his clothes. But there was no odor in them. It was most definitely not there. There were a thousand other odors: the odor of stone, sand, moss, resin, raven's blood—even the odor of the sausage that he had bought years before near Sully was clearly perceptible. Those clothes contained an olfactory diary of the last seven, eight years. Only one odor was not there—his own odor, the odor of the person who had worn them continuously all that time.

And now he began to be truly alarmed. The sun had set. He was standing naked at the entrance to the tunnel, where he had lived in darkness for seven years. The wind blew cold, and he was freezing, but he did not notice that he was freezing, for within him was a counterfrost, fear. It was not the same fear that he had felt in his dream—the ghastly fear of suffocating on himself—which he had had to shake off and flee whatever the cost. What he now felt was the fear of not knowing much of anything about himself. It was the opposite pole of that other fear. He could not flee it, but had to move toward it. He had to know for certain—even if that knowledge proved too terrible— whether he had an odor or not. And he had to know now. At once.

He went back into the tunnel. Within a few yards he was fully engulfed in darkness, but he found his way as if by brightest daylight. He had gone down this path many thousands of times, knew every step and every turn, could smell every low-hanging jut of rock and every tiny protruding stone. It was not hard to find the way. What was hard was fighting back the memory of the claustrophobic dream rising higher and higher within him like a flood tide with every step he took. But he was brave. That is to say, he fought the fear of knowing with the fear of not knowing, and he won the battle, because he knew he had no choice. When he had reached the end of the tunnel, there where the rock slide slanted upwards, both fears fell away from him. He felt calm, his mind was quite clear and his nose sharp as a scalpel. He squatted down, laid his hands over his eyes, and smelled. Here on this spot, in this remote stony grave, he had lain for seven years. There must be some smell of him here, if anywhere in this world. He breathed slowly. He analyzed exactly. He allowed himself time to come to a judgment. He squatted there for a quarter of an hour. His memory was infallible, and he knew precisely how this spot had smelled seven years before: stony and moist, salty, cool, and so pure that no living creature, man or beast, could ever have entered the place . . . which was exactly how it smelled now.

He continued to squat there for a while, quite calm, simply nodding his head gently. Then he turned around and walked, at first hunched down, but when the height of the tunnel allowed it, erect, out into the open air.

Outside he pulled on his rags (his shoes had rotted off him years before), threw the horse blanket over his shoulders, and that same night left the Plomb du Cantal, heading south.

≈ *Thirty* ≈

HE LOOKED AWFUL. His hair reached down to the hollows of his knees, his scraggly beard to his navel. His nails were like talons, and the skin on his arms and legs, where the rags no longer covered his body, was peeling off in shreds.

The first people he met, farmers in a field near the town of Pierrefort, ran off screaming at the sight of him. But in the town itself, he caused a sensation. By the hundreds people came running to gape at him. Many of them believed he was an escaped galley slave. Others said he was not really a human being, but some mixture of man and bear, some kind of forest creature. One fellow, who had been to sea, claimed that he looked like a member of a wild Indian tribe in Cayenne, which lay on the other side of the great ocean. They led him before the mayor. There, to the astonishment of the assembly, he produced his journeyman's papers, opened his mouth, and related in a few gabbled but sufficiently comprehensible words—for these were the first words that he had uttered in seven years—how he had been attacked by robbers, dragged off, and held captive in a cave for seven years.

169

He had seen neither daylight nor another human being during that time, had been fed by an invisible hand that let down a basket in the dark, and finally set free by a ladder—without his ever knowing why and without ever having seen his captors or his rescuer. He had thought this story up, since it seemed to him more believable than the truth; and so it was, for similar attacks by robbers occurred not infrequently in the mountains of the Auvergne and Languedoc, and in the Cévennes. At least the mayor recorded it all without protest and passed his report on to the marquis de La Taillade-Espinasse, liege lord of the town and member of parliament in Toulouse.

At the age of forty, the marquis had turned his back on life at the court of Versailles and retired to his estates, where he lived for science alone. From his pen had come an important work concerning dynamic political economy. In it he had proposed the abolition of all taxes on real estate and agricultural products, as well as the introduction of an upside-down progressive income tax, which would hit the poorest citizens the hardest and so force them to a more vigorous development of their economic activities. Encouraged by the success of his little book, he authored a tract on the raising of boys and girls between the ages of five and ten. Then he turned to experimental agriculture. By spreading the semen of bulls over various grasses, he attempted to produce a milk-yielding animal-vegetable hybrid, a sort of udder flower. After initial successes that enabled him to produce a cheese from his milk grass—described by the Academy of Sciences of Lyon as "tasting of goat, though slightly bitter"—he had to abandon his experiments because of the enormous cost of spewing bull semen by the hundreds of quarts across his fields. In any case, his concern with matters agro-biological had awakened his interest not only in the plowed clod, so to speak, but in the earth in general and its relationship to the biosphere in particular.

He had barely concluded his work with the milk-yielding udder flower when he threw himself with great élan into unflagging research for a grand treatise on the relationship between proximity to the earth and vital energy. His thesis was that life could develop only at a certain distance from the earth, since the earth itself constantly emits a corrupting gas, a so-called *fluidum letale,* which lames vital energies and sooner or later totally extinguishes them. All living creatures therefore endeavor to distance themselves from the earth by growing—that is, they grow away from it and not, for instance, into it; which is why their most valuable parts are lifted heavenwards: the ears of grain, the blossoms of flowers, the head of man; and therefore, as they begin to bend and buckle back toward the earth in old age, they will inevitably fall victim to the lethal gas, into which they are in turn finally changed once they have decomposed after death.

When the marquis de La Taillade-Espinasse received word that in Pierrefort an individual had been found who had dwelt in a cave for seven years—that is, completely encapsulated by the corrupting element of the earth—he was beside himself with delight and immediately had Grenouille brought to his laboratory, where he subjected him to a thorough examination. He found his theories confirmed most graphically: the *fluidum letale* had already so assaulted Grenouille that his twenty-five-year-old body clearly showed the marks of senile deterioration. All that had prevented his death, Taillade-Espinasse declared, was that during his imprisonment Grenouille had been given earth-removed plants, presumably bread and fruits, for nourishment. And now his former healthy condition could be restored only by the wholesale expulsion of the *fluidum,* using a vital ventilation machine, devised by Taillade-Espinasse himself. He had such an apparatus standing in his manor in Montpellier, and if Grenouille was willing to make himself available as the object of a scientific demonstration, he was willing not only to free him from hopeless contamination by earth gas, but he would also provide him with a handsome sum of money. . . .

Two hours later they were sitting in the carriage. Although the roads were in miserable condition, they traveled the sixty-four miles to Montpellier in just under two days, for despite his advanced age, the marquis would not be denied his right personally to whip both driver and horses and to lend a hand whenever, as frequently happened, an axle or spring broke—so excited was he by his find, so eager to present it to an educated audience as soon as possible. Grenouille, however, was not allowed to leave the carriage even once. He was forced to sit there all wrapped up in his rags and a blanket drenched with earth and clay. During the trip he was given raw vegetable roots to eat. The marquis hoped these procedures would preserve the contamination by earth's *fluidum* in its ideal state for a while yet.

Upon their arrival in Montpellier, he had Grenouille taken at once to the cellar of his mansion, and sent out invitations to all the members of the medical faculty, the botanical association, the agricultural school, the chemophysical club, the Freemason lodge, and the other assorted learned societies, of which the city had no fewer than a dozen. And several days later—exactly one week after he had left his mountain solitude—Grenouille found himself on a dais in the great hall of the University of Montpellier and was presented as the scientific sensation of the year to a crowd of several hundred people.

In his lecture, Taillade-Espinasse described him as living proof for the validity of his theory of earth's *fluidum letale*. While he stripped Grenouille of his rags piece by piece, he explained the devastating effect that the corruptive gas had perpetrated on Grenouille's body: one could see the pustules and scars caused by the corrosive gas; there on his breast a giant, shiny-red gas cancer; a general disintegration of the skin; and even clear evidence of fluidal deformation of the bone structure, the visible indications being a clubfoot and a hunchback. The internal organs as well had been damaged by the gas—pancreas, liver, lungs, gallbladder, and intestinal tract—as the analysis of a stool sample (accessible to the public in a basin at the feet of the exhibit) had proved beyond doubt. In summary, it could be said that the paralysis of the vital energies caused by a seven-year contamination with *fluidum letale Taillade* had progressed so far that the exhibit—whose external appearance, by the way, already displayed significant molelike traits —could be described as a creature more disposed toward death than life. Nevertheless, the lecturer pledged that within eight days, using ventilation therapy in combination with a vital diet, he would restore this doomed creature to the point where the signs of a complete recovery would be self-evident to everyone, and he invited those present to return in one week to satisfy themselves of the success of this prognosis, which, of course, would then have to be seen as valid proof that his theory concerning earth's *fluidum* was likewise correct.

The lecture was an immense success. The learned audience applauded the lecturer vigorously and lined up to pass the dais where Grenouille was standing. In his state of preserved deterioration and with all his old scars and deformities, he did indeed look so impressively dreadful that everyone considered him beyond recovery and already half decayed, although he himself felt quite healthy and robust. Many of the gentlemen tapped him up and down in a professional manner, measured him, looked into his mouth and eyes. Several of them addressed him directly and inquired about his life in the cave and his present state of health. But he kept strictly to the instructions the marquis had given him beforehand and answered all such questions with nothing more than a strained death rattle, making helpless gestures with his hands to his larynx, as if to indicate that that too was already rotted away by the *fluidum letale Taillade.*

At the end of the demonstration, Taillade-Espinasse packed him back up and transported him home to the storage room of his manor. There, in the presence of several selected doctors from the medical faculty, he locked Grenouille in his vital ventilation machine, a box made of tightly jointed pine boards, which by means of a suction flue extending far above the house roof could be flooded with air extracted from the higher regions, and thus free of lethal gas. The air could then escape through a leather flap-valve placed in the floor. The apparatus was kept in operation by a staff of servants who tended it day and night, so that the ventilators inside the flue never stopped pumping. And so, surrounded by the constant purifying stream of air, Grenouille was fed a diet of foods from earth-removed regions—dove bouillon, lark pie, ragout of wild duck, preserves of fruit picked from trees, bread made from a special wheat grown at high altitudes, wine from the Pyrenees, chamois milk, and frozen frothy meringue from hens kept in the attic of the mansion—all of which was presented at hourly intervals through the door of a double-walled air lock built into the side of the chamber.

This combined treatment of decontamination and revitalization lasted for five days. Then the marquis had the ventilators stopped and Grenouille brought to a washroom, where he was softened for several hours in baths of lukewarm rainwater and finally waxed from head to toe with nut-oil soap from Potosí in the Andes. His finger- and toenails were trimmed, his teeth cleaned with pulverized lime from the Dolomites, he was shaved, his hair cut and combed, coiffed and powdered. A tailor, a cobbler were sent for, and Grenouille was fitted out in a silk shirt, with white jabot and white ruffles at the cuffs, silk stockings, frock coat, trousers, and vest of blue velvet, and handsome buckled shoes of black leather, the right one cleverly elevated for his crippled foot. The marquis personally applied white talcum makeup to Grenouille's scarred face, dabbed his lips and cheeks with crimson, and gave a truly noble arch to his eyebrows with the aid of a soft stick of linden charcoal. Then he dusted him with his own personal perfume, a rather simple violet fragrance, took a few steps back, and took some time to find words for his delight.

"Monsieur," he began at last, "I am thrilled with myself. I am overwhelmed at my own genius. I have, to be sure, never doubted the correctness of my fluidal theory; of course not; but to find it so gloriously confirmed by an applied therapy overwhelms me. You were a beast, and I have made a man of you. A veritable divine act. Do forgive me, I am so touched! —Stand in front of that mirror there and regard yourself. You will realize for the first time in your life that you are a human being; not a particularly extraordinary or in any fashion distinguished one, but nevertheless a perfectly acceptable human being. Go on, monsieur! Regard yourself and admire the miracle that I have accomplished with you!"

It was the first time that anyone had ever said "monsieur" to Grenouille.

He walked over to the mirror and looked into it.

Before that day he had never seen himself in a mirror. He saw a gentleman in a handsome blue outfit, with a white shirt and silk stockings; and instinctively he ducked, as he had always ducked before such fine gentlemen. The fine gentleman, however, ducked as well, and when Grenouille stood up straight again, the fine gentleman did the same, and then they both stared straight into each other's eyes.

What dumbfounded Grenouille most was the fact that he looked so unbelievably normal. The marquis was right: there was nothing special about his looks, nothing handsome, but then nothing especially ugly either. He was a little short of stature, his posture was a little awkward, his face a little expressionless—in short, he looked like a thousand other people. If he were now to go walking down the street, not one person would turn around to look at him. A man such as he now was, should he chance to meet him, would not even strike him as in any way unusual. Unless, of course, he would smell that the man, except for a hint of violets, had as little odor as the gentleman in the mirror—or himself, standing there in front of it.

And yet only ten days before, farmers had run away screaming at the sight of him. He had not felt any different from the way he did now; and now, if he closed his eyes, he felt not one bit different from then. He inhaled the air that rose up from his own body and smelled the bad perfume and the velvet and the freshly glued leather of his shoes; he smelled the silk cloth, the powder, the makeup, the light scent of the soap from Potosí. And suddenly he knew that it had not been the dove bouillon nor the ventilation hocus-pocus that had made a normal person out of him, but solely these few clothes, the haircut, and the little masquerade with cosmetics.

He blinked as he opened his eyes and saw how the gentleman in the mirror blinked back at him and how a little smile played about his carmine lips, as if signaling to him that he did not find him totally unattractive. And Grenouille himself found that the gentleman in the mirror, this odorless figure dressed and made up like a man, was not all that bad either; at least it seemed to him as if the figure—once its costume had been perfected—might have an effect on the world outside that he, Grenouille, would never have expected of himself. He nodded to the figure and saw that in nodding back it flared its nostrils surreptitiously.

❧ Thirty-one ❧

THE FOLLOWING DAY—the marquis was just about to instruct him in the basic poses, gestures, and dance steps he would need for his coming social debut—Grenouille faked a fainting spell and, as if totally exhausted and in imminent danger of suffocation, collapsed onto a sofa.

The marquis was beside himself. He screamed for servants, screamed for fan bearers and portable ventilators, and while the servants scurried about, he knelt down at Grenouille's side, fanning him with a handkerchief soaked in bouquet of violets, and appealed to him, literally begged him, to get to his feet, and please not to breathe his last just yet, but to wait, if at all possible, until the day after tomorrow, since the survival of the theory of the *fluidum letale* would otherwise be in utmost jeopardy.

Grenouille twisted and turned, coughed, groaned, thrashed at the handkerchief with his arms, and finally, after falling from the sofa in a highly dramatic fashion, crept to the most distant corner of the room. "Not that perfume!" he cried with his last bit of energy. "Not that perfume! It will kill me!" And only when Taillade-Espinasse had tossed the handkerchief out the window and his violet-scented jacket into the next room, did Grenouille allow his attack to ebb, and in a voice that slowly grew calmer explained that as a perfumer he had an occupationally sensitive nose and had always reacted very strongly to certain perfumes, especially so during this period of recuperation. And his only explanation for the fact that the scent of violets in particular—a lovely flower in its own right —should so oppress him was that the marquis's perfume contained a high percentage of violet root extract, which, being of subterranean origin, must have a pernicious effect on a person like himself suffering from the influence of *fluidum letale*. Yesterday, at the first application of the scent, he had felt quite queasy, and today, as he had once again perceived the odor of roots, it had been as if someone had pushed him back into that dreadful, suffocating hole where he had vegetated for several years. His very nature had risen up against it, that was all he could say; and now that his grace the marquis had used his art to restore him to a life free of fluidal air, he would rather die on the spot than once again be at the mercy of the dreaded *fluidum*. At the mere thought of a perfume extracted from roots, he could feel his whole body cramping up. He was firmly convinced, however, that he would recover in an instant if the marquis would permit him to design a perfume of his own, one that would completely drive out the scent of violets. He had in mind an especially light, airy fragrance, consisting primarily of earth-removed ingredients, like *eaux* of almond and orange blossom, eucalyptus, pine, and cypress oils. A splash of such a scent on his clothes, a few drops on his neck and cheeks—and he would be permanently immune to any repetition of the embarrassing seizure that had just overwhelmed him. . . .

179

For clarity's sake, the proper forms of reported speech have been used here, but in reality this was a verbal eruption of uninterrupted blubberings, accompanied by numerous coughs and gasps and struggles for breath, all of which Grenouille accented with quiverings and fidgetings and rollings of the eyes. The marquis was deeply impressed. It was, however, not so much his ward's symptoms of suffering as the deft argumentation, presented totally under the aegis of the theory of *fluidum letale,* that convinced him. Of course it was the violet perfume! An obnoxious, earth-bound—indeed subterranean—product! He himself was probably infected by it after years of use. Had no idea that day in day out he had been bringing himself ever nearer to death by using the scent. His gout, the stiffness in his neck, the enervation of his member, his hemorrhoids, the pressure in his ears, his rotten tooth—all of it doubtless came from the contagious fluidal stench of violet roots. And that stupid little man, that lump of misery there in the corner of the room, had given him the idea. He was touched. He would have loved to have gone over to him, lifted him up, and pressed him to his enlightened heart. But he feared that he still smelled too much of violets, and so he screamed for his servants yet again and ordered that all the violet perfume be removed from the house, the whole mansion aired, his clothes disinfected in the vital-air ventilator, and that Grenouille at once be conveyed in his sedan chair to the best perfumer in the city. And of course this was precisely what Grenouille had intended his seizure to accomplish.

The science of perfumery was an old tradition in Montpellier, and although in more recent times it had lost ground to its competitor, the town of Grasse, there were still several good perfumers and glovers residing in the city. The most prestigious of them, a

certain Runel—well aware of the trade he enjoyed
with the house of the marquis de La Taillade-
Espinasse as its purveyor of soaps, oils, and scents—
declared himself prepared to take the unusual step of
surrendering his studio for an hour to the strange
journeyman perfumer from Paris who had been conveyed thither in a sedan chair. The latter refused all
instructions, did not even want to know where things
were; he knew his way around, he said, would manage
well enough. And he locked himself in the laboratory
and stayed there a good hour, while Runel joined the
marquis's majordomo for a couple of glasses of wine
in a tavern, where he was to learn why his violet
cologne was no longer a scent worth smelling.

Runel's laboratory and shop fell far short of being
so grandly equipped as Baldini's perfume shop in
Paris had been in its day. An average perfumer would
not have made any great progress with its few floral
oils, colognes, and spices. Grenouille, however, recognized with the first inhaled sniff that the ingredients
on hand would be quite sufficient for his purposes. He
did not want to create a great scent; he did not want to
create a prestigious cologne such as he had once made
for Baldini, one that stood out amid a sea of mediocrity and tamed the masses. Nor was even the simple
orange blossom scent that he had promised the marquis his true goal. The customary essences of neroli,
eucalyptus, and cypress were meant only as a cover
for the actual scent that he intended to produce: that
was the scent of humanness. He wanted to acquire the
human-being odor—if only in the form of an inferior
temporary surrogate—that he did not possess himself. True, *the* odor of human being did not exist, any
more than *the* human countenance. Every human
being smelled different, no one knew that better than
Grenouille, who recognized thousands upon thousands of individual odors and could sniff out the

difference of each human being from birth on. And yet—there was a basic perfumatory theme to the odor of humanity, a rather simple one, by the way: a sweaty-oily, sour-cheesy, quite richly repulsive basic theme that clung to all humans equally and above which each individual's aura hovered only as a small cloud of more refined particularity.

That aura, however, the highly complex, unmistakable code of a *personal* odor, was not perceptible for most people in any case. Most people did not know that they even had such a thing, and moreover did everything they could to disguise it under clothes or fashionable artificial odors. Only that basic odor, the primitive human effluvium, was truly familiar to them; they lived exclusively within it and it made them feel secure; and only a person who gave off that standard vile vapor was ever considered one of their own.

It was a strange perfume that Grenouille created that day. There had never before been a stranger one on earth. It did not smell like a scent, but like *a human being who gives off a scent.* If one had smelled this perfume in a dark room, one would have thought a second person was standing there. And if a human being, who smelled like a human being, had applied it, that person would have seemed to have the smell of two people, or, worse still, to be a monstrous double creature, like some figure that you can no longer clearly pinpoint because it looks blurred and out of focus, like something at the bottom of a lake beneath the shiver of waves.

And to imitate this human odor—quite unsatisfactorily, as he himself knew, but cleverly enough to deceive others—Grenouille gathered up the most striking ingredients in Runel's workshop.

There was a little pile of cat shit behind the threshold of the door leading out to the courtyard, still rather fresh. He took a half teaspoon of it and placed it together with several drops of vinegar and finely ground salt in a mixing bottle. Under the worktable he found a thumbnail-sized piece of cheese, apparently from one of Runel's lunches. It was already quite old, had begun to decompose, and gave off a biting, pungent odor. From the lid of a sardine tub that stood at the back of the shop, he scratched off a rancid, fishy something-or-other, mixed it with rotten egg and castoreum, ammonia, nutmeg, horn shavings, and singed pork rind, finely ground. To this he added a relatively large amount of civet, mixed these ghastly ingredients with alcohol, let it digest, and filtered it into a second bottle. The bilge smelled revolting. Its stink was putrid, like a sewer, and if you fanned its vapor just once to mix it with fresh air, it was as if you were standing in Paris on a hot summer day, at the corner of the rue aux Fers and the rue de la Lingerie, where the odors from Les Halles, the Cimetière des Innocents, and the overcrowded tenements converged.

On top of this disgusting base, which smelled more like a cadaver than a human being, Grenouille spread a layer of fresh, oily scents: peppermint, lavender, turpentine, lime, eucalyptus, which he then simultaneously disguised and tamed with the pleasant bouquet of fine floral oils—geranium, rose, orange blossom, and jasmine. After a second dilution with alcohol and a splash of vinegar there was nothing left of the disgusting basic odor on which the mixture was built. The latent stench lay lost and unnoticeable under the fresh ingredients; the nauseous part, pampered by the scent of flowers, had become almost interesting; and, strangely enough, there was no putrefaction left to smell, not the least. On the contrary, the perfume seemed to exhale the robust, vivacious scent of life.

Grenouille filled two flacons with it, stoppered them, and stuck them in his pocket. Then he washed the bottles, mortars, funnels, and spoons carefully with water, rubbed them down with bitter-almond oil to remove all traces of odor, and picked up a second mixing bottle. In it he quickly composed another perfume, a sort of copy of the first, likewise consisting of fresh and floral elements, but containing nothing of the witches' brew as a base, but rather a totally conventional one of musk, ambergris, a tiny bit of civet, and cedarwood oil. By itself it smelled totally different from the first—flatter, more innocent, detoxified—for it lacked the components of the imitation human odor. But once a normal human being applied it and married it to his own odor, it could no longer be distinguished from the one that Grenouille had created exclusively for himself.

After he had poured the second perfume into flacons, he stripped and sprinkled his clothes with the first. Then he dabbed himself in the armpits, between the toes, on the genitals, on the chest, neck, ears, and hair, put his clothes back on, and left the laboratory.

❧ *Thirty-two* ❧

As HE CAME OUT onto the street, he was suddenly afraid, for he knew that for the first time in his life he was giving off a human odor. He found that he stank, stank quite disgustingly. And because he could not imagine that other people would not also perceive his odor as a stench, he did not dare go directly into the tavern where Runel and the marquis's majordomo were waiting for him. It seemed less risky to him first to try out his new aura in an anonymous environment.

He slipped down toward the river through the darkest and narrowest alleyways, where tanners and dyers had their workshops and carried on their stinking business. When someone approached, or if he passed an entryway where children were playing or women were sitting, he forced himself to walk more slowly, bringing his odor with him in a large, compact cloud.

From his youth on, he had been accustomed to people's passing him and taking no notice of him whatever, not out of contempt—as he had once believed—but because they were quite unaware of his

existence. There was no space surrounding him, no
waves broke from him into the atmosphere, as with
other people; he had no shadow, so to speak, to cast
across another's face. Only if he ran right into someone in a crowd or in a street-corner collision would
there be a brief moment of discernment; and the
person encountered would bounce off and stare at
him for a few seconds as if gazing at a creature that
ought not even to exist, a creature that, although
undeniably *there,* in some way or other was not
present—and would take to his heels and have forgotten him, Grenouille, a moment later. . . .

But now, in the streets of Montpellier, Grenouille
sensed and saw with his own eyes—and each time he
saw it anew, a powerful sense of pride washed over
him—that he exerted an effect on people. As he
passed a woman who stood bent down over the edge
of a well, he noticed how she raised her head for a
moment to see who was there, and then, apparently
satisfied, turned back to her bucket. A man who was
standing with his back to him turned around and
gazed after him with curiosity for a good while. The
children he met scooted to one side—not out of fear,
but to make room for him; and even when they came
hurtling out of a side doorway right toward him, they
were not frightened, but simply slipped naturally on
past him as if they had anticipated an approaching
person.

Several such meetings taught him to assess more
precisely the power and effect of his new aura, and he
grew more self-assured and cocky. He moved more
rapidly toward people, passed by them more closely,
even stretched out one arm a little, grazing the arm of
a passerby as if by chance. Once he jostled a man as if
by accident while moving to pass around him. He
stopped, apologized, and the man—who only yesterday would have reacted to Grenouille's sudden ap-

pearance as if to a thunderbolt—behaved as though
nothing had happened, accepted the apology, even
smiled briefly, and clapped Grenouille on the shoulder.

He left the back streets and entered the square
before the cathedral of Saint-Pierre. The bells were
ringing. There was a crush of people at both sides of
the portal. A wedding had just ended. People wanted
to see the bride. Grenouille hurried over and mingled
with the crowd. He shoved, bored his way in to where
he wanted to be, where people were packed together
most densely, where he could be cheek by jowl with
them, rubbing his own scent directly under their
noses. And in the thick of the crush, he spread his
arms, spread his legs, and opened his collar so that the
odor could flow unimpeded from his body . . . and
his joy was boundless when he noticed that the others
noticed nothing, nothing whatever, that all these men,
women, and children standing pressed about him
could be so easily duped, that they could inhale his
concoction of cat shit, cheese, and vinegar as an odor
just like their own and accept him, Grenouille the
cuckoo's egg, in their midst as a human being among
human beings.

He felt a child against his knee, a little girl standing
wedged in among the adults. He lifted her up with
hypocritical concern and held her with one arm so
that she could see better. The mother not only toler-
ated this, she thanked him as well, and the kid yowled
with delight.

Grenouille stood there like that in the bosom of the
crowd for a good quarter of an hour, a strange child
pressed sanctimoniously to his chest. And while the
wedding party passed by—to the accompaniment of
the booming bells and the cheers of the masses and a
pelting shower of coins—Grenouille broke out in a
different jubilation, a black jubilation, a wicked feel-

ing of triumph that set him quivering and excited him like an attack of lechery, and he had trouble keeping from spurting it like venom and spleen over all these people and screaming exultantly in their faces: that he was not afraid of them; that he hardly hated them anymore; but that his contempt for them was profound and total, because they were so dumb they stank; because they could be deceived by him, let themselves be deceived; because they were nothing, and he was everything! And as if to mock them, he pressed the child still closer to him, bursting out and shouting in chorus with the others: "Hurrah for the bride! Long live the bride! Long live the glorious couple!"

When the wedding party had departed and the crowd had begun to disperse, he gave the child back to its mother and went into the church—to recover from his excitement and rest a little. Inside the cathedral the air was still filled with incense billowing up in cold clouds from two thuribles at each side of the altar and lying in a suffocating layer above the lighter odors of the people who had just been sitting there. Grenouille hunched down on a bench behind the choir.

All at once great contentment came over him. Not a drunken one, as in the days when he had celebrated his lonely orgies in the bowels of the mountain, but a very cold and sober contentment, as befits awareness of one's own power. He now knew what he was capable of. Thanks to his own genius, with a minimum of contrivance he had imitated the odor of human beings and at one stroke had matched it so well that even a child had been deceived. He now knew that he could do much more. He knew that he could improve on this scent. He would be able to create a scent that was not merely human, but superhuman, an angel's scent, so indescribably good and vital that whoever smelled it would be enchanted and

188

with his whole heart would have to love him, Grenouille, the bearer of that scent.

Yes, that was what he wanted—they would love him as they stood under the spell of his scent, not just accept him as one of them, but love him to the point of insanity, of self-abandonment, they would quiver with delight, scream, weep for bliss, they would sink to their knees just as if under God's cold incense, merely to be able to smell *him*, Grenouille! He would be the omnipotent god of scent, just as he had been in his fantasies, but this time in the real world and over real people. And he knew that all this was within his power. For people could close their eyes to greatness, to horrors, to beauty, and their ears to melodies or deceiving words. But they could not escape scent. For scent was a brother of breath. Together with breath it entered human beings, who could not defend themselves against it, not if they wanted to live. And scent entered into their very core, went directly to their hearts, and decided for good and all between affection and contempt, disgust and lust, love and hate. He who ruled scent ruled the hearts of men.

Grenouille sat at his ease on his bench in the cathedral of Saint-Pierre and smiled. His mood was not euphoric as he formed his plans to rule humankind. There were no mad flashings of the eye, no lunatic grimace passed over his face. He was not out of his mind, which was so clear and buoyant that he asked himself why he wanted to do it at all. And he said to himself that he wanted to do it because he was evil, thoroughly evil. And he smiled as he said it and was content. He looked quite innocent, like any happy person.

He sat there for a while, with an air of devout tranquillity, and took deep breaths, inhaling the incense-laden air. And yet another cheerful grin crossed his face. How miserable this God smelled!

189

How ridiculously bad the scent that this God let spill from Him. It was not even genuine frankincense fuming up out of those thuribles. A bad substitute, adulterated with linden and cinnamon dust and saltpeter. God stank. God was a poor little stinker. He had been swindled, this God had, or was Himself a swindler, no different from Grenouille—only a considerably worse one!

≫ *Thirty-three* ≪

T HE MARQUIS de La Taillade-Espinasse was thrilled with his new perfume. It was staggering, he said, even for the discoverer of the *fluidum letale,* to note what a striking influence on the general condition of an individual such a trivial and ephemeral item as perfume could have as a result of its being either earth-bound or earth-removed in origin. Grenouille, who but a few hours before had lain pale and near swooning, now appeared as fresh and rosy as any healthy man his age could. Why—even with all the qualifications appropriate to a man of his rank and limited education—one might almost say that he had gained something very like a personality. In any case, he, Taillade-Espinasse, would discuss the case in the chapter on vital dietetics in his soon-to-be-published treatise on the theory of the *fluidum letale.* But first he wished to anoint his own body with this new perfume.

Grenouille handed him both flacons of conventional floral scent, and the marquis sprinkled himself with it. He seemed highly gratified by the effect. He confessed that after years of being oppressed by the leaden scent of violets, a mere dab of this made him feel as if he had sprouted floral wings; and if he was not mistaken, the beastly pain in his knee was already subsiding, likewise the buzzing in his ears. All in all he felt buoyant, revitalized, and several years younger. He approached Grenouille, embraced him, and called him "my fluidal brother," adding that this was in no way a form of social address, but rather a purely spiritual one *in conspectu universalitatis fluidi letalis,* before which—and before which alone!—all men were equal. Also—and this he said as he disengaged himself from Grenouille, in a most friendly disengagement, without the least revulsion, almost as if he were disengaging himself from an equal—he was planning soon to found an international lodge that stood above all social rank and the goal of which would be utterly to vanquish the *fluidum letale* and replace it in the shortest possible time with purest *fluidum vitale*—and even now he promised to win Grenouille over as the first proselyte. Then he had him write the formula for the floral perfume on a slip of paper, pocketed it, and presented Grenouille with fifty louis d'or.

Precisely one week after the first lecture, the marquis de La Taillade-Espinasse once again presented his ward in the great hall of the university. The crush was monstrous. All Montpellier had come, not just scientific Montpellier, but also and in particular social Montpellier, among whom were many ladies desirous of seeing the fabled caveman. And although Taillade's enemies, primarily the champions of the Friends of the University Botanical Gardens and members of the Society for the Advancement of Agriculture, had mobilized all their supporters, the exhibition was a scintillating success. In order to remind his audience of Grenouille's condition of only the week before, Taillade-Espinasse first circulated drawings depicting the caveman in all his ugliness and depravity. He then had them lead in the new Grenouille dressed in a handsome velvet blue coat and silk shirt, rouged, powdered, and coiffed; and merely by the way he walked, so erect and with dainty steps and an elegant swing of the hips, by the way he climbed to the dais without anyone's assistance, bowing deeply and nodding with a smile now to one side now to the other, he silenced every skeptic and critic. Even the friends of the university's botanical garden were embarrassedly speechless. The change was too egregious, the apparent miracle too overwhelming: where but a week ago had cowered a drudge, a brutalized beast, there now stood a truly civilized, properly proportioned human being. An almost prayerful mood spread through the hall, and as Taillade-Espinasse commenced his lecture, perfect silence reigned. He once again set forth his all too familiar theory about earth's *fluidum letale,* explained how and with what mechanical and dietetic means he had driven it from the body of his exhibit, replacing it with *fluidum vitale.* Finally he demanded of all those present, friend and foe alike, that in the face of such overwhelming evidence they abandon their opposition to this new doctrine and make common cause with him, Taillade-Espinasse, against the evil *fluidum* and open themselves to the beneficial *fluidum vitale.* At this he spread his arms wide, cast his eyes heavenwards—and many learned men did likewise, and women wept.

Grenouille stood at the dais but did not listen. He watched with great satisfaction the effect of a totally different fluid, a much realer one: his own. As was appropriate for the size of the great hall, he had doused himself with perfume, and no sooner had he climbed the dais than the aura of his scent began to radiate powerfully from him. He saw—literally saw with his own eyes!—how it captured the spectators sitting closest, was transmitted to those farther back, and finally reached the last rows and the gallery. And whomever it captured—and Grenouille's heart leapt for joy within him—was visibly changed. Under the sway of the odor, but without their being aware of it, people's facial expressions, their airs, their emotions were altered. Those who at first had gawked at him out of pure amazement now gazed at him with a milder eye; those who had made a point of leaning back in their seats with furrowed critical brows and mouths markedly turned down at the corners now leaned forward more relaxed and with a look of childlike ease on their faces. And as his odor reached them, even the faces of the timorous, frightened, and hypersensitive souls who had borne the sight of his former self with horror and beheld his present state with due misgiving now showed traces of amity, indeed of sympathy.

At lecturer's end the entire assemblage rose to its feet and broke into frenetic cheering. "Long live the *fluidum vitale!* Long live Taillade-Espinasse! Hurrah for the fluidal theory! Down with orthodox medicine!"—such were the cries of the learned folk of Montpellier, the most important university town in the south of France, and the marquis de La Taillade-Espinasse experienced the greatest hour of his life.

Grenouille, however, having climbed down from the dais to mingle among the crowd, knew that these ovations were in reality meant for him, for him alone, Jean-Baptiste Grenouille—although not one of those cheering in the hall suspected anything of the sort.

❧ *Thirty-four* ❧

HE STAYED ON in Montpellier for several weeks. He had achieved a certain fame and was invited to salons where he was asked about his life in the cave and about how the marquis had cured him. He had to tell the tale of the robbers over and over, how they had dragged him off, and how the basket was let down, and about the ladder. And every time he added more lovely embellishments and invented new details. And so he gained some facility in speaking—admittedly only a very limited one, since he had never in all his life handled speech well—and, what was even more important to him, a practiced routine for lying.

In essence, he could tell people whatever he wanted. Once they had gained confidence in him—and with the first breath, they gained confidence in him, for they were inhaling his artificial odor—they believed everything. And in time he gained a certain self-assurance in social situations such as he had never known before. This was apparent even in his body. It was as if he had grown. His humpback seemed to disappear. He walked almost completely erect. And when someone spoke to him, he no longer hunched over, but remained erect and returned the look directed at him. Granted, in this short time he did not become a man-of-the-world, no dandy-about-town, no peerless social lion. But his cringing, clumsy manner fell visibly from him, making way for a bearing that was taken for natural modesty or at worst for a slight, inborn shyness that made a sympathetic impression on many gentlemen and many ladies— sophisticated circles in those days had a weakness for everything natural and for a certain unpolished charm.

When March came he packed his things and was off, secretly, so early in the morning that the city gates had only just been opened. He was wearing an inconspicuous brown coat that he had bought secondhand at a market the day before and a shabby hat that covered half his face. No one recognized him, no one saw or noticed him, for he had intentionally gone without his perfume that day. And when around noon the marquis had inquiries made, the watchmen swore by all that's holy that they had seen all kinds of people leaving the city, but not the caveman, whom they knew and would most certainly have noticed. The marquis then had word spread that with his permission Grenouille had left Montpellier to look after family matters in Paris. Privately he was dreadfully annoyed, for he had intended to take Grenouille on a tour through the whole kingdom, recruiting adherents for his fluidal theory.

After a while he calmed down again, for his own fame had spread without any such tour, almost without any action on his part. A long article about the *fluidum letale Taillade* appeared in the *Journal des Sçavans* and even in the *Courier de l'Europe* and fluidally contaminated patients came from far and wide for him to cure them. In the summer of 1764, he founded the first Lodge of the Vital Fluidum, with 120 members in Montpellier, and established branches in Marseille and Lyon. Then he decided to dare the move to Paris and from there to conquer the entire civilized world with his teachings. But first he wanted to provide a propaganda base for his crusade by accomplishing some heroic fluidal feat, one that would overshadow the cure of the caveman, indeed all other experiments. And in early December he had a company of fearless disciples join him on an expedition to the Pic du Canigou, which was on the same longitude with Paris and was considered the highest mountain in the Pyrenees. Though on the threshold of senescence, the man wanted to be borne to the summit at nine thousand feet and left there in the sheerest, finest vital air for three whole weeks, whereupon, he announced, he would descend from the mountain precisely on Christmas Eve as a strapping lad of twenty.

The disciples gave up shortly beyond Vernet, the last human settlement at the foot of the fearsome mountain. But nothing daunted the marquis. Casting his garments from him in the icy cold and whooping in exultation, he began the climb alone. The last that was seen of him was his silhouette: hands lifted ecstatically to heaven and voice raised in song, he disappeared into the blizzard.

His followers waited in vain that Christmas Eve for the return of the marquis de La Taillade-Espinasse. He returned neither as an old man nor a young one. Nor when early summer came the next year and the most audacious of them went in search of him, scaling the still snowbound summit of the Pic du Canigou, did they find any trace of him, no clothes, no body parts, no bones.

His teachings, however, suffered no damage at all. On the contrary. Soon the legend was abroad that there on the mountain peak he had wedded himself to the eternal *fluidum vitale,* merging with it and it with him, and now forever floated—invisible but eternally young—above the peaks of the Pyrenees, and whoever climbed up to him would encounter him there and remain untouched by sickness or the process of aging for one full year. Well into the nineteenth century Taillade's fluidal theory was advocated from many a chair at faculties of medicine and put into therapeutic practice by many an occult society. And even today, on both sides of the Pyrenees, particularly in Perpignan and Figueras, there are secret Tailladic lodges that meet once a year to climb the Pic du Canigou.

There they light a great bonfire, ostensibly for the summer solstice and in honor of St. John—but in reality it is to pay homage to their master, Taillade-Espinasse, and his grand *fluidum,* and to seek eternal life.

PART
❧3❧

❧ Thirty-five ❧

WHEREAS GRENOUILLE had needed seven years for the first stage of his journey through France, he put the second behind him in less than seven days. He no longer avoided busy roads and cities, he made no detours. He had an odor, he had money, he had self-confidence, and he had no time to lose.

By evening of the day he left Montpellier, he had arrived at Le Grau-du-Roi, a small harbor town southwest of Aigues-Mortes, where he boarded a merchant ship for Marseille. In Marseille he did not even leave the harbor, but immediately sought out a ship that brought him farther along the coast to the east. Two days later he was in Toulon, in three more in Cannes. The rest of the way he traveled on foot. He followed a back road that led up into the hills, northward into the interior.

Two hours later he was standing on a rise and before him was spread a valley several miles wide, a kind of basin in the landscape—its surrounding rim made up of gently rising hills and a ridge of steep mountains, its broad bowl covered with fields, gardens, and olive groves. The basin had its own special, intimate climate. Although the sea was so near that one could see it from the tops of the hills, there was nothing maritime, nothing salty and sandy, nothing expansive about this climate; instead, it possessed a secluded tranquillity as if you were many days' journey distant from the coast. And although to the north the high mountains were covered with snow that would remain for a good while yet, it was not in the least raw or barren and no cold wind blew. Spring was further advanced than in Montpellier. A mild haze lay like a glass bell over the fields. Apricot and almond trees were in bloom, and the warm air was infused with the scent of jonquils.

At the other end of the wide basin, perhaps two miles off, a town lay among—or better, clung to—the rising mountains. From a distance it did not make a particularly grand impression. There was no mighty cathedral towering above the houses, just a little stump of a church steeple, no commanding fortress, no magnificent edifice of note. The walls appeared anything but defiant—here and there the houses spilled out from their limits, especially in the direction of the plain, lending the outskirts a somewhat disheveled look. It was as if the place had been overrun and then retaken so often that it was weary of offering serious resistance to any future intruders—not out of weakness, but out of indolence, or maybe even out of a sense of its own strength. It looked as if it had no need to flaunt itself. It reigned above the fragrant basin at its feet, and that seemed to suffice.

This equally homely and self-confident place was the town of Grasse, for decades now the uncontested center for production of and commerce in scents, perfumes, soaps, and oils. Giuseppe Baldini had always uttered the name with enraptured delight. The town was the Rome of scents, the promised land of perfumes, and the man who had not earned his spurs here did not rightfully bear the title of perfumer.

Grenouille gazed very coolly at the town of Grasse. He was not seeking the promised land of perfumers, and his heart did not leap at the sight of this small town clinging to the far slopes. He had come because he knew that he could learn about several techniques for production of scent there better than elsewhere. And he wanted to acquire them, for he needed them for his own purposes. He pulled the flacon with his perfume from his pocket, dabbed himself lightly, and continued on his way. An hour and a half later, around noon, he was in Grasse.

He ate at an inn near the top of the town, on the place aux Aires. The square was divided lengthwise by a brook where tanners washed their hides and afterwards spread them out to dry. The odor was so pungent that many a guest lost his appetite for his meal. But not Grenouille. It was a familiar odor to him; it gave him a sense of security. In every city he always sought out the tanning district first. And then, emerging from that region of stench to explore the other parts of the place, he no longer felt a stranger.

He spent all that afternoon wandering about the town. It was unbelievably filthy, despite—or perhaps directly because of—all the water that gushed from springs and wells, gurgling down through the town in unchanneled rivulets and brooks, undermining the streets or flooding them with muck. In some neighborhoods the houses stood so close together that only a yard-wide space was left for passageways and stairs, forcing pedestrians to jostle one another as they waded through the mire. And even in the squares and along the few broader streets, vehicles could hardly get out of each other's way.

Nevertheless, however filthy, cramped, and slovenly, the town was bursting with the bustle of commerce. During his tour, Grenouille spotted no less than seven soapworks, a dozen master perfumers and glovers, countless small distilleries, pomade studios, and spice shops, and finally some seven wholesalers in scents.

These were in fact merchants who completely controlled the wholesale supply of scent. One would hardly know it by their houses. The facades to the street looked modestly middle class. But what was stored behind them, in warehouses and in gigantic cellars, in kegs of oil, in stacks of finest lavender soaps, in demijohns of floral colognes, wines, alcohols, in bales of scented leather, in sacks and chests and crates stuffed with spices—Grenouille smelled out every detail through the thickest walls—these were riches beyond those of princes. And when he smelled his way more penetratingly through the prosaic shops and storerooms fronting the streets, he discovered that at the rear of these provincial family homes were buildings of the most luxurious sort. Around small but exquisite gardens, where oleander and palm trees flourished and fountains bordered by ornamental flowers leapt, extended the actual residential wings, usually built in a U-shape toward the south: on the upper floors, bedchambers drenched in sunlight, the walls covered with silk; on the ground floor wainscoted salons and dining rooms, sometimes with terraces built out into the open air, where, just as Baldini had said, people ate from porcelain with golden cutlery. The gentlemen who lived behind these modest sham facades reeked of gold and power, of carefully secured riches, and they reeked of it more strongly than anything Grenouille had smelled thus far on his journey through the provinces.

He stopped and stood for a good while in front of one of these camouflaged palazzi. The house was at the beginning of the rue Droite, a main artery that traversed the whole length of the city, from west to east. It was nothing extraordinary to look at, perhaps the front was a little wider and ampler than its neighbors', but certainly not imposing. At the gateway stood a wagon from which kegs were being unloaded down a ramp. A second vehicle stood waiting. A man with some papers went into the office, came back out with another man, both of them disappeared through the gateway. Grenouille stood on the opposite side of the street and watched the comings and goings. He was not interested in what was happening. And yet he stood there. Something else was holding him fast.

He closed his eyes and concentrated on the odors that came floating to him from the building across the way. There were the odors of the kegs, vinegar and wine, then the hundredfold heavy odors of the warehouse, then the odors of wealth that the walls exuded like a fine golden sweat, and finally the odors of a garden that had to lie on the far side of the building. It was not easy to catch the delicate scents of the garden, for they came only in thin ribbons from over the house's gables and down into the street. Grenouille discerned magnolia, hyacinth, daphne, and rhododendron . . . but there seemed to be something else besides, something in the garden that gave off a fatally wonderful scent, a scent so exquisite that in all his life his nose had never before encountered one like it—or, indeed, only once before. . . . He had to get closer to that scent.

He considered whether he ought simply to force his way through the gate and onto the premises. But meanwhile so many people had become involved in unloading and inventorying the kegs that he was sure to be noticed. He decided to walk back down the street and find an alley or passageway that would perhaps lead him along the far side of the house. Within a few yards he had reached the town gate at the start of the rue Droite. He walked through it, took a sharp left, and followed the town wall downhill. He had not gone far before he smelled the garden, faintly at first, blended with the air from the fields, but then ever more strongly. Finally he knew that he was very close. The garden bordered on the town wall. It was directly beside him. If he moved back a bit, he could see the top branches of the orange trees just over the wall.

Again he closed his eyes. The scents of the garden descended upon him, their contours as precise and clear as the colored bands of a rainbow. And that one, that precious one, that one that mattered above all else, was among them. Grenouille turned hot with rapture and cold with fear. Blood rushed to his head as if he were a little boy caught red-handed, and then it retreated to his solar plexus, and then rushed up again and retreated again, and he could do nothing to stop it. This attack of scent had come on too suddenly. For a moment, for a breath, for an eternity it seemed to him, time was doubled or had disappeared completely, for he no longer knew whether now was now and here was here, or whether now was not in fact then and here there—that is, the rue des Marais in Paris, September 1753. The scent floating out of the garden was the scent of the redheaded girl he had murdered that night. To have found that scent in this world once again brought tears of bliss to his eyes— and to know that it could not possibly be true frightened him to death.

He was dizzy, he tottered a little and had to support himself against the wall, sinking slowly down against it in a crouch. Collecting himself and gaining control of his senses, he began to inhale the fatal scent in short, less dangerous breaths. And he established that, while the scent from behind the wall bore an extreme resemblance to the scent of the redheaded girl, it was

not completely the same. To be sure, it also came from
a redheaded girl, there was no doubt of that. In his
olfactory imagination, Grenouille saw this girl as if in
a picture: she was not sitting still, she was jumping
about, warming up and then cooling off, apparently
playing some game in which she had to move quickly
and then just as quickly stand still—with a second
person, by the way, someone with a totally insignificant odor. She had dazzlingly white skin. She had
green eyes. She had freckles on her face, neck, and
breasts . . . that is—and Grenouille's breath stopped
for a moment, then he sniffed more vigorously and
tried to suppress the memory of the scent of the girl
from the rue des Marais—that is, this girl did not
even have breasts in the true sense of the word! She
barely had the rudimentary start of breasts. Infinitely
tender and with hardly any fragrance, sprinkled with
freckles, just beginning to expand, perhaps only in the
last few days, perhaps in the last few hours, perhaps
only just at this moment—such were the little cupped
breasts of this girl. In a word: the girl was still a child.
But what a child!

The sweat stood out on Grenouille's forehead. He
knew that children did not have an exceptional scent,
any more than green buds of flowers before they
blossom. This child behind the wall, however, this
bud still almost closed tight, which only just now was
sending out its first fragrant tips, unnoticed by anyone
except by him, Grenouille—this child already had a
scent so terrifyingly celestial that once it had unfolded
its total glory, it would unleash a perfume such as the
world had never smelled before. She already smells
better now, Grenouille thought, than that girl did
back then in the rue des Marais—not as robust, not as
voluminous, but more refined, more richly nuanced,
and at the same time more natural. In a year or two
this scent will be ripened and take on a gravity that no

one, man or woman, will be able to escape. People will be overwhelmed, disarmed, helpless before the magic of this girl, and they will not know why. And because people are stupid and use their noses only for blowing, but believe absolutely anything they see with their eyes, they will say it is because this is a girl with beauty and grace and charm. In their obtuseness, they will praise the evenness of her features, her slender figure, her faultless breasts. And her eyes, they will say, are like emeralds and her teeth like pearls and her limbs smooth as ivory—and all those other idiotic comparisons. And they will elect her Queen of the Jasmine, and she will be painted by stupid portraitists, her picture will be ogled, and people will say that she is the most beautiful woman in France. And to the strains of mandolins, youths will howl the nights away sitting beneath her window . . . rich, fat old men will skid about on their knees begging her father for her hand . . . and women of every age will sigh at the sight of her and in their sleep dream of looking as alluring as she for just one day. And none of them will know that it is truly not how she looks that has captured them, not her reputed unblemished external beauty, but solely her incomparable, splendid scent! Only he would know that, only Grenouille, he alone. He knew it already in fact.

Ah! He wanted to have that scent! Not in the useless, clumsy fashion by which he had had the scent of the girl in the rue des Marais. For he had merely sucked that into himself and destroyed it in the process. No, he wanted truly to possess the scent of this girl behind the wall; to peel it from her like skin and to make her scent his own. How that was to be done, he did not know yet. But he had two years in which to learn. Ultimately it ought to be no more difficult than robbing a rare flower of its perfume.

He stood up, almost reverently, as if leaving behind

something sacred or someone in deep sleep. He moved on, softly, hunched over, so that no one might see him, no one might hear him, no one might be made aware of his precious discovery. And so he fled along the wall to the opposite end of the town, where he finally lost the girl's scent and reentered by way of the Porte des Fénéants. He stood in the shadow of the buildings. The stinking vapors of the streets made him feel secure and helped him to tame the passions that had overcome him. Within fifteen minutes he had grown perfectly calm again. To start with, he thought, he would not again approach the vicinity of the garden behind the wall. That was not necessary. It excited him too much. The flower would flourish there without his aid, and he knew already in what manner it would flourish. He dared not intoxicate himself with that scent prematurely. He had to throw himself into his work. He had to broaden his knowledge and perfect the techniques of his craft in order to be equipped for the time of harvest. He had a good two years.

❧ *Thirty-six* ❦

NOT FAR FROM the Porte des Fénéants, in the rue de la Louve, Grenouille discovered a small perfumer's workshop and asked for a job.

It turned out that the proprietor, *maître parfumeur* Honoré Arnulfi, had died the winter before and that his widow, a lively, black-haired woman of perhaps thirty, was managing the business alone, with the help of a journeyman.

After complaining at length about the bad times and her own precarious financial situation, Madame Arnulfi declared that she really could not afford a second journeyman, but on the other hand she needed one for all the upcoming work; that she could not possibly put up a second journeyman here in the house, but on the other hand she did have at her disposal a small cabin in an olive grove behind the Franciscan cloister—not ten minutes away—in which a young man of modest needs could sleep in a pinch; further, that as an honest mistress she certainly knew that she was responsible for the physical well-being of her journeymen, but that on the other hand she did not see herself in a position to provide two warm meals a day—in short (as Grenouille had of course smelled for some time already): Madame Arnulfi was a woman of solid prosperity and sound business sense. And since he was not concerned about money and declared himself satisfied with a salary of two francs a week and with the other niggardly provisions, they quickly came to an agreement. The first journey-man was called in, a giant of a man named Druot. Grenouille at once guessed that he regularly shared Madame's bed and that she apparently did not make certain decisions without first consulting him. With legs spread wide and exuding a cloud of spermy odor, he planted himself before Grenouille, who looked ridiculously frail in the presence of this Hun, and inspected him, looked him straight in the eye—as if this technique would allow him to recognize any improper intentions or a possible rival—finally grinned patronizingly, and signaled his agreement with a nod.

That settled it. Grenouille got a handshake, a cold evening snack, a blanket, and a key to the cabin—a windowless shack that smelled pleasantly of old sheep dung and hay, where he made himself at home as well as he could. The next day he began work for Madame Arnulfi.

It was jonquil season. Madame Arnulfi had the flowers grown on small parcels of land that she owned in the broad basin below the city, or she bought them from farmers, with whom she haggled fiercely over every ounce. The blossoms were delivered very early in the morning, emptied out in the workshop by the basketfuls into massive but lightweight and fragrant piles. Meanwhile, in a large caldron Druot melted pork lard and beef tallow to make a creamy soup into which he pitched shovelfuls of fresh blossoms, while Grenouille constantly had to stir it all with a spatula as long as a broom. They lay on the surface for a

moment, like eyes facing instant death, and lost all
color the moment the spatula pushed them down into
the warm, oily embrace. And at almost the same
moment they wilted and withered, and death apparently came so rapidly upon them that they had no
choice but to exhale their last fragrant sighs into the
very medium that drowned them; for—and Grenouille observed this with indescribable fascination
—the more blossoms he stirred under into the caldron, the sweeter the scent of the oil. And it was not
that the dead blossoms continued to give off scent
there in the oil—no, the oil itself had appropriated
the scent of the blossoms.

Now and then the soup got too thick, and they had
to pour it quickly through a sieve, freeing it of
macerated cadavers to make room for fresh blossoms.
Then they dumped and mixed and sieved some more,
all day long without pause, for the procedure allowed
no delays, until, as evening approached, all the piles
of blossoms had passed through the caldron of oil.
Then—so that nothing might be wasted—the refuse
was steeped in boiling water and wrung out to the last
drop in a screw press, yielding still more mildly
fragrant oil. The majority of the scent, however, the
soul of the sea of blossoms, had remained in the
caldron, trapped and preserved in an unsightly, slowly
congealing grayish white grease.

The following day, the maceration, as this procedure was called, continued—the caldron was heated
once again, the oil melted and fed with new blossoms.
This went on for several days, from morning till
evening. It was tiring work. Grenouille had arms of
lead, calluses on his hands, and pains in his back as he
staggered back to his cabin in the evening. Although
Druot was at least three times as strong as he, he did
not once take a turn at stirring, but was quite content
to pour in more feather-light blossoms, to tend the

fire, and now and then, because of the heat, to go out for a drink. But Grenouille did not mutiny. He stirred the blossoms into the oil without complaint, from morning till night, and hardly noticed the exertion of stirring, for he was continually fascinated by the process taking place before his eyes and under his nose: the sudden withering of the blossoms and the absorption of their scent.

After a while, Druot would decide that the oil was finally saturated and could absorb no more scent. He would extinguish the fire, sieve the viscous soup one last time, and pour it into stoneware crocks, where almost immediately it solidified to a wonderfully fragrant pomade.

This was the moment for Madame Arnulfi, who came to assay the precious product, to label it, and to record in her books the exact quality and quantity of the yield. After she had personally capped the crocks, had sealed them and borne them to the cool depths of her cellar, she donned her black dress, took out her widow's veil, and made the rounds of the city's wholesalers and vendors of perfume. In touching phrases she described to these gentlemen her situation as a woman left all on her own, let them make their offers, compared the prices, sighed, and finally sold— or did not sell. Perfumed pomades, when stored in a cool place, keep for a long time. And when the price leaves something to be desired, who knows, perhaps it will climb again come winter or next spring. Also you had to consider whether instead of selling to these hucksters you ought not to join with other small producers and together ship a load of pomade to Genoa or share in a convoy to the autumn fair in Beaucaire—risky enterprises, to be sure, but extremely profitable when successful. Madame Arnulfi carefully weighed these various possibilities against one another, and sometimes she would indeed sign a contract, selling a portion of her treasure, but hold another portion of it in reserve, and risk negotiating for a third part all on her own. But if during her inquiries she had got the impression that there was a glut on the pomade market and that in the foreseeable future there would be no scarcity to her advantage, she would hurry back home, her veil wafting behind her, and give Druot instructions to subject the whole yield to a lavage and transform it into an *essence absolue.*

And the pomade would be brought up again from the cellar, carefully warmed in tightly covered pots, diluted with rectified spirits, and thoroughly blended and washed with the help of a built-in stirring apparatus that Grenouille operated. Returned to the cellar, this mixture quickly cooled; the alcohol separated from the congealed oil of the pomade and could be drained off into a bottle. A kind of perfume had been produced, but one of enormous intensity, while the pomade that was left behind had lost most of its fragrance. Thus the fragrance of the blossoms had been transferred to yet another medium. But the operation was still not at an end. After carefully filtering the perfumed alcohol through gauze that retained the least little clump of oil, Druot filled a small alembic and distilled it slowly over a minimum flame. What remained in the matrass was a tiny quantity of a pale-hued liquid that Grenouille knew quite well, but had never smelled in such quality and purity either at Baldini's or Runel's: the finest oil of the blossom, its polished scent concentrated a hundred times over to a little puddle of *essence absolue.* This essence no longer had a sweet fragrance. Its smell was almost painfully intense, pungent, and acrid. And yet one single drop, when dissolved in a quart of alcohol, sufficed to revitalize it and resurrect a whole field of flowers.

The yield was frightfully small. The liquid from the matrass filled three little flacons and no more. Nothing was left from the scent of hundreds of thousands of blossoms except those three flacons. But they were worth a fortune, even here in Grasse. And worth how much more once delivered to Paris or Lyon, to Grenoble, Genoa, or Marseille! Madame Arnulfi's glance was suffused with beauty when she looked at the little bottles, she caressed them with her eyes; and when she picked them up and stoppered them with snugly fitting glass stoppers, she held her breath to prevent even the least bit of the precious contents from being blown away. And to make sure that after stoppering not the tiniest atom would evaporate and escape, she sealed them with wax and encapsulated them in a fish bladder tightly tied around the neck of the bottle. Then she placed them in a crate stuffed with wadded cotton and put them under lock and key in the cellar.

❧ *Thirty-seven* ❧

IN April **they** macerated broom and orange blossoms, in May a sea of roses, the scent from which submerged the city in a creamy, sweet, invisible fog for a whole month. Grenouille worked like a horse. Self-effacing and as acquiescent as a slave, he did every menial chore Druot assigned him. But all the while he stirred, spatulated, washed out tubs, cleaned the workshop, or lugged firewood with apparent mindlessness, nothing of the essential business, nothing of the metamorphosis of scent, escaped his notice. Grenouille used his nose to observe and monitor more closely than Druot ever could have the migration of scent of the flower petals—through the oil and then via alcohol to the precious little flacons. Long before Druot noticed it, he would smell when the oil was overheated, smell when the blossoms were exhausted, when the broth was impregnated with scent. He could smell what was happening in the interior of the mixing pots and the precise moment when the distilling had to be stopped. And occasionally he let this be known—of course, quite unassumingly and without abandoning his submissive demeanor. It

216

seemed to him, he said, that the oil might possibly be getting too hot; he almost thought that they could filter shortly; he somehow had the feeling that the alcohol in the alembic had evaporated now. . . . And in time Druot, who was not fabulously intelligent, but not a complete idiot either, came to realize that his decisions turned out for the best when he did or ordered to be done whatever Grenouille "almost thought" or "somehow had a feeling about." And since Grenouille was never cocky or know-it-all when he said what he thought or felt, and because he never—particularly never in the presence of Madame Arnulfi!—cast Druot's authority and superior position of first journeyman in doubt, not even ironically, Druot saw no reason not to follow Grenouille's advice or, as time went on, not to leave more and more decisions entirely to his discretion.

It was increasingly the case that Grenouille did not just do the stirring, but also the feeding, the heating, and the sieving, while Druot stepped round to the Quatre Dauphins for a glass of wine or went upstairs to check out how things were doing with Madame. He knew that he could depend on Grenouille. And although it meant twice the work, Grenouille enjoyed being alone, perfecting himself in these new arts and trying an occasional experiment. And with malicious delight, he discovered that the pomades he made were incomparably finer, that his *essence absolue* was several percent purer than those that he produced together with Druot.

Jasmine season began at the end of July, August was for tuberoses. The perfume of these two flowers was both so exquisite and so fragile that not only did the blossoms have to be picked before sunrise, but they also demanded the most gentle and special handling. Warmth diminished their scent; suddenly to plunge them into hot, macerating oil would have completely destroyed it. The souls of these noblest of blossoms could not be simply ripped from them, they had to be methodically coaxed away. In a special impregnating room, the flowers were strewn on glass plates smeared with cool oil or wrapped in oil-soaked cloths; there they would die slowly in their sleep. It took three or four days for them to wither and exhale their scent into the adhering oil. Then they were carefully plucked off and new blossoms spread out. This procedure was repeated a good ten, twenty times, and it was September before the pomade had drunk its fill and the fragrant oil could be pressed from the cloths. The yield was considerably less than with maceration. But in purity and verisimilitude, the quality of the jasmine paste or the *huile antique de tubéreuse* won by such a cold enfleurage exceeded that of any other product of the perfumer's art. Particularly with jasmine, it seemed as if the oiled surface were a mirror image that radiated the sticky-sweet, erotic scent of the blossom with lifelike fidelity—*cum grano salis,* of course. For Grenouille's nose obviously recognized the difference between the odor of the blossoms and their preserved scent: the specific odor of the oil—no matter how pure—lay like a gossamer veil over the fragrant tableau of the original, softening it, gently diluting its bravado—and, perhaps, only then making its beauty bearable for normal people. . . . But in any case, cold enfleurage was the most refined and effec-. tive method to capture delicate scents. There was no better. And even if the method was not good enough completely to satisfy Grenouille's nose, he knew quite well that it would suffice a thousand times over for duping a world of numbed noses.

Just as with maceration, after only a brief time he had likewise surpassed his tutor Druot in the art of cold perfumery—and had made this clear to him in the approved, discreet, and groveling fashion. Druot gladly left it to him to go to the slaughterhouse and buy the most suitable fats, to purify and render them, to filter them and adjust their proportions—a terribly difficult task that Druot himself was always skittish about performing, since an adulterated or rancid fat, or one that smelled too much of pig, sheep, or cow, could ruin the most expensive pomade. He let Grenouille decide how to arrange the oiled plates in the impregnating room, when to rotate the blossoms, and whether the pomade was sufficiently impregnated. Druot soon let Grenouille make all the delicate decisions that he, just as Baldini before him, could only approximate with rules of thumb, but which Grenouille made by employing the wisdom of his nose—something Druot, of course, did not suspect.

"He's got a fine touch," said Druot. "He's got a good feel for things." And sometimes he also thought: Really and truly, he is more talented than me, a hundred times a better perfumer. And all the while he considered him to be a total nitwit, because Grenouille—or so he believed—did not cash in at all on his talent, whereas he, Druot, even with his more modest gifts, would soon become a master perfumer. And Grenouille encouraged him in this opinion, displaying doltish drudgery and not a hint of ambition, acting as if he comprehended nothing of his own genius and were merely executing the orders of the more experienced Druot, without whom he would be a cipher. After their fashion, they got along quite well.

Then came autumn and winter. Things were quieter in the workshop. The floral scents lay captive in their crocks and flacons in the cellar, and if Madame did not wish some pomade or other to be washed or for a sack of dried spices to be distilled, there was not all that much to do. There were still the olives, a couple of basketfuls every week. They pressed the virgin oil from them and put what was left through the oil mill.

And wine, some of which Grenouille distilled to rectified spirit.

Druot made himself more and more scarce. He did his duty in Madame's bed, and when he did appear, stinking of sweat and semen, it was only to head off at once for the Quatre Dauphins. Nor did Madame come downstairs often. She was busy with her investments and with converting her wardrobe for the period that would follow her year of mourning. For days, Grenouille might often see no one except the maid who fixed his midday soup and his evening bread and olives. He hardly went out at all. He took part in corporate life—in the regular meetings and processions of the journeymen—only just often enough as to be conspicuous neither by his absence nor by his presence. He had no friends or close acquaintances, but took careful pains not to be considered arrogant or a misfit. He left it to the other journeymen to find his society dull and unprofitable. He was a master in the art of spreading boredom and playing the clumsy fool—though never so egregiously that people might enjoy making fun of him or use him as the butt of some crude practical joke inside the guild. He succeeded in being considered totally uninteresting. People left him alone. And that was all he wanted.

❧ *Thirty-eight* ❧

H E SPENT HIS time in the workshop. He explained to Druot that he was trying to invent a formula for a new cologne. In reality, however, he was experimenting with scents of a very different sort. Although he had used it very sparingly, the perfume that he had mixed in Montpellier was slowly running out. He created a new one. But this time he was not content simply to imitate basic human odor by hastily tossing together some ingredients; he made it a matter of pride to acquire a personal odor, or better yet, a number of personal odors.

First he made an odor for inconspicuousness, a mousy, workaday outfit of odors with the sour, cheesy smell of humankind still present, but only as if exuded into the outside world through a layer of linen and wool garments covering an old man's dry skin. Bearing this smell, he could move easily among people. The perfume was robust enough to establish the olfactory existence of a human being, but at the same time so discreet that it bothered no one. Using it, Grenouille was not actually present, and yet his presence was justified in the most modest sort of way—a bastard state that was very handy both in the Arnulfi household and on his occasional outings in the town.

On certain occasions, to be sure, this modest scent proved inconvenient. When he had errands to run for Druot or wanted to buy his own civet or a few musk pods from a merchant, he might prove to be so perfectly inconspicuous that he was either ignored and no one waited on him, or was given the wrong item or forgotten while being waited on. For such occasions he had blended a somewhat more redolent, slightly sweaty perfume, one with a few olfactory edges and hooks, that lent him a coarser appearance and made people believe he was in a hurry and on urgent business. He also had good success with a deceptive imitation of Druot's *aura seminalis,* which he learned to produce by impregnating a piece of oily linen with a paste of fresh duck eggs and fermented wheat flour and used whenever he needed to arouse a certain amount of notice.

Another perfume in his arsenal was a scent for arousing sympathy that proved effective with middle-aged and elderly women. It smelled of watery milk and fresh, soft wood. The effect Grenouille created with it—even when he went out unshaved, scowling, and wrapped in a heavy coat—was of a poor, pale lad in a frayed jacket who simply had to be helped. Once they caught a whiff of him, the market women filled his pockets with nuts and dried pears because he seemed to them so hungry and helpless. And the butcher's wife, an implacably callous old hag if there ever was one, let him pick out, for free, smelly old scraps of meat and bone, for his odor of innocence touched her mother's heart. He then took these scraps, digested them directly in alcohol, and used them as the main component for an odor that he applied when he wanted to be avoided and left completely alone. It surrounded him with a slightly nauseating aura, like the rancid breath of an old slattern's mouth when she awakens. It was so effective that even Druot, hardly a squeamish sort, would automatically turn aside and go in search of fresh air, without any clear knowledge, of course, of what had actually driven him away. And sprinkling a few drops of the repellent on the threshold of his cabin was enough to keep every intruder, human or animal, at a distance.

Protected by these various odors, which he changed like clothes as the situation demanded and which permitted him to move undisturbed in the world of men and to keep his true nature from them, Grenouille devoted himself to his real passion: the subtle pursuit of scent. And because he had a great goal right under his nose and over a year still left to him, he not only went about the task with burning zeal, but he also systematically planned how to sharpen his weapons, polish his techniques, and gradually perfect his methods. He began where he had left off at Baldini's, with extracting the scent from inert objects: stone, metal, glass, wood, salt, water, air. . . .

What before had failed so miserably using the crude process of distillation succeeded now, thanks to the strong absorptive powers of oil. Grenouille took a brass doorknob, whose cool, musty, brawny smell he liked, and wrapped it in beef tallow for a few days. And sure enough, when he peeled off the tallow and examined it, it smelled quite clearly like the doorknob, though very faintly. And even after a lavage in alcohol, the odor was still there, infinitely delicate, distant, overshadowed by the vapor of the spirits, and in this world probably perceptible only to Grenouille's nose—but it was certainly there. And that meant, in principle at least, at his disposal. If he had ten thousand doorknobs and wrapped them in tallow for a thousand days, he could produce a tiny drop of brass-doorknob *essence absolue* strong enough for anyone to have the indisputable illusion of the original under his nose.

He likewise succeeded with the porous chalky dust from a stone he found in the olive grove before his cabin. He macerated it and extracted a dollop of stone pomade, whose infinitesimal odor gave him indescribable delight. He combined it with other odors taken from all kinds of objects lying around his cabin, and painstakingly reproduced a miniature olfactory model of the olive grove behind the Franciscan cloister. Carrying it about with him bottled up in a tiny flacon, he could resurrect the grove whenever he felt like it.

These were virtuoso odors, executed as wonderful little trifles that of course no one but he could admire or would ever take note of. He was enchanted by their meaningless perfection; and at no time in his life, either before or after, were there moments of such truly innocent happiness as in those days when he playfully and eagerly set about creating fragrant landscapes, still lifes, and studies of individual objects. For he soon moved on to living subjects.

He hunted for winter flies, for maggots, rats, small cats, and drowned them in warm oil. At night he crept into stalls to drape cows, goats, and piglets for a few hours in cloths smeared with oil or to wrap them in greasy bandages. Or he sneaked into sheepfolds and stealthily sheared a lamb and then washed the redolent wool in rectified spirit. At first the results were not very satisfactory. For in contrast to the patient things, doorknobs and stones, animals yielded up their odor only under protest. The pigs scraped off the bandages by rubbing against the posts of their sties. The sheep bleated when he approached them by night with a knife. The cows obstinately shook the greasy cloths from their udders. Some of the beetles that he caught gave off foully stinking secretions while he was trying to work with them, and the rats, probably out of fear, would shit in the olfactorily sensitive pomades. Unlike flowers, the animals he tried to macerate would not yield up their scent without complaints or with only a mute sigh—they fought desperately against death, absolutely did not want to be stirred under, but kicked and struggled, and in their fear of death created large quantities of sweat whose acidity ruined the warm oil. You could not, of course, do sound work under such conditions. The objects would have to be quieted down, and so suddenly that they would have no time to become afraid or to resist. He would have to kill them.

He first tried it with a puppy. He enticed it away from its mother with a piece of meat, all the way from the slaughterhouse to the laboratory, and as the animal panted excitedly and lunged joyfully for the meat in Grenouille's left hand, he gave one quick, hard blow to the back of its head with a piece of wood he held in his right. Death descended on the puppy so suddenly that the expression of happiness was still on its mouth and in its eyes long after Grenouille had bedded it down in the impregnating room on a grate between two greased plates, where it exuded its pure doggy scent, unadulterated by the sweat of fear. To be sure, one had to be careful! Carcasses, just as plucked blossoms, spoiled quickly. And so Grenouille stood guard over his victim, for about twelve hours, until he noticed that the first wisps of carrion scent—not really unpleasant, but adulterating nevertheless—rose up from the dog's body. He stopped the enfleurage at once, got rid of the carcass, and put the impregnated oil in a pot, where he carefully rinsed it. He distilled the alcohol down to about a thimbleful and filled a tiny glass tube with these few remaining drops. The perfume smelled clearly of dog—moist, fresh, tallowy, and a bit pungent. It smelled amazingly like dog. And when Grenouille let the old bitch at the slaughterhouse sniff at it, she broke out in yelps of joy and whimpered and would not take her nose out of the glass tube. Grenouille closed it up tight and put it in his pocket and bore it with him for a long time as a souvenir of his day of triumph, when for the first time he had succeeded in robbing a living creature of its aromatic soul.

Then, very gradually and with utmost caution, he went to work on human beings. At first he stalked them from a safe distance with a wide-meshed net, for he was less concerned with bagging large game than with testing his hunting methods.

Disguised by his faint perfume for inconspicuousness, he mingled with the evening's guests at the Quatre Dauphins inn and stuck tiny scraps of cloth drenched in oil and grease under the benches and tables and in hidden nooks. A few days later he collected them and put them to the test. And indeed, along with all sorts of kitchen odors, tobacco smoke, and wine smells, they exhaled a little human odor. But it remained very vague and masked, was more the suggestion of general exhalations than a personal odor. A similar mass aura, though purer and more sublimely sweaty, could be gleaned from the cathedral, where on December 24 Grenouille hung his experimental flags under the pews and gathered them in again on the twenty-sixth, after no less than seven masses had been sat through just above them. A ghastly conglomerate of odor was reproduced on the impregnated swatches: anal sweat, menstrual blood, moist hollows of knees, and clenched hands, mixed with the exhaled breath of thousands of hymn-singing and Ave Maria–mumbling throats and the oppressive fumes of incense and myrrh. A horrible concen-

tration of nebulous, amorphous, nauseating odors—
and yet unmistakably human.

Grenouille garnered his first individual odor in the
Hôpital de la Charité. He managed to pilfer sheets
that were supposed to be burned because the journeyman sackmaker who had lain wrapped in them for
two months had just died of consumption. The cloth
was so drenched in the exudations of the sackmaker
that it had absorbed them like an enfleurage paste and
could be directly subjected to lavage. The result was
eerie: right under Grenouille's nose, the sackmaker
rose olfactorily from the dead, ascending from the
alcohol solution, hovering there—the phantom slightly distorted by the peculiar methods of reproduction
and the countless miasmas of his disease—but perfectly recognizable in space as an olfactory personage.
A small man of about thirty, blond, with a bulbous
nose, short limbs, flat, cheesy feet, swollen genitalia,
choleric temperament, and a stale mouth odor—not a
handsome man, aromatically speaking, this sackmaker, not worth being held on to for any length of
time, like the puppy. And yet for one whole night
Grenouille let the scent-specter flutter about his cabin
while he sniffed at him again and again, happy and
deeply satisfied with the sense of power that he had
won over the aura of another human being. He
poured it out the next day.

He tried one more experiment during these winter
days. He discovered a deaf-mute beggar woman wandering through the town and paid her one franc to
wear several different sets of rags smeared with oils
and fats against her naked skin. It turned out that
lamb suet, pork lard, and beef tallow, rendered many
times over, combined in a ratio of two to five to
three—with the addition of a small amount of virgin
oil—was best for absorbing human odor.

Grenouille let it go at that. He refrained from

overpowering some whole, live person and processing him or her perfumatorily. That sort of thing would have meant risks and would have resulted in no new knowledge. He knew he now was master of the techniques needed to rob a human of his or her scent, and he knew it was unnecessary to prove this fact anew.

Indeed, human odor was of no importance to him whatever. He could imitate human odor quite well enough with surrogates. What he coveted was the odor of *certain* human beings: that is, those rare humans who inspire love. These were his victims.

❧Thirty-nine❧

IN JANUARY THE widow Arnulfi married her first journeyman, Dominique Druot, who was thus promoted to *maître gantier et parfumeur*. There was a great banquet for the guild masters and a more modest one for the journeymen; Madame bought a new mattress for her bed, which she now shared officially with Druot, and took her gay finery from the armoire. Otherwise, everything remained as it was. She retained the fine old name of Arnulfi and retained her fortune for herself, as well as the management of the finances and the keys to the cellar; Druot fulfilled his sexual duties daily and refreshed himself afterwards with wine; and although he was now the one and only journeyman, Grenouille took care of most of the work at hand in return for the same small salary, frugal board, and cramped quarters.

The year began with a yellow flood of cassias, then hyacinths, violet petals, and narcotic narcissus. One Sunday in March—it was about a year now since his arrival in Grasse—Grenouille set out to see how things stood in the garden behind the wall at the other end of town. He was ready for the scent this time,

229

knew more or less exactly what awaited him . . . and nevertheless, as he caught a whiff of it, at the Porte Neuve, no more than halfway to the spot beside the wall, his heart beat more loudly and he felt the blood in his veins tingle with pleasure: she was still there, the incomparably beautiful flower, she had survived the winter unblemished, her sap was running, she was growing, expanding, driving forth the most exquisite ranks of buds! Her scent had grown stronger, just as he had expected, without losing any of its delicacy. What a year before had been sprinkled and dappled about was now blended into a faint, smooth stream of scent that shimmered with a thousand colors and yet bound each color to it and did not break. And this stream, Grenouille recognized blissfully, was fed by a spring that grew ever fuller. Another year, just one more year, just twelve more months, and that spring would gush over, and he could come to cap it and imprison the wild flow of its scent.

He walked along the wall to the spot behind which he knew the garden was located. Although the girl was apparently not in the garden but in the house, in her room behind closed windows, her scent floated down to him like a steady, gentle breeze. Grenouille stood quite still. He was not intoxicated or dizzy as he had been the first time he had smelled it. He was filled with the happiness of a lover who has heard or seen his darling from afar and knows that he will bring her home within the year. It was really true—Grenouille, the solitary tick, the abomination, Grenouille the Monster, who had never felt love and would never be able to inspire it, stood there beside the city wall of Grasse on that day in March and loved and was profoundly happy in his love.

True, he did not love another human being, certainly not the girl who lived in the house beyond the wall. He loved her scent—that alone, nothing else, and only inasmuch as it would one day be his alone. He would bring it home within the year, he swore it by his very life. And after this strange oath, or betrothal, this promise of loyalty given to himself and to his future scent, he left the place light of heart and returned to town through the Porte du Cours.

That night, as he lay in his cabin, he conjured up the memory of the scent—he could not resist the temptation—and immersed himself in it, caressed it, and let it caress him, so near to it, as fabulously close as if he possessed it already in reality, his scent, his own scent; and he made love to it and to himself through it for an intoxicatingly, deliciously long time. He wanted this self-loved feeling to accompany him in his sleep. But at the very instant when he closed his eyes, in the moment of the single breath it takes to fall asleep, it deserted him, was suddenly gone, and in its place the room was filled with the cold, acrid smell of goat stall.

Grenouille was terrified. What happens, he thought, if the scent, once I possess it . . . what happens if it runs out? It's not the same as it is in your memory, where all scents are indestructible. The real thing gets used up in this world. It's transient. And by the time it has been used up, the source I took it from will no longer exist. And I will be as naked as before and will have to get along with surrogates, just like before. No, it will be even worse than before! For in the meantime I will have known it and possessed it, my own splendid scent, and I will not be able to forget it, because I never forget a scent. And for the rest of my life I will feed on it in my memory, just as I was feeding right now from the premonition of what I will possess. . . . What do I need it for at all?

This was a most unpleasant thought for Grenouille. It frightened him beyond measure to think that once he did possess the scent that he did not yet possess, he must inevitably lose it. How long could he keep it? A few days? A few weeks? Perhaps a whole month, if he perfumed himself very sparingly with it? And then? He saw himself shaking the last drops from the bottle, rinsing the flacon with alcohol so that the last little bit would not be lost, and then he saw, smelled, how his beloved scent would vanish in the air, irrevocably, forever. It would be like a long slow death, a kind of suffocation in reverse, an agonizing gradual self-evaporation into the wretched world.

He felt chilled. He was overcome with a desire to abandon his plans, to walk out into the night and disappear. He would wander across the snow-covered mountains, not pausing to rest, hundreds of miles into the Auvergne, and there creep into his old cave and fall asleep and die. But he did not do it. He sat there and did not yield to his desire, although it was strong. He did not yield, because that desire was an old one of his, to run away and hide in a cave. He knew about that already. What he did not yet know was what it was like to possess a human scent as splendid as the scent of the girl behind the wall. And even knowing that to possess that scent he must pay the terrible price of losing it again, the very possession *and* the loss seemed to him more desirable than a prosaic renunciation of both. For he had renounced things all his life. But never once had he possessed and lost.

Gradually the doubts receded and with them the chill. He sensed how the warmth of his blood revitalized him and how the will to do what he had intended to do again took possession of him. Even more powerfully than before in fact, for that will no longer originated from simple lust, but equally from a well-considered decision. Grenouille the tick, presented the choice between drying up inside himself or letting himself drop, had decided for the latter, knowing full well that this drop would be his last. He lay back on his makeshift bed, cozy in his straw, cozy under his blanket, and thought himself very heroic.

Grenouille would not have been Grenouille, however, if he had long been content with a fatalist's heroic feelings. His will to survive and conquer was too tough, his nature too cunning, his spirit too crafty for that. Fine—he had decided to possess the scent of the girl behind the wall. And if he lost it again after a few weeks and died of the loss, that was fine too. But better yet would be not to die and still possess the scent, or at least to delay its loss as long as humanly possible. One simply had to preserve it better. One must subdue its evanescence without robbing it of its character—a problem of the perfumer's art.

There are scents that linger for decades. A cupboard rubbed with musk, a piece of leather drenched with cinnamon oil, a glob of ambergris, a cedar chest—they all possess virtually eternal olfactory life. While other things—lime oil, bergamot, jonquil and tuberose extracts, and many floral scents—evaporate within a few hours if they are exposed to the air in a pure, unbound form. The perfumer counteracts this fatal circumstance by binding scents that are too volatile, by putting them in chains, so to speak, taming their urge for freedom—though his art consists of leaving enough slack in the chains for the odor seemingly to preserve its freedom, even when it is tied so deftly that it cannot flee. Grenouille had once succeeded in performing this feat perfectly with some tuberose oil, whose ephemeral scent he had chained with tiny quantities of civet, vanilla, labdanum, and cypress—only then did it truly come into its own. Why should not something similar be possible with the scent of this girl? Why should he have to use, to waste, this most precious and fragile of all scents in pure form? How crude! How extraordinarily unsophisticated! Did one leave diamonds uncut? Did one

wear gold in nuggets around one's neck? Was he,
Grenouille, a primitive pillager of scents like Druot or
these other maceraters, distillers, and blossom crush-
ers? Or was he not, rather, the greatest perfumer in
the world?

He banged his fist against his brow—to think he
had not realized this before. But of course this unique
scent could not be used in a raw state. He must set it
like the most precious gemstone. He must design a
diadem of scent, and at its sublime acme, intertwined
with the other scents and yet ruling over them, *his*
scent would gleam. He would make a perfume using
all the precepts of the art, and the scent of the girl
behind the wall would be the very soul of it.

As the adjuvants, as bass, tenor, and soprano, as
zenith and as fixative, musk and civet, attar of roses or
neroli were inappropriate—that was certain. For such
a perfume, for a human perfume, he had need of other
ingredients.

≫ *Forty* ≪

IN MAY OF that same year, the naked body of a fifteen-year-old girl was found in a rose field, halfway between Grasse and the hamlet of Opio east of town. She had been killed by a heavy blow to the back of the head. The farmer who discovered her was so disconcerted by the gruesome sight that he almost ended up a suspect himself, when in a quivering voice he told the police lieutenant that he had never seen anything so beautiful—when he had really wanted to say that he had never seen anything so awful.

She was indeed a girl of exquisite beauty. She was one of those languid women made of dark honey, smooth and sweet and terribly sticky, who take control of a room with a syrupy gesture, a toss of the hair, a single slow whiplash of the eyes—and all the while remain as still as the center of a hurricane, apparently unaware of the force of gravity by which they irresistibly attract to themselves the yearnings and the souls of both men and women. And she was young, so very young, that the flow of her allure had not yet grown viscous. Her full limbs were still smooth and solid, her breasts plump and pert as hard-boiled eggs, and

235

the planes of her face, brushed by her heavy black hair, still had the most delicate contours and secret places. Her hair, however, was gone. The murderer had cut it off and taken it with him, along with her clothes.

People suspected the gypsies. Gypsies were capable of anything. Gypsies were known to weave carpets out of old clothes and to stuff their pillows with human hair and to make dolls out of the skin and teeth of the hanged. Only gypsies could be involved in such a perverse crime. There were, however, no gypsies around at the time, not a one near or far; gypsies had last come through the area in December.

For lack of gypsies, people decided to suspect the Italian migrant workers. But there weren't any Italians around either, it was too early in the year for them; they would first arrive in the region in June, at the time of the jasmine harvest, so it could not have been the Italians either. Finally the wigmakers came under suspicion, and they were searched for the hair of the murdered girl. To no avail. Then it was the Jews who were suspect, then the monks of the Benedictine cloister, reputedly a lecherous lot—although all of them were well over seventy—then the Cistercians, then the Freemasons, then the lunatics from the Charité, then the charcoal burners, then the beggars, and last but not least the nobility, in particular the marquis of Cabris, for he had already been married three times and organized—so it was said—orgiastic black masses in his cellars, where he drank the blood of virgins to increase his potency. Of course nothing definite could be proved. No one had witnessed the murder, the clothes and hair of the dead woman were not found. After several weeks the police lieutenant halted his investigation.

In mid-June the Italians arrived, many with families, to hire themselves out as pickers. The farmers put them to work as usual, but, with the murder still on their minds, forbade their wives and daughters to have anything to do with them. You couldn't be too cautious. For although the migrant workers were in fact not responsible for the actual murder, they could have been responsible for it on principle, and so it was better to be on one's guard.

Not long after the beginning of the jasmine harvest, two more murders occurred. Again the victims were very lovely young girls, again of the languid, raven-haired sort, again they were found naked and shorn and lying in a flower field with the backs of their heads bludgeoned. Again there was no trace of the perpetrator. The news spread like wildfire, and there was a threat that hostile action might be taken against the migrants—when it was learned that both victims were Italians, the daughters of a Genoese day laborer.

And now fear spread over the countryside. People no longer knew against whom to direct their impotent rage. Although there were still those who suspected the lunatics or the cryptic marquis, no one really believed that, for the former were under guard day and night, and the latter had long since departed for Paris. So people huddled closer together. The farmers opened up their barns for the migrants, who until then had slept in the open fields. The townsfolk set up nightly patrols in every neighborhood. The police lieutenant reinforced the watch at the gates. But all these measures proved useless. A few days after the double murder, they found the body of yet another girl, abused in the same manner as the others. This time it was a Sardinian washerwoman from the bishop's palace; she had been struck down near the great basin of the Fontaine de la Foux, directly before the gates of the town. And although at the insistence of the citizenry the consuls initiated still further measures—the tightest possible control at the gates, a

PERFUME

reinforced nightwatch, a curfew for all female persons after nightfall—all that summer not a single week went by when the body of a young girl was not discovered. And they were always girls just approaching womanhood, and always very beautiful and usually dark, sugary types. Soon, however, the murderer was no longer rejecting the type of girl more common among the local population: soft, pale-skinned, and somewhat more full-bodied. Even brown-haired girls and some dark blondes—as long as they weren't too skinny—were among the later victims. He tracked them down everywhere, not just in the open country around Grasse, but in the town itself, right in their homes. The daughter of a carpenter was found slain in her own room on the fifth floor, and no one in the house had heard the least noise, and although the dogs normally yelped the moment they picked up the scent of any stranger, not one of them had barked. The murderer seemed impalpable, incorporeal, like a ghost.

People were outraged and reviled the authorities. The least rumor caused mob scenes. A traveling salesman of love potions and other nostrums was almost massacred, for word spread that one of the ingredients in his remedies was female hair. Fires were set at both the Cabris mansion and the Hôpital de la Charité. A servant returning home one night was shot down by his own master, the woolen draper Alexandre Misnard, who mistook him for the infamous murderer of young girls. Whoever could afford it sent his adolescent daughters to distant relatives or to boarding schools in Nice, Aix, or Marseille. The police lieutenant was removed from office at the insistence of the town council. His successor had the college of medicine examine the bodies of the shorn beauties to determine the state of their virginity. It was found that they had all remained untouched.

PERFUME

Strangely enough, this knowledge only increased the sense of horror, for everyone had secretly assumed that the girls had been ravished. People had at least known the murderer's motive. Now they knew nothing at all, they were totally perplexed. And whoever believed in God sought succor in the prayer that at least his own house should be spared this visitation from hell.

The town council was a committee of thirty of the richest and most influential commoners and nobles in Grasse. The majority of them were enlightened and anticlerical, paid not the least attention to the bishop, and would have preferred to turn the cloisters and abbeys into warehouses or factories. In their distress, the proud, powerful men of the town council condescended to write an abject petition begging the bishop to curse and excommunicate this monster who murdered young girls and yet whom temporal powers could not capture, just as his illustrious predecessor had done in the year 1708, when terrible locusts had threatened the land. And indeed, at the end of September, the slayer of the young women of Grasse, having cut down no fewer than twenty-four of its most beautiful virgins out of every social class, was made anathema and excommunicated both in writing and from all the pulpits of the city, including a ban spoken by the bishop himself from the pulpit of Notre-Dame-du-Puy.

The result was conclusive. From one day to the next, the murders ceased. October and November passed with no corpses. At the start of December, reports came in from Grenoble that a murderer there was strangling young girls, then tearing their clothes to shreds and pulling their hair out by the handfuls. And although these coarse methods in no way squared with the cleanly executed crimes of the Grasse murderer, everyone was convinced that it was one and the

239

same person. In their relief that the beast was no longer among them but instead ravaging Grenoble a good seven days' journey distant, the citizens of Grasse crossed themselves three times over. They organized a torchlight procession in honor of the bishop and celebrated a mass of thanksgiving on December 24. On January 1, 1766, the tighter security measures were relaxed and the nighttime curfew for women was lifted. Normality returned to public and private life with incredible speed. Fear had melted into thin air, no one spoke of the terror that had ruled both town and countryside only a few months before. Not even the families involved still spoke of it. It was as if the bishop's curse had not only banned the murderer, but every memory of him. And the people were pleased that it was so.

But any man who still had a daughter just approaching that special age did not, even now, allow her to be without supervision; twilight brought misgivings, and each morning, when he found her healthy and cheerful, he rejoiced—though of course without actually admitting the reason why.

❧ Forty-one ❧

THERE WAS one man in Grasse, however, who did not trust this peace. His name was Antoine Richis, he held the title of second consul, and he lived in a grand residence at the entrance to the rue Droite.

Richis was a widower and had a daughter named Laure. Although not yet forty years old and of undiminished vigor, he intended to put off a second marriage for some time yet. First he wanted to find a husband for his daughter. And not the first comer, either, but a man of rank. There was a baron de Bouyon who had a son and an estate near Vence, a man of good reputation and miserable financial situation, with whom Richis had already concluded a contract concerning the future marriage of their children. Once he had married Laure off, he planned to put out his own courting feelers in the direction of the highly esteemed houses of Drée, Maubert, or Fontmichel—not because he was vain and would be damned if he didn't get a noble bedmate, but because he wanted to found a dynasty and to put his own posterity on a track leading directly to the highest social and political influence. For that he needed at

241

least two sons, one to take over his business, the other
to pursue a law career leading to the parliament in Aix
and advancement to the nobility. Given his present
rank, however, he could hold out hopes for such
success only if he managed intimately to unite his own
person and family with provincial nobility.

Only one thing justified such high-soaring plans: his
fabulous wealth. Antoine Richis was far and away the
wealthiest citizen anywhere around. He possessed
latifundia not only in the area of Grasse, where he
planted oranges, oil, wheat, and hemp, but also near
Vence and over toward Antibes, where he leased out
his farms. He owned houses in Aix and houses in the
country, owned shares in ships that traded with India,
had a permanent office in Genoa, and was the largest
wholesaler for scents, spices, oils, and leathers in
France.

The most precious thing that Richis possessed,
however, was his daughter. She was his only child, just
turned sixteen, with auburn hair and green eyes. She
had a face so charming that visitors of all ages and
both sexes would stand stock-still at the sight of her,
unable to pull their eyes away, practically licking that
face with their eyes, the way tongues work at ice
cream, with that typically stupid, single-minded expression on their faces that goes with concentrated
licking. Even Richis would catch himself looking at
his daughter for indefinite periods of time, a quarter
of an hour, a half hour perhaps, forgetting the rest of
the world, even his business—which otherwise did
not happen even in his sleep—melting away in con-
templation of this magnificent girl and afterwards
unable to say what it was he had been doing. And of
late—he noticed this with uneasiness—of an evening,
when he brought her to her bed or sometimes of a
morning when he went in to waken her and she still
lay sleeping as if put to rest by God's own hand and

242

the forms of her hips and breasts were molded in the veil of her nightgown and her breath rose calm and hot from the frame of bosom, contoured shoulder, elbow, and smooth forearm in which she had laid her face—then he would feel an awful cramping in his stomach and his throat would seem too tight and he would swallow and, God help him, would curse himself for being this woman's father and not some stranger, not some other man, before whom she lay as she lay now before him, and who then without scruple and full of desire could lie down next to her, on her, in her. And he broke out in a sweat, and his arms and legs trembled while he choked down this dreadful lust and bent down to wake her with a chaste fatherly kiss.

During the year just past, at the time of the murders, these fatal temptations had not yet come over him. The magic that his daughter worked on him then—or so at least it seemed to him—had still been a childish magic. And thus he had not been seriously afraid that Laure would be one of the murderer's victims, since everyone knew that he attacked neither children nor grown women, but exclusively ripening but virginal girls. He had indeed augmented the watch of his home, had had new grilles placed at the windows of the top floor, and had directed Laure's maid to share her bedchamber with her. But he was loath to send her away as his peers had done with their daughters, some even with their entire families. He found such behavior despicable and unworthy of a member of the town council and second consul, who, he suggested, should be a model of composure, courage, and resolution to his fellow citizens. Besides which, he was a man who did not let his decisions be made for him by other people, nor by a crowd thrown into panic, and certainly not by some anonymous piece of criminal trash. And so all during those terrible days, he had been one of the few people in the town who were immune to the fever of fear and kept a cool head. But, strange to say, this had now changed. While others publicly celebrated the end of the rampage as if the murderer were already hanged and had soon fully forgotten about those dreadful days, fear crept into Antoine Richis's heart like a foul poison. For a long time he would not admit that it was fear that caused him to delay trips that ought to have been made some time ago, or to be reluctant merely to leave the house, or to break off visits and meetings just so that he could quickly return home. He gave himself the excuse that he was out of sorts or overworked, but admitted as well that he was a bit concerned, as every father with a daughter of marriageable age is concerned, a thoroughly normal concern. . . . Had not the fame of her beauty already gone out to the wider world? Did not people stretch their necks even now when he accompanied her to church on Sundays? Were not certain gentlemen on the council already making advances, in their own names or in those of their sons . . . ?

❧ *Forty-two* ❦

But, then, one day in March, Richis was sitting in the salon and watched as Laure walked out into the garden. She was wearing a blue dress, her red hair falling down over it and blazing in the sunlight—he had never seen her look so beautiful. She disappeared behind a hedge. And it took about two heartbeats longer than he had expected before she emerged again—and he was frightened to death, for during those two heartbeats he thought he had lost her forever.

That same night he awoke out of a terrifying dream, the details of which he could no longer remember, but it had had to do with Laure, and he burst into her room convinced that she was dead, lay there in her bed murdered, violated, and shorn—and found her unharmed.

He went back to his chamber, bathed in sweat and trembling with agitation, no, not with agitation, but with fear, for he finally admitted it to himself: it was naked fear that had seized him, and in admitting it he grew calmer and his thoughts clearer. To be honest, he had not believed in the efficacy of the bishop's anathe-

245

ma from the start, nor that the murderer was now prowling about Grenoble, nor that he had ever left town. No, he was still living here, among the citizens of Grasse, and at some point he would strike again. Richis had seen several of the girls murdered during August and September. The sight had horrified him, and at the same time, he had to admit, fascinated him, for they all, each in her own special way, had been of dazzling beauty. He never would have thought that there was so much unrecognized beauty in Grasse. The murderer had opened his eyes. The murderer possessed exquisite taste. And he had a system. It was not just that all the murders had been carried out in the same efficient manner, but the very choice of victims betrayed intentions almost economical in their planning. To be sure, Richis did not know *what* the murderer actually craved from his victims, since he could not have robbed them of the best that they offered—their beauty and the charm of youth . . . or could he? In any case, it seemed to him, as absurd as it sounded, that the murderer was not a destructive personality, but rather a careful collector. For if one imagined—and so Richis imagined—all the victims not as single individuals, but as parts of some higher principle and thought of each one's characteristics as merged in some idealistic fashion into a unifying whole, then the picture assembled out of such mosaic pieces would be the picture of absolute beauty, and the magic that radiated from it would no longer be of human, but of divine origin. (As we can see, Richis was an enlightened thinker who did not shrink from blasphemous conclusions, and though he was not thinking in olfactory categories, but rather in visual ones, he was nevertheless very near the truth.)

Assuming then—Richis continued in his thoughts —that the murderer was just such a collector of beauty and was working on the picture of perfection, even if only in the fantasy of his sick brain; assuming, moreover, that he was the man of sublime taste and perfect methods that he indeed appeared to be—then one could not assume that he would waive claim to the most precious component on earth needed for his picture: the beauty of Laure. His entire previous homicidal work would be worth nothing without her. She was the keystone to his building.

As he drew this horrifying conclusion, Richis was sitting in his nightshirt on the edge of his bed, and he was amazed at how calm he had become. He no longer felt chilled, was no longer trembling. The vague fear that had plagued him for weeks had vanished and was replaced by the awareness of a specific danger: Laure had quite obviously been the goal of all the murderer's endeavors from the beginning. And all the other murders were adjuncts to the last, crowning murder. It remained quite unclear what material purpose these murders were intended to serve or if they even had one at all. But Richis had perceived the essence of the matter: the murderer's systematic method and his idealistic motive. The longer he thought about it, the better both of these pleased him and the greater his admiration for the murderer—an admiration, admittedly, that reflected back upon him as would a polished mirror, for after all, it was he, Richis, who had picked up his opponent's trail with his own refined and analytical powers of reasoning.

If he, Richis, had been the murderer and were himself possessed by the murderer's passions and ideas, he would not have been able to proceed in any other fashion than had been employed thus far, and like him, he would do his utmost to crown his mad work with the murder of the unique and splendid Laure.

This last thought appealed to him especially. Because he was in the position to put himself inside the mind of the would-be murderer of his daughter, he had made himself vastly superior to the murderer. For all his intelligence, that much was certain, the murderer was not in the position to put himself inside Richis's mind—if only because he could not even begin to suspect that Richis had long since imagined himself in the murderer's own situation. This was fundamentally no different from how things worked in business—*mutatis mutandis,* to be sure. You were master of a competitor whose intentions you had seen through; there was no way he could get the better of you—not if your name was Antoine Richis, and you were a natural fighter, a seasoned fighter. After all, the largest wholesale perfume business in France, his wealth, his office as second consul, these had not fallen into his lap as gracious gifts, but he had fought for them, with doggedness and deceit, recognizing dangers ahead of time, shrewdly guessing his competitors' plans, and outdistancing his opponents. And in just the same way he would achieve his future goals, power and noble rank for his heirs. And in no other way would he counter the plans of the murderer, his competitor for the possession of Laure—if only because Laure was also the keystone in the edifice of his, of Richis's, own plans. He loved her, certainly; but he needed her as well. And he would let no one wrest from him whatever it was he needed to realize his own highest ambitions—he would hold on tooth and claw to that.

He felt better now. Having succeeded by these nocturnal deliberations in bringing his struggle with the demon down to the level of a business rivalry, he felt fresh courage, indeed arrogance, take hold of him.

PERFUME

The last remnants of fear were gone, the despondency and anxious care that had tormented him into doddering senility had vanished, the fog of gloomy forebodings in which he had tapped about for weeks had lifted. He found himself on familiar terrain and felt himself equal to every challenge.

❧ Forty-three ❧

RELIEVED, ALMOST elated, he sprang from his bed, pulled the bell rope, and ordered the drowsy valet who staggered into his room to pack clothes and provisions because at daybreak he intended to set out for Grenoble in the company of his daughter. Then he dressed and chased the rest of the servants from their beds.

In the middle of the night, the house on the rue Droite awoke and bustled with life. The fire blazed up in the kitchen, excited maids scurried along the corridors, servants dashed up and down the stairs, in the vaulted cellars the keys of the steward rattled, in the courtyard torches shone, grooms ran among the horses, others tugged mules from their stalls, there was bridling and saddling and running and loading—one would have almost believed that the Austro-Sardinian hordes were on the march, pillaging and torching, just as in 1746, and that the lord of the manor was mobilizing to flee in panic. Not at all! The lord of the manor was sitting at his office desk, as sovereign as a marshal of France, drinking *café au lait*, and providing instructions for the constant stream of domestics barging in on him. All the while, he wrote letters to the mayor, to the first consul, to his secretary, to his solicitor, to his banker in Marseille, to the baron de Bouyon, and to diverse business partners.

By around six that morning, he had completed his correspondence and given all the orders necessary to carry out his plans. He tucked away two small traveling pistols, buckled on his money belt, and locked his desk. Then he went to awaken his daughter.

By eight o'clock, the little caravan was on the move. Richis rode at its head; he was a splendid sight in his gold-braided, burgundy coat beneath a black riding coat and black hat with jaunty feathers. He was followed by his daughter, dressed less showily, but so radiantly beautiful that the people along the street and at the windows had eyes only for her, their fervent ah's and oh's passing through the crowd while the men doffed their hats—apparently for the second consul, but in reality for her, the regal woman. Then, almost unnoticed, came her maid, then Richis's valet with two packhorses—the notoriously bad condition of the road to Grenoble meant that a wagon could not be used—and the end of the parade was drawn up by a dozen mules laden with all sorts of stuff and supervised by two grooms. At the Porte du Cours the watch presented arms and only let them drop when the last mule had tramped by. Children ran behind them for a good little while, waving at the baggage crew as they slowly moved up the steep, winding road into the mountains.

The departure of Antoine Richis and his daughter made a strange but deep impression on people. It was as if they had witnessed some archaic sacrificial procession. The word spread that Richis was going to Grenoble, to the very city where the monster who murdered young girls was now residing. People did not know what to think about that. Did what Richis was doing show criminal negligence or admirable courage? Was he daring or placating the gods? They had only the vague foreboding that they had just seen this beautiful girl with the red hair for the last time. They suspected that Laure Richis might be lost.

This suspicion would prove correct, although the presumptions it was based upon were completely false. Richis was not heading for Grenoble at all. The pompous departure was nothing but a diversionary tactic. A mile and a half northwest of Grasse, near the village of Saint-Vallier, he ordered a halt. He handed his valet letters of attorney and transmittal and ordered him to bring the mule train and grooms to Grenoble by himself.

He, however, turned off with Laure and her maid in the direction of Cabris, where they rested at midday, and then rode straight across the mountains of the Tanneron toward the south. The path was an extremely arduous one, but it allowed them to circumvent Grasse and its basin in a great arc and to arrive on the coast by evening without being recognized. . . . The following day—according to Richis's plan—he would ferry across with Laure to the Iles de Lérins, on the smaller of which was located the well-fortified monastery of Saint-Honorat. It was managed by a handful of elderly but quite able-bodied monks whom Richis knew very well, since for years he had bought and resold the monastery's total production of eucalyptus cordial, pine nuts, and cypress oil. And there in the monastery of Saint-Honorat—which except for the prison of Château d'If and the state prison on the Ile Sainte-Marguerite was probably the safest place in the Provence—he intended to lodge his daughter for the present. But he would immediately return to the mainland, this time circumventing Grasse on the east via Antibes and Cagnes, and arrive in Vence by evening of the same day. He had ordered his secretary to proceed there in order to prepare the agreement with baron de Bouyon concerning the marriage of their children Laure and Alphonse. He hoped to make Bouyon an offer that he could not refuse: assumption of his debts up to forty thousand livres, a dowry consisting of an equal sum as well as diverse landholdings and an oil mill near Maganosc, a yearly income of three thousand livres for the young couple. Richis's only conditions were that the marriage should take place within ten days and be consummated on the wedding day, and that the couple should thereafter take up residence in Vence.

Richis knew that in acting so hastily he was driving the price excessively high for the union of his house with the house of Bouyon. He would have got it cheaper had he waited longer. The baron would have begged for permission to raise the social rank of the daughter of a bourgeois wholesaler through a marriage to his son, for the fame of Laure's beauty would only grow, just as would Richis's wealth and Bouyon's financial miseries. But what did that matter! His opponent in this deal was not the baron, but the unknown murderer. He was the one whose business had to be spoiled. A married woman, deflowered and if possible already pregnant, would no longer fit into his exclusive gallery. The last mosaic stone would be tarnished, Laure would have lost all value for the murderer, his enterprise would have failed. And he was to feel his defeat! Richis wanted to hold the wedding ceremony in Grasse, with great pomp and open to the public. And even if he could not know his adversary, would never know him, he would take personal pleasure in knowing that he was in attendance at the event and would have to watch with his own eyes as that which he most desired was snatched away from under his nose.

The plan was nicely thought out. And once again we must admire Richis's acumen for coming so close to the truth. For in point of fact the marriage of Laure Richis to the son of the baron de Bouyon would have meant a devastating defeat for the murderer of the maidens of Grasse. But the plan was not yet carried out. Richis had not yet rescued his daughter by marrying her off. He had not yet ferried her across to the safety of the monastery of Saint-Honorat. The three riders were still passing through the inhospitable mountains of the Tanneron. Sometimes the path was so bad that they had to dismount from their horses. It was all going too slowly. By evening, they hoped to reach the sea near La Napoule, a small town west of Cannes.

❧ Forty-four ❧

AT THE SAME time that Laure Richis and her father were leaving Grasse, Grenouille was at the other end of town in the Arnulfi workshop macerating jonquils. He was alone and he was in good spirits. His days in Grasse were coming to an end. His day of triumph was imminent. Out in his cabin was a crate padded with cotton, in it were twenty-four tiny flacons filled with drops of the congealed aura of twenty-four virgins—precious essences that Grenouille had produced over the last year by cold-oil enfleurage of their bodies, digestion of their hair and clothes, lavage, and distillation. And the twenty-fifth, the most precious and important of all, he planned to fetch today. For his final fishing expedition, he had at the ready a small pot of oils purified several times over, a cloth of finest linen, and a demijohn of high-proof alcohol. The terrain had been studied down to the last detail. The moon was new.

He knew that any attempt to break into the well-protected mansion on the rue Droite was pointless. Which was why he planned, just as dusk fell and before the doors were closed, to sneak in under his

cover of odorlessness, which like a magic cape deprived man and beast of their perceptive faculties,
and there to hide in some nook of the house. Then
later, when everyone was asleep, he would follow the
compass of his nose through the darkness and climb
up to the chamber that held his treasure. He would set
to work on it with his oil-drenched cloths right then
and there. All that he would take with him would be,
as usual, the hair and clothes, since these could be
washed directly in rectified spirit, which could be
done more conveniently in the workshop. He esti-
mated it would take an additional night to complete
the production of the pomade and to distill the
concentrate. And if everything went well—and he had
no reason to doubt that everything would go well—
then by the day after tomorrow he would possess all of
the essences needed for the best perfume in the world,
and he would leave Grasse as the world's most fragrant human being.

Around noon he was finished with his jonquils. He
doused the fire, covered the pot of oil, and stepped
outside the workshop to cool off. The wind was from
the west.

With his very first breath, he knew something was
wrong. The atmosphere was not as it should be. In the
town's aromatic garb, that veil of many thousands of
woven threads, the golden thread was missing. During
the last few weeks the fragrance of that thread had
grown so strong that Grenouille had clearly discerned
it from his cabin on the far side of the town. Now it
was gone, vanished, untraceable despite the most
intensive sniffing. Grenouille was almost paralyzed
with fright.

She is dead, he thought. Then, more terrifying still:
Someone else has got to her before me. Someone else
has plucked my flower and taken its odor for himself!
He could not so much as scream, the shock was too

great for that, but he could produce tears that welled up in the corners of his eyes and suddenly streamed down both sides of his nose.

Then Druot, returning home from the Quatre Dauphins for lunch, remarked in passing that early this morning the second consul had left for Grenoble together with twelve mules and his daughter. Grenouille forced back the tears and ran off, straight through town to the Porte du Cours. He stopped to sniff in the square before the gate. And in the pure west wind, unsullied by the odors of the town, he did indeed find his golden thread again, thin and fragile, but absolutely unmistakable. The precious scent, however, was not blowing from the northwest, where the road leads toward Grenoble, but more from the direction of Cabris—if not directly out of the southwest.

Grenouille asked the watch which road the second consul had taken. The guard pointed north. Not the road to Cabris? Or the other one, that went south toward Auribeau and La Napoule? Definitely not, said the guard, he had watched with his own eyes.

Grenouille ran back through town to his cabin, packed linen, pomade pot, spatula, scissors, and a small, smooth club of olivewood into his knapsack and promptly took to the road—not the road to Grenoble, but the one to which his nose directed him: to the south.

This road, the direct road to La Napoule, led along the foothills of the Tanneron, through the river valleys of the Frayère and Siagne. It was an easy walk. Grenouille made rapid progress. As Auribeau emerged on his right, clinging to the mountains above him, he could smell that he had almost caught up with the runaways. A little later and he had drawn even with them. He could now smell each one, could smell the aroma of their horses. At most they were no more

257

than a half mile west of him, somewhere in the forests
of the Tanneron. They were holding course south-
wards, toward the sea. Just as he was.

Around five o'clock that evening, Grenouille
reached La Napoule. He went to the inn, ate, and
asked for cheap lodging. He was a journeyman tanner
from Nice, he said, on his way to Marseille. He could
spend the night in a stall, they told him. There he lay
down in a corner and rested. He could smell the three
riders approaching. He need only wait.

Two hours later—it was deep dusk by then—they
arrived. To preserve their disguise, they had changed
costumes. The two women now wore dark cloaks and
veils, Richis a black frock coat. He identified himself
as a nobleman on his way from Castellane; in the
morning he wanted to be ferried over to the Iles de
Lérins, the innkeeper should make arrangements for a
boat to be ready by sunrise. Were there any other
guests in the house besides himself and his people?
No, said the innkeeper, only a journeyman tanner
from Nice who was spending the night in a stall.

Richis sent the women to their room. He was going
out to the stalls, he said, to get something from the
saddlebags. At first he could not find the journeyman
tanner, he had to ask a groom to give him a lantern.
Then he saw him, lying on some straw and an old
blanket in one corner, his head resting on his knapsack, sound asleep. He looked so totally insignificant
that for a moment Richis had the impression that he
was not even there, but was merely a chimera cast by
the swaying shadow of the lantern candle. At any rate,
Richis was immediately convinced that there was no
danger whatever to fear from this almost touchingly
harmless creature, and he left very quietly so as not to
disturb his sleep and went back into the inn.

He took his evening meal in his own room along
with his daughter. He had not explained the purpose

and goal of their journey to her and did not do it even now, although she asked him. Tomorrow he would let her in on the secret, he said, but she could be certain that everything that he was planning and doing was for her good and would work toward her future happiness.

After their meal they played a few games of *l'hombre*, which he lost because he was forever gazing at her face to delight in her beauty instead of looking at his cards. Around nine o'clock he brought her to her room, directly across from his own, kissed her good night, and locked the door from the outside. Then he went to bed himself.

He was suddenly very tired from the exertions of the day and of the night before and equally very satisfied with himself and how things had gone. Without the least thought of care, without any of the gloomy suspicions that until yesterday had plagued him and kept him awake every time he had put out his light, he instantly fell asleep and slept without a dream, without a moan, without a twitch or a nervous toss of his body back and forth. For the first time in a good while, Richis found deep, peaceful, refreshing sleep.

Around the same time, Grenouille got up from his bed in the stall. He too was satisfied with how things were going and felt completely refreshed, although he had not slept a single second. When Richis had come to the stall looking for him, he had only feigned sleep, augmenting the impression of obvious harmlessness he already exuded with his odor of inconspicuousness. Moreover, in contrast to the way in which Richis had perceived him, he had observed Richis with utmost accuracy, olfactory accuracy, and Richis's relief at the sight of him had definitely not escaped him.

And so at their meeting each had convinced himself

of the other's harmlessness, both correctly and falsely, and that was how it should be, Grenouille thought, for his apparent and Richis's true harmlessness made it much easier for him, Grenouille, to go about his work—an opinion that, to be sure, Richis would definitely have shared had the situation been reversed.

❧*Forty-five*❧

GRENOUILLE SET to work with professional circumspection. He opened his knapsack, took out the linen, pomade, and spatula, spread the cloth over the blanket on which he had lain, and began to brush on the fatty paste. This job took time, for it was important that the oil be applied in thinner or thicker layers depending on what part of the body would end up lying on a particular patch of the cloth. The mouth and armpits, breasts, genitals, and feet gave off greater amounts of scent than, for instance, shins, back, and elbows; the palms more than the backs of the hands; eyebrows more than eyelids, etc.—and therefore needed to be provided with a heavier dose of oil. Grenouille was creating a model, as it were, transferring onto the linen a scent diagram of the body to be treated, and this part of the job was actually the one that satisfied him most, for it was a matter of an artistic technique that incorporated equally one's knowledge, imagination, and manual dexterity, while at the same time it anticipated on an ideal plane the enjoyment awaiting one from the final results.

Once he had applied the whole potful of pomade,

261

he dabbed about here and there, removing a bit of oil from the cloth here, adding another there, retouching, checking the greasy landscape he had modeled one last time—with his nose, by the way, not with his eyes, for the whole business was carried on in total darkness, which was perhaps yet another reason for Grenouille's equally cheerful mood. There was nothing to distract him on this night of new moon. The world was nothing but odor and the soft sound of surf from the sea. He was in his element. Then he folded the cloth together like a tapestry, so that the oiled surfaces lay against one another. This was a painful procedure for him, because he knew well that despite the utmost caution certain parts of the sculpted contours would be flattened or shifted. But there was no other way to transport the cloth. After he had folded it up small enough to be carried under his arm without all too much difficulty, he tucked spatula, scissors, and the little olivewood club in his pockets and crept out into the night.

The sky was clouded over. There were no lights burning in the inn. The only glimmer on this pitch-dark night was the winking of the lighthouse at the fort on the Ile Sainte-Marguerite, over a mile away to the east, a tiny bright needlepoint in a raven-black cloth. A light, fishy wind was blowing from the bay. The dogs were asleep.

Grenouille walked to the back dormer of the threshing shed, where a ladder stood propped. He picked the ladder up, and balancing it vertically, three rungs clamped under his free right arm, the rest of it pressed against his right shoulder, he moved across the courtyard until he was under her window. The window stood half ajar. As he climbed the ladder, as easily as a set of stairs, he congratulated himself on the circumstances that made it possible for him to harvest the girl's scent here in La Napoule. In Grasse, where the house had barred windows and was tightly guarded, all this would have been much more difficult. She was even sleeping by herself here. He would not have to bother with eliminating the maid.

He pushed up the casement, slipped into the room, and laid down his cloth. Then he turned to the bed. The dominant scent came from her hair, for she was lying on her stomach with her head pressed into the pillow and framed by the crook of her arm—presenting the back of her head in an almost ideal position for the blow by the club.

The sound of the blow was a dull, grinding thud. He hated it. He hated it solely because it was a sound, a sound in the midst of his otherwise soundless procedure. He could bear that gruesome sound only by clenching his teeth, and, after it was all over, standing off to one side stiff and implacable, as if he feared the sound would return from somewhere as a resounding echo. But it did not return, instead stillness returned to the room, an increased stillness in fact, for now even the shuffle of the girl's breathing had ceased. And at once Grenouille's tenseness dissolved (one might have interpreted it more as a posture of reverence or some sort of crabbed moment of silence) and his body fell back to a pliable ease.

He tucked the club away and from here on was all bustle and business. First he unfolded the impregnating cloth, spread it loosely on its back over the table and chairs, taking care that the greased side not be touched. Then he pulled back the bedclothes. The glorious scent of the girl, welling up so suddenly warm and massive, did not stir him. He knew that scent, of course, and would savor it, savor it to intoxication, later on, once he truly possessed it. But now the main thing was to capture as much of it as possible, let as little of it as possible evaporate; for now the watch-words were concentration and haste.

With a few quick snips of his scissors, he cut open her nightgown, pulled it off, grabbed the oiled linen, and tossed it over her naked body. Then he lifted her up, tugged the overhanging cloth under her, rolled her up in it as a baker rolls strudel, tucking in the corners, enveloping her from toes up to brow. Only her hair still stuck out from the mummy clothes. He cut it off close to her scalp and packed it inside her nightgown, which he then tied up into a bundle. Finally he took a piece of cloth still dangling free and flapped it over the shaved skull, smoothed down the overlapping ends, gently pressed it tight with a finger. He examined the whole package. Not a slit, not a hole, not one bulging pleat was left through which the girl's scent could have escaped. She was perfectly packed. There was nothing to do but wait, for six hours, until the gray of dawn.

He took the little armchair on which her clothes lay, dragged it to the bed, and sat down. The gentle breath of her scent still clung to the ample black cloak, blending with the odor of aniseed cakes she had put in her pocket as a snack for the journey. He put his feet up on the end of the bed, near her feet, covered himself with her dress, and ate aniseed cakes. He was tired. But he did not want to fall asleep, because it was improper to sleep on the job, even if your job was merely to wait. He recalled the nights he had spent distilling in Baldini's workshop: the soot-blackened alembic, the flickering fire, the soft spitting sound the distillate made as it dripped from the cooling tube into the Florentine flask. From time to time you had to tend the fire, pour in more distilling water, change Florentine flasks, replace the exhausted stuff you were distilling. And yet it had always seemed to him that you stayed awake not so that you could take care of these occasional tasks, but because being awake had its own unique purpose. Even here in this bedchamber, where the process of enfleurage was proceeding all on its own, where in fact premature checking, turning, or poking the fragrant package could only cause trouble—even here, it seemed to Grenouille, his waking presence was important. Sleep would have endangered the spirit of success.

It was not especially difficult for him to stay awake and wait, despite his weariness. He loved *this* waiting. He had also loved it with the twenty-four other girls, for it was not a dull waiting-till-it's-over, not even a yearning, expectant waiting, but an attendant, purposeful, in a certain sense active, waiting. Something was happening while you waited. The most essential thing was happening. And even if he himself was doing nothing, it was happening through him nevertheless. He had done his best. He had employed all his artistic skill. He had made not one single mistake. His performance had been unique. It would be crowned with success. . . . He need only wait a few more hours. It filled him with profound satisfaction, this waiting. He had never felt so fine in all his life, so peaceful, so steady, so whole and at one with himself—not even back inside his mountain—as during these hours when a craftsman took his rest sitting in the dark of night beside his victim, waiting and watching. They were the only moments when something like cheerful thoughts formed inside his gloomy brain.

Strangely enough, these thoughts did not look toward the future. He did not think of the scent that he would glean in a few hours, nor of the perfume made of the auras of twenty-five maidens, nor of future plans, happiness, and success. No, he thought of his past. He remembered the stations of his life, from

265

Madame Gaillard's house and the moist, warm wood-pile in front of it to his journey today to the little village of La Napoule, which smelled like fish. He thought of Grimal the tanner, of Giuseppe Baldini, of the marquis de La Taillade-Espinasse. He thought of the city of Paris, of its great effluvium, that evil smell of a thousand iridescences; he thought of the red-headed girl in the rue des Marais, of open country, of the spare wind, of forests. He thought, too, of the mountain in the Auvergne—he did not avoid such memories in the least—of his cave, of the air void of human beings. He thought of his dreams. And he thought of all these things with great satisfaction. Yes, it seemed to him as he looked back over it that he was a man to whom fortune had been especially kind, and that fate had led him down some tortuous paths, but that ultimately they had proved to be the right ones—how else would it have been possible for him to have found his way here, into this dark chamber, at the goal of his desires? He was, now that he really considered it, a truly blessed individual!

Feelings of humility and gratitude welled up within him. "I thank you," he said softly, "I thank you, Jean-Baptiste Grenouille, for being what you are!" So touched was he by himself.

Then his eyelids closed—not for sleep, but so that he could surrender himself completely to the peace of this holy night. The peace filled his heart. But it seemed also as if it reigned all about him. He smelled the peaceful sleep of the maid in the adjoining room, the deep contentment of Antoine Richis's sleep on the other side of the corridor; he smelled the peaceful slumber of the innkeeper and his servants, of the dogs, of the animals in their stalls, of the whole village, and of the sea. The wind had died away. Everything was still. Nothing disturbed the peace.

Once he turned his foot to one side and ever so softly touched Laure's foot. Not actually her foot, but simply the cloth that enveloped it and beneath that the thin layer of oil drinking up her scent, her glorious scent, his scent.

≈ *Forty-six* ≈

As the birds began to squawk—that is, a good while before the break of dawn—he got up and finished his task. He threw open the cloth and pulled it from the dead woman like a bandage. The fat peeled off nicely from her skin. Little scraps of it were left hanging only in the smallest crannies, and these he had to scrape off with his spatula. The remaining streaks of pomade he wiped off with her undershirt, using it to rub down her body from head to foot one last time, so thoroughly that even the oil in her own pores pearled from her skin, and with it the last flake and filament of her scent. Only now was she really dead for him, withered away, pale and limp as a fallen petal.

He tossed the undershirt into the large scent-impregnated cloth—the only place where she had life now—placed her nightgown and her hair in it as well, and rolled it all up into a small, firm package that he clamped under his arm. He did not even take the trouble to cover the body on the bed. And although the black of night had already become the blue gray of dawn and objects in the room had begun to regain

268

their contours, he did not cast a single glance at the bed to rest his eyes on her at least once in his life. Her form did not interest him. She no longer existed for him as a body, but only as a disembodied scent. And he was carrying that under his arm, taking it with him.

Softly he swung out over the windowsill and climbed down the ladder. The wind had come up again outside, and the sky was clearing, pouring a cold, dark blue light over the land.

A half hour later, the scullery maid started the fire in the kitchen. As she came out of the house to fetch wood she saw the ladder leaning there, but was still too sleepy to make any rhyme or reason of it. Shortly after six the sun rose. Gigantic and golden red, it lifted up out of the sea between the Iles de Lérins. Not a cloud was in the sky. A radiant spring day had begun.

With his room facing west, Richis did not awaken until seven. He had slept truly splendidly for the first time in months, and contrary to his custom lay there yet another quarter of an hour, stretching and sighing with enjoyment as he listened to the pleasant hubbub rising up from the kitchen below. When he finally did get up and open the window wide, taking in the beautiful weather outside and breathing in the fresh morning air and listening to the sound of the surf, his good mood knew no bounds, and he puckered his lips and whistled a bright melody.

While he dressed, he went on whistling, and was whistling still as he left his room and on winged feet approached the door to his daughter's room across the hall. He rapped. And rapped again, very softly, so as not to frighten her. There was no answer. He smiled. He could well understand that she was still sleeping.

Carefully he inserted the key in the lock and turned the bolt, softly, very softly, considerately, not wanting

269

to wake her, eager almost to find her still sleeping, wanting to kiss her awake once again—one last time, before he must give her to another man.

The door sprang open, he entered, and the sunlight fell full into his eyes. Everything in the room sparkled, as if it were filled with glittering silver, and for a moment he had to shut his eyes against the pain of it.

When he opened them again, he saw Laure lying on her bed, naked and dead and shorn clean and sparkling white. It was like his nightmare, the one he had dreamt in Grasse the night before last and had forgotten again. Every detail came back to him now as if in a blazing flash. In that instant everything was exactly as it had been in the dream, only very much brighter.

⊰ Forty-seven ⊱

THE NEWS OF Laure Richis's murder spread through the region of Grasse as fast as if the message had been "The king is dead!" or "War's been declared!" or "Pirates have landed on the coast!"—and the awful sense of terror it triggered was similar as well. All at once the fear that they had so carefully forgotten was back again, as virulent as it had been last autumn and with all the accompanying phenomena: panic, outrage, anger, hysterical suspicions, desperation. People stayed in their houses at night, locked up their daughters, barricaded themselves in, mistrusted one another, and slept no more. Everyone assumed it would continue this time as it had before, a murder a week. The calendar seemed to have been set back six months.

The dread was more paralyzing, however, than six months earlier, for people felt helpless at the sudden return of a danger that they had thought well behind them. If even the bishop's anathema had proved useless! If even Antoine Richis, the great Richis, the richest man in town, the second consul, a powerful, prudent man who had every kind of assistance available, if even he could not protect his child! If the murderer's hand was not be deterred even by the hallowed beauty of Laure—for indeed she seemed a saint to everyone who had known her, especially now, afterwards, now that she was dead—what hope was there of escaping this murderer? He was more cruel than the plague, for you could flee before the plague, but not before this murderer, as the case of Richis had proved. Apparently he possessed supernatural powers. He was most certainly in league with the devil, if he was not the devil himself. And so many people, especially the simpler souls, knew no better course than to go to church and pray, every tradesman to his patron: the locksmiths to St. Aloysius, the weavers to St. Crispin, the gardeners to St. Anthony, the perfumers to St. Joseph. And they took their wives and daughters with them, praying together, eating and sleeping in the church; they did not leave during the day themselves now, convinced that the only possible refuge from this monster—if any refuge was to be had—was under the protection of the despairing parish and the gaze of the Madonna.

Seeing that the church had failed once already, other, quicker wits banded together in occult groups. Hiring at great expense a certified witch from Gourdon, they crept into one of the many limestone grottoes of subterranean Grasse and celebrated black masses to curry the Old Gentleman's favor. Still others, in particular members of the upper middle class and the educated nobility, put their money on the most modern scientific methods, magnetizing their houses, hypnotizing their daughters, gathering in their salons for secret fluidal meetings, and employing telepathy to drive off the murderer's spirit with communal thought emissions. The guilds organized a penitential procession from Grasse to La Napoule and back. The monks from the town's five monasteries established services of perpetual prayer and ceaseless chants, so that soon unbroken lamentation was heard day and night, now on one street corner, now on another. Hardly anyone worked.

Thus, with feverish passivity and something very like impatience, the people of Grasse awaited the murderer's next blow. No one doubted that it would fall. And secretly everyone yearned to hear the horrible news, if only in the hope that it would not be about him, but someone else.

This time, however, the civil, regional, and provincial authorities did not allow themselves to be infected by the hysterical mood of the citizenry. For the first time since the murderer of maidens had appeared on the scene, well-planned and effective cooperative efforts were instituted among the prefectures of Grasse, Draguignan, and Toulon, among magistrates, police, commissaries, parliament, and the navy.

This cooperation among the powerful arose partly from fear of a general civil uprising, partly from the fact that only since Laure Richis's murder did they have clues that made systematic pursuit of the murderer possible for the first time. The murderer had been seen. Obviously they were dealing with the ominous journeyman tanner who had spent the night of the murder in the inn stables and disappeared the next morning without a trace. According to the joint testimony of the innkeeper, the groom, and Richis, he was a nondescript, shortish fellow with a brownish coat and a coarse linen knapsack. Although in other respects the recollections of the three witnesses remained unusually vague—they had been unable to describe the man's face, hair color, or manner of speech—the innkeeper did add that, if he was not mistaken, he had noticed something awkward or limping about the stranger's posture and gait, as if he had a wounded leg or a crippled foot.

Armed with these clues, two mounted troops had taken up pursuit of the murderer by noon of the same day, following the Maréchaussée in the direction of Marseille—one along the coast, the other taking the inland road. The environs of La Napoule were combed by volunteers. Two commissioners from the provincial court at Grasse traveled to Nice to make inquiries about journeyman tanners. All ships departing from the ports of Fréjus, Cannes, and Antibes were checked; the roads leading across the border into Savoy were blocked and travelers required to identify themselves. For those who could read, an arrest warrant and description of the culprit appeared on all the town gates of Grasse, Vence, and Gourdon, and on village church doors. Town criers made three announcements daily. The report of a suspected clubfoot, of course, merely confirmed the view that the culprit was none other than the devil himself and tended more to arouse panic among the populace than to bring in useful information.

But only after the presiding judge of the court in Grasse had, on Richis's behalf, offered a reward of no less than two hundred livres for information leading to the apprehension of the murderer did denunciations bring about the arrest of several journeyman tanners in Grasse, Opio, and Gourdon—one of whom indeed had the rotten luck of limping. They were already considering subjecting the man to torture despite a solid alibi supported by several witnesses, when, ten days after the murder, a man from the city watch appeared at the magistrate's office and gave the following deposition: At noon on the day in question, he, Gabriel Tagliasco, captain of the guard, while engaged in his customary duties at the Porte du Cours, had been approached by an individual, who, as he now realized, fit the description in the warrant almost exactly, and had been questioned repeatedly

274

and insistently concerning the road by which the second consul and his caravan had departed the city that same morning. He had ascribed no importance to the incident, neither then nor later, and would most certainly have been unable to recall the individual purely on the basis of his own memory—so thoroughly unremarkable was the man—had he not seen him by chance only yesterday, right here in Grasse, in the rue de la Louve, in front of the studio of Maître Druot and Madame Arnulfi, on which occasion he had noticed that as the man walked back into the workshop he had a definite limp.

Grenouille was arrested an hour later. The innkeeper and his groom from La Napoule, who were in Grasse to identify the other suspects, immediately recognized him as the journeyman tanner who had spent the night with them: it was he, and no other—this must be the wanted murderer.

They searched the workshop, they searched the cabin in the olive grove behind the Franciscan cloister. In one corner, hardly hidden, lay the shredded nightgown, the undershirt, and the red hair of Laure Richis. And when they dug up the floor, piece by piece the clothes and hair of the other twenty-four girls came to light. The wooden club used to kill the victims was found, and the linen knapsack. The evidence was overwhelming. The order was given to toll the church bells. The presiding judge announced by proclamation and public notice that the infamous murderer of young girls, sought now for almost one year, had finally been captured and was in custody.

❧ *Forty-eight* ❧

AT FIRST people did not believe the report. They assumed it was a ruse by which the officials were covering up their own incompetence and attempting to calm the dangerously explosive mood of the populace. People remembered only too well when the word had been that the murderer had departed for Grenoble. This time fear had set its jaws too firmly into their souls.

Not until the next day, when the evidence was displayed on the church square in front of the provost court—and it was a ghastly sight to behold, twenty-five garments with twenty-five crops of hair, all mounted like scarecrows on poles set up across the top of the square opposite the cathedral—did public opinion change.

Hundreds of people filed by the macabre gallery. The victims' relatives would recognize the clothes and collapse screaming. The rest of the crowd, partly because they were sensation seekers, partly because they wanted to be totally convinced, demanded to see the murderer. The call soon became so loud, the unrest of the churning crowd in the small square so menacing, that the presiding judge decided to have Grenouille brought up out of his cell and to exhibit him at the window on the second floor of the provost court.

As Grenouille appeared at the window, the roar turned to silence. All at once it was as totally quiet as if this were noon on a hot summer day, when everyone is out in the fields or has crept into the shade of his own home. Not a footfall, not a cough, not a breath was to be heard. The crowd was all eyes and one mouth agape, for minutes on end. Not a soul could comprehend how this short, paltry, stoopshouldered man there at the window—this mediocrity, this miserable nonentity, this cipher—could have committed more than two dozen murders. He simply did not look like a murderer. No one could have said just *how* he had imagined the murderer, the devil himself, ought to look, but they were all agreed: not like this! And nevertheless—although the murderer did not in the least match their conception, and the exhibition, one would presume, could not have been less convincing—simply because of the physical reality of this man at the window, because he and no other was presented to them as the murderer, the effect was paradoxically persuasive. They all thought: It simply can't be true!—and at the very same moment knew that it had to be true.

To be sure, only after the guards had led the mannikin back into the shadows of the room, only after he was no longer present and visible but existed, if for the briefest time, merely as a memory, one might almost say as a concept, the concept of an abominable murderer within people's brains, only then did the crowd's bewilderment subside and make away for an appropriate reaction: the mouths closed tight, the thousand eyes came alive again. And then there rang out as if in one voice a thundering cry of rage and revenge: "We want him!" And they set about to storm the provost court, to strangle him with their own hands, to tear him apart and scatter the pieces. It was all the guards could do to barricade the gate and force the mob back. Grenouille was promptly returned to his dungeon. The presiding judge appeared at the window and promised a trial remarkable for its swift and implacable justice. It took several hours, however, for the crowd to disperse, and several days for the town to quiet down to any extent.

The proceedings against Grenouille did indeed move at an extraordinarily rapid pace, not only because the evidence was overwhelming, but also because the accused himself freely confessed to all the murders charged against him.

But when asked about his motives, he had no convincing answer to give them. His repeated reply was that he had needed the girls and that was why he had slain them. What had he needed them for or what was that supposed to mean, "he needed them"?—to that he was silent. They then subjected him to torture, hanged him by his feet for hours, pumped him full of seven pints of water, put clamps on his feet—without the least success. The man seemed immune to physical pain, did not utter a sound, and when questioned again replied with nothing more than: "I needed them." The judges considered him insane. They discontinued the torture and decided to bring the case to an end without further interrogation.

The only delay that occurred after that was a legal squabble with the magistrate of Draguignan, in whose jurisdiction La Napoule was located, and with the parliament in Aix, both of whom wanted to take over the trial themselves. But the judges of Grasse would not let the matter be wrested from them now. They were the ones who had arrested the culprit, the overwhelming majority of the murders had been committed in the area under their jurisdiction, and if they handed the murderer over to another court, there was the threat of the pent-up anger of the citizenry. His blood would have to flow in Grasse.

On April 15, 1766, a verdict was rendered and read to the accused in his cell: "The journeyman perfumer, Jean-Baptiste Grenouille," it stated, "shall within the next forty-eight hours be led out to the parade ground before the city gates and there be bound to a wooden cross, his face toward heaven, and while still alive be dealt twelve blows with an iron rod, breaking the joints of his arms, legs, hips, and shoulders, and then, still bound to the cross, be raised up to hang until death." The customary act of mercy, by which the offender was strangled with a cord once his body had been crushed, was expressly forbidden the executioner, even if the agonies of death should take days. The body was to be buried by night in an unmarked grave in the knacker's yard.

Grenouille received the verdict without emotion. The bailiff asked him if he had a last wish. "No, nothing," Grenouille said; he had everything he needed.

A priest entered the cell to hear his confession, but came out again after fifteen minutes with nothing accomplished. When he had mentioned the name of God, the condemned man had looked at him with total incomprehension, as if he had heard the name for the first time, had then stretched out on his plank bed and sunk at once into a deep sleep. To have said another word would have been pointless.

During the next two days, many people came to see the famous murderer at close range. The guards let them peek through the shutter in the door and demanded six sol per peek. An etcher, who wanted to prepare a sketch, had to pay two francs. His subject, however, was rather a disappointment. The prisoner, bound at his wrists and ankles, lay on his plank bed the whole time and slept. His face was turned to the wall, and he responded to neither knocks nor shouts. Visitors were strictly banned from the cell, and despite some tempting offers, the guards did not dare disregard this prohibition. It was feared the prisoner might be murdered ahead of time by a relative of one of his victims. For the same reason no one was allowed to offer him food. It might have been poisoned. During the whole period of imprisonment, Grenouille's food came from the servants' kitchen in the bishop's palace and had first to be tasted by the prison warden. The last two days, however, he ate nothing at all. He lay on his bed and slept. Occasionally his chains rattled, and if the guard hurried over to the shutter, he could watch Grenouille take a drink from his canteen, then throw himself back on his plank bed, and go back to sleep. It seemed as if the man was so tired of life that he did not want to experience his last hours awake.

Meanwhile the parade grounds were readied for the execution. Carpenters built a scaffold, nine feet by nine feet square and six feet high, with a railing and a sturdy set of stairs—Grasse had never had one as fine as this. Plus a wooden grandstand for local notables and a fence to separate them from the common people, who were to be kept at some distance. In the buildings to the left and right of the Porte du Cours and in the guardhouse itself, places at the windows had long since been rented out at exorbitant rates. The executioner's assistants had even leased the rooms of the patients in the Charité, which was located off to one side, and resold them to curious spectators at a handsome profit. The lemonade vendors stocked up with pitcherfuls of licorice water, the etcher printed up several hundred copies of the sketch he had made of the murderer in prison—touched up a bit from his own imagination—itinerant peddlers streamed into town by the dozens, the bakers baked souvenir cookies.

The executioner, Monsieur Papon, who had not had an offender to smash for years now, had a heavy, squared iron rod forged for him and went off to the slaughterhouse to practice blows on carcasses. He was permitted only twelve hits, and he had to strike true, crushing all twelve joints without damaging the vital body parts, like the chest or head—a difficult business that demanded a fine touch and good timing.

The citizens readied themselves for the event as if for a high holiday. That there would be no work that day went without saying. The women ironed their holiday dresses, the men dusted off their frock coats and had their boots polished to a high gloss. Whoever held military rank or occupied public office, whoever was a guild master, an attorney-at-law, a notary, a head of a fraternal order, or held any other position of importance, donned his uniform or official garb, along with his medals, sashes, chains, and periwig powdered to a chalky white. Pious folk intended to assemble immediately afterwards for religious services, the disciples of Satan planned a hearty Luciferian mass of thanksgiving, the educated aristocracy were going to gather for magnetic séances at the manors of the Cabris, Villeneuves, and Fontmichels. The roasting and baking had begun in the kitchens, the wine had been fetched from the cellars, the floral displays from the market, and the organist and choir were practicing in the cathedral.

In the Richis household on the rue Droite everything remained quiet. Richis had forbidden any preparations for the "Day of Liberation," as people were calling the murderer's execution day. It all disgusted him. The sudden eruption of renewed fear among the populace had disgusted him, their feverish joy of anticipation disgusted him. The people themselves, every one of them, disgusted him. He had not participated in the presentation of the culprit and his victims in the cathedral square, nor in the trial, nor in the obscene procession of sensation seekers filing past the cell of the condemned man. He had requested that the court come to his home for him to identify his daughter's hair and clothing, had given his testimony briefly and calmly, and had asked that they leave him those items as keepsakes, which they did. He carried them to Laure's room, laid the shredded nightgown and undershirt on her bed, spread the red hair over the pillow, sat down beside them, and did not leave the room again day or night, as if by pointlessly standing guard now, he could make good what he had neglected to do that night in La Napoule. He was so full of disgust, disgust at the world and at himself, that he could not weep.

He was also disgusted by the murderer. He did not want to regard him as a human being, but only as a victim to be slaughtered. He did not want to see him until the execution, when he would be laid on the cross and the twelve blows crashed down upon him— then he would want to see him, want to see him from up close, and he had had a place reserved for himself in the front row. And when the crowd had wandered off after a few hours, he wanted to climb up onto the bloody scaffold and crouch next to him, keeping watch, by night, by day, for however long he had to, and look into the eyes of this man, the murderer of his daughter, and drop by drop to trickle the disgust within him into those eyes, to pour out his disgust like burning acid over the man in his death agonies—until the beast perished. . . .

And after that? What would he do after that? He did not know. Perhaps resume his normal life, perhaps get married, perhaps father a son, perhaps do nothing at all, perhaps die. It made no difference whatever to him. To think about it seemed to him as pointless as to think about what he would do after his own death: nothing, of course. Nothing that he could know at this point.

⊱ Forty-nine ⊰

THE EXECUTION was scheduled for five in the afternoon. The first spectators had arrived by morning
and secured themselves places. They brought chairs
and footstools with them, pillows, food, wine, and
their children. Around noon, masses of country
people streamed in from all directions, and the parade grounds were soon so packed that new arrivals
had to camp along the road to Grenoble and on the
terracelike gardens and fields that rose at the far end
of the area. Vendors were already doing a brisk
business—people ate, people drank, everything
hummed and simmered as at a country fair. Soon
there were a good ten thousand people gathered, more
than for the crowning of the Queen of the Jasmine,
more than for the largest guild procession, more than
Grasse had ever seen before. They stood far up on the
slopes. They hung in the trees, they squatted atop
walls and on the roofs, they pressed together ten or
twelve to a window. Only in the center of the grounds,
protected by the fence barricade, as if stamped and
cut from the dough of the crowd, was there still an

284

open space for the grandstand and the scaffold, which suddenly appeared very small, like a toy or the stage of a puppet theater. And one pathway was left open, leading from the place of execution to the Porte du Cours and into the rue Droite.

Shortly after three, Monsieur Papon and his henchmen appeared. The applause swept forward like thunder. They carried two wooden beams forming a St. Andrew's cross to the scaffold and set it at a good working height by propping it up on four carpenter's horses. A journeyman carpenter nailed it down. Every move, every gesture of the deputy executioners and the carpenter was greeted by the crowd's applause. And when Papon stepped forward with his iron rod, walked around the cross, measuring his steps, striking an imaginary blow now on one side, now on the other, there was an eruption of downright jubilation.

At four, the grandstand began to fill. There were many fine folk to admire, rich gentlemen with lackeys and fine manners, beautiful women, big hats, shimmering clothes. The whole of the nobility from both town and country was on hand. The gentlemen of the council appeared in closed rank, the two consuls at their head. Richis was dressed in black, with black stockings and a black hat. Behind the council the magistrates marched in, led by the presiding judge of the court. Last of all, in an open sedan chair came the bishop, wearing gleaming purple vestments and a little green hat. Whoever still had his cap on doffed it now to be sure. This was awe-inspiring.

Then nothing happened for about ten minutes. The lords and ladies had taken their places, the common folk waited impassively; no one was eating now, they all waited. Papon and his henchmen stood on the scaffold platform as if they too had been nailed down. The sun hung large and yellow over the Esterel. From the valley of Grasse a warm wind came up, bearing with it the scent of orange blossoms. It was very warm and almost implausibly still.

Finally, when it seemed the tension could last no longer without its bursting into a thousand-voiced scream, into a tumult, a frenzy, or some other mob scene, above the stillness they heard the clatter of horses and the creaking of wheels.

Down the rue Droite came a carriage drawn by a pair of horses, the police lieutenant's carriage. It drove through the city gate and reappeared for all to see in the narrow path leading to the scaffold. The police lieutenant had insisted on this manner of arrival, since otherwise he could not guarantee the safety of the convicted man. It was certainly not the customary practice. The prison was hardly five minutes away from the place of execution, and if a condemned man, for whatever reason, could not have managed the short distance on foot, then he would have traveled it in an open donkey cart. That a man should be driven to his own execution in a coach, with a driver, liveried footmen, and a mounted guard—no one had ever seen anything like that.

And nevertheless, there was no sign of unrest or displeasure among the crowd—on the contrary. People were satisfied that at least something was happening, considered the idea of the coach a clever stroke, just as at the theater people enjoy a familiar play when it is presented in some surprisingly new fashion. Many even thought the grand entrance appropriate. Such an extraordinarily abominable criminal deserved extraordinary treatment. You couldn't drag him to the scaffold in chains like a common thief and kill him. There would have been nothing sensational about that. But to lead him from his upholstered equipage to the St. Andrew's cross—that was an incomparably imaginative bit of cruelty.

The carriage stopped midway between the scaffold and the grandstand. The footmen jumped down, opened the carriage door, and folded down the steps. The police lieutenant climbed out, behind him an officer of the guard, and finally Grenouille. He was wearing a blue frock coat, a white shirt, white silk stockings, and buckled black shoes. He was not bound. No one led him by the arm. He got out of the carriage as if he were a free man.

And then a miracle occurred. Or something very like a miracle, or at least something so incomprehensible, so unprecedented, and so unbelievable that everyone who witnessed it would have called it a miracle afterwards if they had taken the notion to speak of it at all—which was not the case, since afterwards every single one of them was ashamed to have had any part in it whatever.

What happened was that from one moment to the next, the ten thousand people on the parade grounds and on the slopes surrounding it felt themselves infused with the unshakable belief that the man in the blue frock coat who had just climbed out of the carriage *could not possibly be a murderer*. Not that they doubted his identity! The man standing there was the same one whom they had seen just a few days before at the window of the provost court on the church square and whom, had they been able to get their hands on him, they would have lynched with savage hatred. The same one who only two days before had been lawfully condemned on the basis of overwhelming evidence and his own confession. The same one whose slaughter at the hands of the executioner they had eagerly awaited only a few minutes before. It was he—no doubt of it!

And yet—it was not he either, it could not be he, he could not be a murderer. The man who stood at the scaffold was innocence personified. All of them—

from the bishop to the lemonade vendor, from the marquis to the little washerwoman, from the presiding judge to the street urchin—knew it in a flash.

Papon knew it too. And his great hands, still clutching the iron rod, trembled. All at once his strong arms were as weak, his knees as wobbly, his heart as anxious as a child's. He would not be able to lift that rod, would never in his life have the strength to lift it against this little, innocent man—oh, he dreaded the moment when they would lead him forward; he tottered, had to prop himself up with his death-dealing rod to keep from sinking feebly to his knees, the great, the mighty Papon!

The ten thousand men and women, children and patriarchs assembled there felt no different—they grew weak as young maidens who have succumbed to the charms of a lover. They were overcome by a powerful sense of goodwill, of tenderness, of crazy, childish infatuation, yes, God help them, of love for this little homicidal man, and they were unable, unwilling to do anything about it. It was like a fit of weeping you cannot fight down, like tears that have been held back too long and rise up from deep within you, dissolving whatever resists them, liquefying it, and flushing it away. These people were now pure liquid, their spirits and minds were melted; nothing was left but an amorphous fluid, and all they could feel was their hearts floating and sloshing about within them, and they laid those hearts, each man, each woman, in the hands of the little man in the blue frock coat, for better or worse. They loved him.

Grenouille had been standing at the open carriage door for several minutes now, not moving at all. The footman next to him had sunk to his knees, and sank farther still until achieving the fully prostrate position customary in the Orient before a sultan or Allah. And even in this posture, he still quivered and swayed, trying to sink even farther, to lie flat upon the earth, to lie within it, under it. He wanted to sink to the opposite side of the world out of pure subservience. The officer of the guard and the police lieutenant, doughty fellows both, whose duty it was now to lead the condemned man to the scaffold and hand him over to his executioner, could no longer manage anything like a coordinated action. They wept and removed their hats, put them back on, cast themselves to the ground, fell into each other's arms, withdrew again, flapped their arms absurdly in the air, wrung their hands, twitched and grimaced like victims of St. Vitus's dance.

The noble personages, being somewhat farther away, abandoned themselves to their emotions with hardly more discretion. Each gave free rein to the urges of his or her heart. There were women who with one look at Grenouille thrust their fists into their laps and sighed with bliss; and others who, in their burning desire for this splendid young man—for so he appeared to them—fainted dead away without further ado. There were gentlemen who kept springing up and sitting down and leaping up again, snorting vigorously and grasping the hilts of their swords as if to draw them, and then when they did, each thrusting his blade back in so that it rattled and clattered; and others who cast their eyes mutely to heaven and clenched their hands in prayer; and there was Monseigneur the Bishop, who, as if he had been taken ill, slumped forward and banged his forehead against his knees, sending his little green hat rolling—when in fact he was not ill at all, but rather for the first time in his life basking in religious rapture, for a miracle had occurred before their very eyes, the Lord God had personally stayed the executioner's hand by disclosing as an angel the very man who had for all the world appeared a murderer. Oh, that such a thing had

happened, here in the eighteenth century. How great
was the Lord! And how small and petty was he
himself, who had spoken his anathema, without himself believing it, merely to pacify the populace! Oh,
what presumption! Oh, what lack of faith! And now
the Lord had performed a miracle! Oh, what splendid
humiliation, what sweet abasement, what grace to be
a bishop thus chastised by God.

Meanwhile the masses on the other side of the
barricade were giving themselves over ever more
shamelessly to the uncanny rush of emotion that
Grenouille's appearance had unleashed. Those who at
the start had merely felt sympathy and compassion
were now filled with naked, insatiable desire, and
those who had at first admired and desired were now
driven to ecstasy. They all regarded the man in the
blue frock coat as the most handsome, attractive, and
perfect creature they could imagine: to the nuns he
appeared to be the Savior in person, to the satanists as
the shining Lord of Darkness, to those who were
citizens of the Enlightenment as the Highest Principle, to young maidens as a fairy-tale prince, to men as
their ideal image of themselves. And they all felt as if
he had seen through them at their most vulnerable
point, grasped them, touched their erotic core. It was
as if the man had ten thousand invisible hands and
had laid a hand on the genitals of the ten thousand
people surrounding him and fondled them in just the
way that each of them, whether man or woman,
desired in his or her most secret fantasies.

The result was that the scheduled execution of one
of the most abominable criminals of the age degenerated into the largest orgy the world had seen since the
second century before Christ. Respectable women
ripped open their blouses, bared their breasts, cried
out hysterically, threw themselves on the ground with
skirts hitched high. The men's gazes stumbled madly

over this landscape of straddling flesh; with quivering fingers they tugged to pull from their trousers their members frozen stiff by some invisible frost; they fell down anywhere with a groan and copulated in the most impossible positions and combinations: grandfather with virgin, odd-jobber with lawyer's spouse, apprentice with nun, Jesuit with Freemason's wife—all topsy-turvy, just as opportunity presented. The air was heavy with the sweet odor of sweating lust and filled with loud cries, grunts, and moans from ten thousand human beasts. It was infernal.

Grenouille stood there and smiled. Or rather, it seemed to the people who saw him that he was smiling, the most innocent, loving, enchanting, and at the same time most seductive smile in the world. But in fact it was not a smile, but an ugly, cynical smirk that lay upon his lips, reflecting both his total triumph and his total contempt. He, Jean-Baptiste Grenouille, born with no odor of his own on the most stinking spot in this world, amid garbage, dung, and putrefaction, raised without love, with no warmth of a human soul, surviving solely on impudence and the power of loathing, small, hunchbacked, lame, ugly, shunned, an abomination within and without—he had managed to make the world admire him. To hell with admire! Love him! Desire him! Idolize him! He had performed a Promethean feat. He had persevered until, with infinite cunning, he had obtained for himself that divine spark, something laid gratis in the cradle of every other human being but withheld from him alone. And not merely that! He had himself actually struck that spark upon himself. He was even greater than Prometheus. He had created an aura more radiant and more effective than any human being had ever possessed before him. And he owed it to no one—not to a father, nor a mother, and least of all to a gracious God—but to *himself* alone. He was in very truth his own God, and a more splendid God than the God that stank of incense and was quartered in churches. A flesh-and-blood bishop was on his knees before him, whimpering with pleasure. The rich and the mighty, proud ladies and gentlemen, were fawning in adoration, while the common folk all around—among them the fathers, mothers, brothers, and sisters of his victims—celebrated an orgy in his honor and in his name. A nod of his head and they would all renounce their God and worship him, Grenouille the Great.

Yes, he *was* Grenouille the Great! Now it had become manifest. It was he, just as in his narcissistic fantasies of old, but now in reality. And in that moment he experienced the greatest triumph of his life. And he was terrified.

He was terrified because he could not enjoy one second of it. In that moment as he stepped out of the carriage into the bright sunlight of the parade grounds, clad in the perfume that made people love him, the perfume on which he had worked for two years, the perfume that he had thirsted to possess his whole life long . . . in that moment, as he saw and smelled how irresistible its effect was and how with lightning speed it spread and made captives of the people all around him—in that moment his whole disgust for humankind rose up again within him and completely soured his triumph, so that he felt not only no joy, but not even the least bit of satisfaction. What he had always longed for—that other people should love him—became at the moment of its achievement unbearable, because he did not love them himself, he hated them. And suddenly he knew that he had never found gratification in love, but always only in hatred —in hating and in being hated.

But the hate he felt for people remained without an echo. The more he hated them at this moment, the more they worshiped him, for they perceived only his counterfeit aura, his fragrant disguise, his stolen perfume, and it was indeed a scent to be worshiped.

He would have loved right now to have exterminated these people from the earth, every stupid, stinking, eroticized one of them, just as he had once exterminated alien odors from the world of his raven-black soul. And he wanted them to realize how much he hated them and for them, realizing that it was the only emotion that he had ever truly felt, to return that hate and exterminate him just as they had originally intended. For once in his life, he wanted to empty himself. For once in his life, he wanted to be like other people and empty himself of what was inside him— what they did with their love and their stupid adoration, he would do with his hate. For once, just for once, he wanted to be apprehended in his true being, for other human beings to respond with an answer to his only true emotion, hatred.

But nothing came of that. Nothing could ever come of it. And most certainly not on this day. For after all, he was masked with the best perfume in the world, and beneath his mask there was no face, but only his total odorlessness. Suddenly he was sick to his stomach, for he felt the fog rising again.

Just as it had back then in his cave, in his dream, in his sleep, in his heart, in his fantasy, all at once fog was rising, the dreadful fog from his own odor, which he could not smell, because he was odorless. And just as then, he was filled with boundless fear and terror, felt as if he were going to suffocate. But this time it was different, this was no dream, no sleep, but naked reality. And different, too, because he was not lying alone in a cave, but standing in a public place before ten thousand people. And different because here no scream would help to wake and free him, no flight would rescue him and bring him into the good, warm world. For here and now, this *was* the world, and this, here and now, was his dream come true. And he had wanted it thus.

The horrible, suffocating fog rose up from the morass of his soul, while all around him people moaned in orgiastic and orgasmic rapture. A man came running up to him. He had leapt up out of the first row of the notables' grandstand so violently that his black hat toppled from his head, and now with his black frock coat billowing, he fluttered across the parade grounds like a raven or an avenging angel. It was Richis.

He is going to kill me, thought Grenouille. He is the only one who has not let himself be deceived by my mask. He won't let himself be deceived. The scent of his daughter is clinging to me, betraying me as surely as blood. He has got to recognize me and kill me. He has got to do it.

And he spread his arms wide to receive the angel storming down upon him. He already could feel the thrust of the dagger or sword tickling so wonderfully at his breast, and the blade passing through his armor of scent and the suffocating fog, right to the middle of his cold heart—finally, finally, something in his heart, something other than himself! And he sensed his deliverance already at hand.

And then, suddenly, there was Richis at his breast, no avenging angel, but a shaken, pitiably sobbing Richis, who threw his arms around him, clutching him very tight, as if he could find no other footing in a sea of bliss. No liberating thrust of the dagger, no prick to the heart, not even a curse or a cry of hatred. Instead, Richis's cheek wet with tears glued to his, and quivering lips that whimpered to him: "Forgive me, my son, my dear son, forgive me!"

With that, everything within him went white before his eyes, while the world outside turned raven black.

The trapped fog condensed to a raging liquid, like frothy, boiling milk. It inundated him, pressed its unbearable weight against the inner shell of his body, could find no way out. He wanted to flee, for God's sake, to flee, but where. . . . He wanted to burst, to explode, to keep from suffocating on himself. Finally he sank down and lost consciousness.

⊰ *Fifty* ⊱

WHEN HE again came to, he was lying in Laure Richis's bed. The reliquary of clothes and hair had been removed. A candle was burning on the night table. The window was ajar, and he could hear the exultation of the town's revels in the distance. Antoine Richis was sitting on a footstool beside the bed watching him. He had placed Grenouille's hand in his own and was stroking it.

Even before he opened his eyes, Grenouille had checked the atmosphere. Everything was quiet within him. There was no more boiling or bursting. His soul was again dominated as usual by cold night, just what he needed for a frosty and clear conscious mind to be directed to the outside world: there he smelled his perfume. It had changed. Its peaks had leveled off so that the core of Laure's scent emerged more splendidly than ever—a mild, dark, glowing fire. He felt secure. He knew that he was unassailable for a few hours yet, and he opened his eyes.

Richis's gaze rested on him. An infinite benevolence lay in that gaze: tenderness, compassion, the empty, fatuous profundity of a lover.

296

He smiled, pressed Grenouille's hand more tightly, and said, "It will all turn out all right. The magistrate has overturned the verdict. All the witnesses have recanted. You are free. You can do whatever you want. But I would like you to stay here with me. I have lost a daughter, but I want to gain you as my son. You're very much like her. You are beautiful like her, your hair, your mouth, your hand . . . I have been holding your hand all this time, your hand is like hers. And when I look into your eyes, it's as if she were looking at me. You are her brother, and I want you to become my son, my friend, my pride and joy, my heir. Are your parents still alive?"

Grenouille shook his head, and Richis's face turned beet red for joy. "Then will you be my son?" he stammered, jumping up from his stool to sit on the edge of the bed and clasp Grenouille's other hand as well. "Will you? Will you? Will you have me for a father?—Don't say anything! Don't speak! You are still too weak to talk. Just nod."

Grenouille nodded. And joy erupted from Richis's every pore like scarlet sweat, and he bent down to Grenouille and kissed him on the mouth.

"Sleep now, my dear son!" he said, standing back up again. "I will keep watch over you until you have fallen asleep." And after he had observed him in mute bliss for a long time: "You have made me very, very happy."

Grenouille pulled the corners of his mouth apart, the way he had noticed people do when they smile. Then he closed his eyes. He waited a while before letting his respiration grow easy and deep like a sleeper's. He could feel Richis's loving gaze on his face. At one point he felt Richis bending forward again to kiss him, but then refraining for fear of waking him. Finally the candle was blown out, and Richis slipped on tiptoe from the room.

297

Grenouille lay there until he could no longer hear a sound in the house or the town. When he got up, it was already dawn. He dressed and stole away, softly down the hall, softly down the stairs, and through the salon out onto the terrace.

From there you could see over the city wall, out across the valley surrounding Grasse—in clear weather probably as far as the sea. A light fog, or better a haze, hung now over the fields, and the odors that came from them—grass, broom, and rose—seemed washed clean, comfortably plain and simple. Grenouille crossed the garden and climbed over the wall.

Out on the parade grounds he had to fight his way through human effluvia before he reached open country. The whole area and the slopes looked like a gigantic, debauched army camp. Drunken forms by the thousands lay all about, exhausted by the dissipations of their nocturnal festivities, many of them naked, many half exposed, half covered by their clothes, which they had used as a sort of blanket to creep under. It stank of sour wine, of brandy, of sweat and piss, of baby shit and charred meat. The campfires where they had roasted, drunk, and danced were still smoking here and there. Now and then a murmur or a snigger would gurgle up from the thousands of snores. It was possible that a few people were still awake, guzzling away the last scraps of consciousness from their brains. But no one saw Grenouille, who carefully but quickly climbed over the scattered bodies as if moving across a swamp. And those who saw him did not recognize him. He no longer had any scent. The miracle was over.

Once he had crossed the grounds, he did not take the road toward Grenoble, nor the one to Cabris, but walked straight across the fields toward the west, never once turning to look back. When the sun rose, fat and yellow and scorching hot, he had long since vanished.

The people of Grasse awoke with a terrible hangover. Even those who had not drunk had heads heavy as lead and were wretchedly sick to their stomachs and wretchedly sick at heart. Out on the parade grounds, by bright sunlight, simple peasants searched for the clothes they had flung off in the excesses of their orgy; respectable women searched for their husbands and children; total strangers unwound themselves in horror from intimate embraces; acquaintances, neighbors, spouses were suddenly standing opposite each other painfully embarrassed by their public nakedness.

For many of them the experience was so ghastly, so completely inexplicable and incompatible with their genuine moral precepts that they had literally erased it from their memories the moment it happened and as a result truly could not recall any of it later. Others, who were not in such sovereign control of their faculties of perception, tried to shut their eyes, their ears, their minds to it—which was not all that easy, for the shame of it was too obvious and too universal. As soon as someone had found his effects and his kin, he beat as hasty and inconspicuous a retreat as possible. By noon the grounds were as good as swept clean.

The townspeople did not emerge from their houses until evening, if at all, to pursue their most pressing errands. Their greetings when they met were of the most cursory sort; they made nothing but small talk. Not a word was said about the events of the morning and the previous night. They were as modest now as they had been uninhibited and brash yesterday. And they were all like that, for they were all guilty. Never was there greater harmony among the citizens of

Grasse than on that day—people lived packed in cotton.

Of course, many of them, because of the offices they held, were forced to deal directly with what had happened. The continuity of public life, the inviolability of law and order demanded that swift measures be taken. The town council was in session by afternoon. The gentlemen—the second consul among them—embraced one another mutely as if by this conspiratorial gesture the body were newly constituted. Then without so much as mentioning the events themselves or even the name Grenouille, they unanimously resolved "immediately to have the scaffold and grandstand on the parade grounds dismantled and to have the trampled fields surrounding them restored to their former orderly state." For this purpose, 160 livres were appropriated.

At the same time the judges met at the provost court. The magistrates agreed without debate to regard the "case of G." as settled, to close the files, to place them in the archives without registry, and to open new proceedings against the thus-far unidentified murderer of twenty-five maidens in the region around Grasse. The order was passed to the police lieutenant to begin his investigation immediately.

By the next day, he had already made new discoveries. On the basis of incontrovertible evidence, he arrested Dominique Druot, *maître parfumeur* in the rue de la Louve, since, after all, it was in his cabin that the clothes and hair of all the victims had been found. The judges were not deceived by the lies he told at first. After fourteen hours of torture, he confessed everything and even begged to be executed as soon as possible—which wish was granted and the execution set for the following day. They strung him up by the gray light of dawn, without any fuss, without scaffold or grandstand, with only the hangman, a magistrate of the court, a doctor, and a priest in attendance. Once death had occurred, had been verified and duly recorded, the body was promptly buried. With that the case was closed.

The town had forgotten it in any event, forgotten it so totally that travelers who passed through in the days that followed and casually inquired about Grasse's infamous murderer of young maidens found not a single sane person who could give them any information. Only a few fools from the Charité, notorious lunatics, babbled something or other about a great feast on the place du Cours, on account of which they had been forced to vacate their rooms.

And soon life had returned completely to normal. People worked hard and slept well and went about their business and behaved decently. Water gushed as it always had from the fountains and wells, sending muck floating down the streets. Once again the town clung shabbily but proudly to its slopes above the fertile basin. The sun shone warmly. Soon it was May. They harvested roses.

PART
❧4❧

✥ Fifty-one ✥

GRENOUILLE TRAVELED by night. As he had done at the beginning of his journeys, he steered clear of cities, avoided highways, lay down to sleep at daybreak, arose in the evening, and walked on. He fed on whatever he found on the way: grasses, mushrooms, flowers, dead birds, worms. He marched through the Provence; south of Orange he crossed the Rhône in a stolen boat, followed the Ardèche deep into the Cévennes and then the Allier northwards.

In the Auvergne he drew close to the Plomb du Cantal. He saw it lying to the west, huge and silver gray in the moonlight, and he smelled the cool wind that came from it. But he felt no urge to visit it. He no longer yearned for his life in the cave. He had experienced that life once and it had proved unlivable. Just as had his other experience—life among human beings. He was suffocated by both worlds. He no longer wanted to live at all. He wanted to go to Paris and die. That was what he wanted.

From time to time he reached in his pocket and closed his hand around the little glass flacon of his perfume. The bottle was still almost full. He had used

305

only a drop of it for his performance in Grasse. There was enough left to enslave the whole world. If he wanted, he could be feted in Paris, not by tens of thousands, but by hundreds of thousands of people; or could walk out to Versailles and have the king kiss his feet; write the pope a perfumed letter and reveal himself as the new Messiah; be anointed in Notre-Dame as Supreme Emperor before kings and emperors, or even as God come to earth—if there was such a thing as God having Himself anointed . . .

He could do all that, if only he wanted to. He possessed the power. He held it in his hand. A power stronger than the power of money or the power of terror or the power of death: the invincible power to command the love of mankind. There was only one thing that power could not do: it could not make him able to smell himself. And though his perfume might allow him to appear before the world as a god—if he could not smell himself and thus never know who he was, to hell with it, with the world, with himself, with his perfume.

The hand that had grasped the flacon was fragrant with a faint scent, and when he put it to his nose and sniffed, he grew wistful and forgot to walk on and stood there smelling. No one knows how good this perfume really is, he thought. No one knows how *well made* it is. Other people are merely conquered by its effect, don't even know that it's a perfume that's working on them, enslaving them. The only one who has ever recognized it for its true beauty is me, because I created it myself. And at the same time, I'm the only one that it cannot enslave. I am the only person for whom it is meaningless.

And on another occasion—he was already in Burgundy: When I was standing there at the wall below the garden where the redheaded girl was playing and her scent came floating down to me . . . or, better, the promise of her scent, for the scent she would carry later did not even exist yet—maybe what I felt that day is like what the people on the parade grounds felt when I flooded them with my perfume . . . ? But then he cast the thought aside: No, it was something else. Because I knew that I desired the scent, not the girl. But those people believed that they desired *me*, and what they really desired remained a mystery to them.

Then he thought no more, for thinking was not his strong point, and then, too, he was already in the Orléanais.

He crossed the Loire at Sully. The next day he had the odor of Paris in his nose. On June 25, 1766, at six in the morning, he entered the city via the rue Saint-Jacques.

It turned out to be a hot day, the hottest of the year thus far. The thousands of odors and stenches oozed out as if from thousands of festering boils. Not a breeze stirred. The vegetables in the market stalls shriveled up. Meat and fish rotted. Tainted air hung in the narrow streets. Even the river seemed to have stopped flowing, to have stagnated. It stank. It was a day like the one on which Grenouille was born.

He walked across the Pont-Neuf to the right bank, and then down to Les Halles and the Cimetière des Innocents. He sat down in the arcades of the charnel house bordering the rue aux Fers. Before him lay the cemetery grounds like a cratered battlefield, burrowed and ditched and trenched with graves, sown with skulls and bones, not a tree, bush, or blade of grass, a garbage dump of death.

Not a soul was to be seen. The stench of corpses was so heavy that even the gravediggers had retreated. Only after the sun had gone down did they come out again to scoop out holes for the dead by torchlight until late into the night.

But then after midnight—the gravediggers had left

by then—the place came alive with all sorts of riffraff: thieves, murderers, cutthroats, whores, deserters, young desperadoes. A small campfire was lit for cooking and in the hope of masking the stench.

When Grenouille came out of the arcades and mixed in with these people, they at first took no notice of him. He was able to walk up to the fire unchallenged, as if he were one of them. That later helped confirm the view that they must have been dealing with a ghost or an angel or some other supernatural being. Because normally they were very touchy about the approach of any stranger.

The little man in the blue frock coat, however, had suddenly simply been there, as if he had sprouted out of the ground, and he had had a little bottle in his hand that he unstoppered. That was the first thing that any of them could recall: that he had stood there and unstoppered a bottle. And then he had sprinkled himself all over with the contents of the bottle and all at once he had been bathed in beauty like blazing fire.

For a moment they fell back in awe and pure amazement. But in the same instant they sensed their falling back was more like preparing for a running start, that their awe was turning to desire, their amazement to rapture. They felt themselves drawn to this angel of a man. A frenzied, alluring force came from him, a riptide no human could have resisted, all the less because no human would have wanted to resist it, for what that tide was pulling under and dragging away was the human will itself: straight to him.

They had formed a circle around him, twenty, thirty people, and their circle grew smaller and smaller. Soon the circle could not contain them all, they began to push, to shove, and to elbow, each of them trying to be closest to the center.

And then all at once the last inhibition collapsed

within them, and the circle collapsed with it. They
lunged at the angel, pounced on him, threw him to the
ground. Each of them wanted to touch him, wanted to
have a piece of him, a feather, a bit of plumage, a
spark from that wonderful fire. They tore away his
clothes, his hair, his skin from his body, they plucked
him, they drove their claws and teeth into his flesh,
they attacked him like hyenas.

But the human body is tough and not easily dis-
membered, even horses have great difficulty accomplishing it. And so the flash of knives soon followed,
thrusting and slicing, and then the swish of axes and
cleavers aimed at the joints, hacking and crushing the
bones. In very short order, the angel was divided into
thirty pieces, and every animal in the pack snatched a
piece for itself, and then, driven by voluptuous lust,
dropped back to devour it. A half hour later, Jean-
Baptiste Grenouille had disappeared utterly from the
earth.

When the cannibals found their way back together
after disposing of their meal, no one said a word.
Someone would belch a bit, or spit out a fragment of
bone, or softly smack with his tongue, or kick a
leftover shred of blue frock coat into the flames. They
were all a little embarrassed and afraid to look at one
another. They had all, whether man or woman, committed a murder or some other despicable crime at
one time or another. But to eat a human being? They
would never, so they thought, have been capable of
anything that horrible. And they were amazed that it
had been so very easy for them and that, embarrassed
as they were, they did not feel the tiniest bite of
conscience. On the contrary! Though the meal lay
rather heavy on their stomachs, their hearts were
definitely light. All of a sudden there were delightful,
bright flutterings in their dark souls. And on their
faces was a delicate, virginal glow of happiness. Per-

haps that was why they were shy about looking up and gazing into one another's eyes.

When they finally did dare it, at first with stolen glances and then candid ones, they had to smile. They were uncommonly proud. For the first time they had done something out of love.